A novel by Snunit Liss

Producer & International Distributor
eBookPro Publishing
www.ebook-pro.com

Someone's Secret
Snunit Liss

Translation from Hebrew: Rona Mendelson
Editor: Michal Heruti
Contact: snunitliss@gmail.com
ISBN 9798391848820

Someone's Secret

A novel by
Snunit Liss

To Geva, my children and my parents –
my wings, my sun, my roots

Subject: Hello Eliza

You don't know me. I recently bought a used laptop at a second-hand electronics store and discovered your life within it. I spent the last few days engrossed in your world and thus, I most likely know you better than you know me.

Before you begin to wonder, let me clarify: I am now in possession of all your files. Your computer, laden with letters and diary entries, has presented me with an entire life. You write profusely! When do you have the time? You write much more than I do, and I'm a man of words – writing is my profession (there, you already know a tad about me).

If I gather correctly, your laptop was stolen before it reached my hands and I am currently the sole proprietor of your digital footprint – your files, passwords (that, fortunately for me, you were in no rush to update), bank account details (that are no use to me, in your case), your search history, and your favorites. It's all here. I could take over your virtual identity if I wanted to do so. In fact, if you care to check, you'll find that I took the liberty of deleting a particularly interesting selection of emails from your Gmail account and various messages from your Facebook groups. I didn't bother with your Twitter account; your witty remarks hold no interest for me.

Before you hurry to warn your contacts and the robotic gatekeepers of your digital wailing walls that someone has

stolen your identity, or desperately change all your passwords – keep reading, or else you may regret it.

I'm about to offer you a deal. If you agree to it and meet my terms, you'll receive your laptop back, your life back, the letters, the passwords, and the scattered notes you wrote to yourself, and those that others have written to you in recent years. If you don't reply within a week, if you don't agree to my offer or reject its terms, you shall lose all your precious letters and memories – a neatly arranged archive, a testament to your diligence. You alone know how meaningful these all are to you. From what I've read thus far, I gather they carry a great significance.

Here are the terms of my offer: you must write and send me 40 letters, each consisting of at least 500 words – candid letters in which you honestly and truly describe your experiences, your activities, observations, feelings, and thoughts.

The letters should arrive at this email address at least once a week. Every so often, I will ask you questions and you will be expected to answer honestly and completely. Sometimes, I will reply to your letters and at times I may not. Either way, you must continue to send the letters regularly.

If you update your passwords, and/or confide in another person regarding our deal or any of our future correspondence and/or attempt to uncover my identity, contact the authorities, block me from accessing your digital activities, try to track me, or take any other action that I deem an attempt to conceal information from me, you will lose all your writings and memories.

I'm intrigued to meet you in my inbox, one on one – textually naked, clean of digital makeup, without all the social, public,

Facebooky bullshit. I want you long in word, sentence, and thought. And don't try to sell me anything you've written in the past – I'm sure to recognize it.

I have nothing to lose in this deal. You, on the other hand, stand to lose everything, and I think we both understand why. Your reply, according to this amicable covenant made between us, shall reach me in no more than a week's time. I look forward to it.

As proof that your computer is, indeed, in my possession, I attach a nice little letter I deleted from your inbox. Someone called Yasmin Dahan sent it to you in 2009. I'm certain you'll recognize it.

Send me your response, Eliza. I'd hate to permanently delete such letters.

Warm regards,
Someone

Attachment: My dearest rectum, what's up???

I finally got around to writing you a proper letter after all our idle chitchats on the phone and Facebook. I have soooo many things that I simply must tell you, so let me know when you're home and we'll Skype.

So, how've you been darling??? Have you managed to save the world yet? I desperately miss your juicy, camouflaged ass. I can't believe I'm here while you're there, defending our country with your gorgeously fit figure. I'm trying to imagine you in your Welfare Officer role and I'm sure all the soldiers at the base are already lining up to cry on your delicate shoulder, and that they spend their nights dreaming about all the lewd things they want to do to you and those purple officer braid on your uniform.

I'm not sure the honorable Chief of Staff of the army knows how fucked up my sista really is, though maybe I should let him in on some secrets from your dubious past, then you too can be discharged for incompatibility and we'll form our own army of Amazons. Oh well, I hope the IDF enjoys the use of your shoulder, just as long as you and the Chief of Staff remember that, as soon as I return, I'll be the rightful owner of that shoulder! At least you're helping people and not shooting them. Given your sense of direction, I'm sure everyone's better off.

I'm just kidding with you, babe, I simply miss you to death and it hurts not having you here with me. But that's life.

I hope it's not too hard for you out there. I doubt I could've managed to stay sane, and if the army hadn't predetermined that I'm not a right fit, I'd have been tossed out within a week, tops, for posing a threat to the nation or whatever that tight-assed psychotechnical evaluator wrote about me on all those rustling paper forms of hers.

Last time we talked, you said you were actually having a pretty interesting time. Like, thrilling even, so you feel like an actress in some distorted war movie that takes you to new and exciting places. I hope you haven't caught the dreary military blues in the meantime, but if you ever do, just give me a buzz (but don't get buzzed because, unfortunately, that's not allowed in the army). Got it?!

Anyway, New York is amazing, everything we imagined, only a thousand times better!!! I don't understand why I haven't been here before. It's so like my mom to live in every possible hole-in-the-wall town in the U.S. of fucking A. and never get around to New York. I'm just walking the streets, feeling so high (and not in the way you're thinking). Everything here is so... much, and so big, but in a good way!

If you even wore a strange-colored shirt back in the kibbutz, people would stare as if you were an alien (not to mention if you hugged another girl, ahem ahem). So, out here it's exactly the opposite. There's nothing you can do that could appear strange to anyone, and even if it does, who fucking cares? At any rate, there are more weirdos here than regular people. You can be A-N-Y-thing!! Whoever you really are. Whoever you're not. Reinvent yourself every day. It's so freeing.

Yesterday I was walking down the street and, all of a sudden, an old man in tattered clothing approached me and asked if I wanted to buy one of his invisible cats.

"Invisible cat?" I asked.

So, he leads me to a pile of empty, rusty cages that had been tossed on the sidewalk and tells me in all seriousness which invisible cat lives in each cage: "This is Cheesy, he's cowardly but very clever. This is Tails, he's mischievous, always trying to run away," and he goes on and on. I really pitied him so I agreed to buy one invisible cat, and then he began interrogating me: "Do you know what invisible cats like to eat?"

"Hmmm, invisible food?" I tried.

"No! Thoughts! But don't try to feed them with the wrong thoughts because they'll choke on them! And do you know what invisible cats like to drink?"

"Errr, feelings?" I guessed.

"Yes!" He was surprised. "But only my feelings. They mustn't drink anyone else's feelings. That could poison them!"

And suddenly he started screaming at me with all his might: "Get away from here! You want to steal my invisible cats and get rid of them! I can see your filthy, dark thoughts... get out of here!"

I was so shocked, I just turned around and ran away. I'm still not used to these kinds of things, but it seems it's not such a big deal for people who've lived here for a while. You get it?!

So that was an extremely surreal incident, but most of the time it's a good kind of crazy here. I stroll through streets lit by so many neon lights that it seems like nighttime never

comes. There are countless ideas soaring in my head like the flocks of fucking birds that gather near the kibbutz reservoirs in springtime. I'm filled with the sensation that everything's going to be great. It sucks you're not here, my darling fallopian tube! But what can we do about it? We'll smoke what we've got. In the meantime, I'll earn us some money (if I have anything left over after the monstrous rent I'm paying), and patiently wait for you to cater to the welfare of every soldier in the army. Then we can finally take that trip we were planning and God Bless America! Just know that there's a ton of fun awaiting us, and invisible cats, and birds in your head, and inspiration.

Okay, I gotta go, my delusional roommate is back and she's standing outside my bedroom door yelling something unintelligible. I'll tell you all about her in my next email or when we get a chance to speak again. She's some piece of work.

Love you to death, miss you!

From me, your darling leg,

Jazz

Subject: WTF?!

Whoever you are, I have no idea how to respond to the email you just sent me. It sounds like some kind of prank, but I can't think of anyone who would want to play such an elaborate prank on me and go through the trouble of sending me such a fucked-up, sick letter.

If this email is real, then you're probably just as unlucky as you are a crazy bastard. I don't know what impression you received from what you read on my laptop, but I'm far from the walking advertisement for a twenty-three-year-old that you think you found. If you plan to produce some kind of private reality show viewing party, then the joke's on you because you just happened to fall on the dullest contestant you could've hoped for. You're not going to get anything sexy or arousing out of this, so go back to your porn sites and give me back my laptop, you demented s.o.b! I don't know what your problem is (and I'm sure you have many of them) but fuck you and your shit and leave me alone! I have no idea, nor am I interested in knowing why you decided to play hide-and-seek with someone whose home was broken into in the middle of the night and her laptop stolen, but believe me, there's nothing here that you need.

Why threaten and force your way into the life of a girl whose files just happened to fall into your hands? Do you realize what I've been through since my computer was stolen?? Do you even

know how much I need it??? How can you live with yourself, wake up in the morning, walk around and breathe while you're holding a virtual gun to someone's head? Does it make you feel good, you piece of shit? Do you need this to feel powerful? Loser! You must know that what you're doing is considered a criminal act, and what if I do end up filing a complaint with the police? I'm pretty sure they have a department that deals with this kind of thing. I have a feeling you're going to enjoy prison, you nobody.

So my response is this: Go fuck yourself! I don't know who you are, what your problems are, and why you're playing this game, but this is not a game to me. The materials on this laptop are more valuable to me than anything a wretched creature like yourself could ever imagine. Don't you dare delete anything. Do you hear me??? You have no right to do that. It's not yours to do with as you please. It's my life! Give it back to me!!!

And since you're so into threats, here's one of my own: if I even think you've deleted anything on my laptop, I'll contact the police and do everything I can to find out who you are and delete your life! You wrote that you know I don't have much money, but I'll scrounge as much as I can and I'm willing to pay you for the return of my laptop. Forget about this nonsense and I promise not to attempt to track you down or ever tell anyone about this. Now enough is enough! Give me back what belongs to me!!!

Liz Fine

Subject: A Cry for Help

Eliza, Alissa, Alice, Liz. In one of your letters, please tell me about the meaning behind your name. It's not a common name for someone born in the 1990s, you know.

You may find it hard to believe, but I'm doing this because I ran out of options. I, too, have lost people in my life, and I can imagine how treasured these memories can be when the someone you cared about is now gone. I turned to you because it seems that, much like me, you don't underestimate the value of words and memories.

Please don't take my request as a threat. See it as a cry for help. I've never had much talent for communicating with people. I always have a feeling there's some sort of distorting mirror standing between me and others. Messages that I try to convey in a delicate matter are construed as aggressive, yet when I'm angry I'm perceived as reserved and detached.

In the past, words were my kingdom – a clear level of separation from those distorting mirrors – whereupon I was able to arrange thoughts and ideas in my own way. If we'd happened to meet several years ago, I would probably have introduced myself as an author. I wrote two quite successful books that have been received with rather ridiculous and flattering superlatives. I define this as my past, since the distorting mirror also seized

my last stronghold; standing between me and my words, and it's thicker than ever.

It's been years since I've produced a worthy piece of literary text. My attempts to send any such excerpts to my publisher have been met with polite and awkward requests for rewrites. As I continued to miss my deadlines, the publishing house suspended my contract and the rumors began to spread – a genuine disgrace for someone once considered "a rising star in the Israeli literary world," a title bestowed upon me in one of those dazzling profile articles at the onset of my career.

You are angry with me, Eliza, and rightly so, but I must admit that when I came across your laptop, I was angry at you! When I flipped it open and found the thousands of texts, lists, letters, and diary entries, my jaw dropped. Among the strokes of your keyboard, I discovered the literary flow that had gone missing from my own. Tell me – how is it that you write so prolifically?! And quite well, I might add. Rather unpolished, but certainly of a certain raw value. Does the muse of inspiration sit on your shoulder a dozen hours a day? If so – release her for a while. Allow her to visit me on occasion. You imprison your words in your outdated hard drive, posting only a rare few online, so I found. Perhaps you're the one holding your words hostage and I'm their redeemer?

My dear Eliza, your words did not only incite my wrath, but they also awakened something inside me that has long been in an incurable, comatose state. Thus, I turn to you, not as one seeking amusement, but as someone desperate for help. I am hoping that my proposal will facilitate my writing and help me

return to the only place in this world that I have ever felt at home. Write to me. Help me reclaim my life – and I will let you reclaim yours.

You are interested, and justly so, in assurances that I will not delete your content while we correspond with each other. I therefore suggest sending you collateral of my own – something worthless in itself but of irreplaceable value to me. You may keep it until I return your life to you. What do you think? Would you like to hold on to one of my internal organs for the time being?

As a peace offering, I attach the following letter sent to you from New York, I believe, by that same Yasmin Dahan.

I've opened my heart to you, yet this doesn't mean that the terms of my offer have changed. Reply within a week or else I shall delete your keepsakes.

Warm regards,
Someone

Attachment: How are you, my darling kidneys?

I keep walking around in constant awe like I'm tripping but I don't really care. I'm simply in love with this city! Sometimes I feel like a solar panel, walking the streets with my face up, arms outstretched to each side just to absorb the flickering lights that cause everything inside my head and body to heat up and bubble.

I didn't even get a chance to tell you about the apartment Joe set up for me! It's relatively decent, I mean, it exists. It's falling apart and tiny but I wasn't expecting the Hilton. What's really odd about it is the roommate who came with it. He didn't even tell me anything about her! I already wrote to him about it and he replied that it was his little surprise for me. I think he was just afraid of my reaction and preferred to let me find out on my own. That's so typical of him, the sweet, cowardly cookie that he is. Give him a kiss from me!

Anyway, this roommate thinks she's fucking Beyoncé and sings to herself every day. All day long! She has a beautiful voice and all, but she bellows it out and plows into my brain with the most horrible songs you can imagine, top 40 crap that'd kill you. I feel like I'm hosting the auditions for American Idol, only I can't give her the red slip (or whatever color they give you when you don't make it and you're sent packing home). Whatever.

She's a dog walker. She takes dogs out for long walks for clients who aren't home all day (which means pretty much every New Yorker since these people work crazy hours). So, she goes out several times a day, picks up dogs from around the neighborhood, takes them for a walk, and brings them back. Remember when I wrote to you that I heard her screaming outside my door? I went out to the living room to find her holding a tiny dog and crying, "No, Dexter, no!!!" Totally hysterical. She tried to resuscitate it and massaged its chest like in some over-dramatic episode of Grey's fucking Anatomy! It turns out, that screw-up forgot one of her dogs and left it tied up to a tree at the park all day, and the heat here in summer is no joke! The dog dehydrated! You get it? I Googled the nearest vet and rushed there with her and poor Dexter. They hooked the dog up to an IV and she told its owner that the dog just suddenly got sick in the middle of their walk. She didn't tell them what really happened to avoid being fired, but Jesus! Like, think, woman!

But forget all that, I have much bigger news... I found a job! Thank you, Mommy dearest, for my American citizenship. The truth is, I haven't told you about it yet because I'm kinda worried about how you'll react, so remember to take it in your stride, sister, okay? Like, I'm keeping myself safe and everything, alright? You know I can take care of myself and all that, right?

All right, take a deep breath, here we go. Well... I'm a vagina model! Yes, you heard correctly!!! And you must admit it tears you up laughing. Well, it tears me up too (relax, there's no tearing of the vagina involved).

You haven't fainted, right? What happened was that I ran across an ad looking for open-minded models somewhere in SoHo that pays very, very well. I checked it out and it looked legit. Anyhoo, I took the subway and got lost for an hour searching for the place. So I go in to be greeted by a receptionist in a posh lobby and I feel like I'm in a tampon commercial. The room's filled with attractive girls, gorgeously dressed, sitting with crossed legs, waiting, fiddling with their phones. Every ten minutes they call one in and another comes out. When it's my turn, I go in and see an art studio, paintings and that sort of thing hanging on the walls, abstracts, not bad actually – powerful, mesmerizing stuff. And there's a strange-looking guy in the middle of the room sitting in front of a gynecologist's examination table! A few feet behind him, there's an uptight prude in a business suit. I know it sounds creepy, but the strange-looking guy wasn't scary. On the contrary, he seemed more intimidated than intimidating. I felt I shouldn't speak too loudly or the windows in his studio would shatter or something. So, he introduces himself and the prude, who turns out to be his lawyer, and asks if I know what this job entails, so I reply, "Modeling" and he says, "Yes, but this is a more intimate kind of modeling."

He starts speaking to me in a soft, quiet voice, almost apologetic, explaining how he's an artist who's now working on a project where he's "channeling the vagina." Yes, he actually said those exact words, I'm not paraphrasing, right? And he's looking for a model whose vagina will uniquely speak to him and will serve as a "basis for inspiration" for his project. Yes, my

darling conjunctiva, I swear to God that's what he said. Then he looked at me to see I haven't freaked out or anything. Honestly, it was all I could do to keep myself from bursting out laughing because, you must admit, it sounds like the sort of situation that you're like... What?!!!!?

It's so bizarre and surreal that I just scrutinize his face trying to figure out if this guy's for real. The truth is – he looks rather miserable, a bit wary, as if he's uncomfortable even talking about it. I feel sorry for him, so I say, "Hey, it's fine," and all this time his uptight lawyer is just standing there without even twitching a muscle in her face. And then he takes on this formal tone and asks me what his lawyer probably worded for him: "Are you okay with what you've just heard? If you prefer to leave at this point, it will be perfectly understandable."

I'm fine with it. So he tells me he's now going to say various terms related to sex and if I agree to hear them I must sign a waiver stating that I understand this isn't sexual harassment. Okay, so I sign it. The prude still hasn't moved an inch. I began to wonder if she isn't suffering from some kind of seizure... Jesus!

Then he says to me, "The next step in our interview is observation. I need to look at your vagina. If I feel she's the right subject for my project and we resolve to work together, you'll be required to expose your vagina to me for several hours per day. The sessions don't involve any contact, and for the record, I should note that I'm not sexually attracted to women. The sessions will include breaks for eating, drinking, and freshening up. If you agree to show me your vagina, we can move on to the next step."

I say, "No problem," and he asks me to sign another legal waiver stating that I'm not going to sue him for this either. I sign the papers and then he motions me over to the examination table and asks in that prim, American, over-polite manner, to please bare the lower part of my body. He shows me where to put my clothes and it's obvious he's dying of awkwardness. I swear – I was feeling much more comfortable than he was. Like, are we in kindergarten?

He turns around and goes to the other corner of the room (!!!) while I undress and lie down on the table with my legs spread apart and he says, "Tell me when you're ready." He approaches me, not daring to make any eye contact. He just advances over to my snatch and looks at it like when you approach a dog, trying to show it that you're friendly and it shouldn't be afraid of you. It was almost as if he was going to reach out his hand for my pussy to sniff.

Actually, it's kind of weird because he's just hypnotized. He murmurs, "What an extraordinary vagina. Where did you say you're from?"

I tell him my mother was American and I was born in the US but grew up in Israel.

"Oh," he mutters, continuing to stare at my pussy in silence for several more moments until finally mumbling, "Okay, you can get dressed now."

Once I'm dressed, he walks over to me, lowers his eyes, and says, "As far as I'm concerned, you're hired, but only if you're comfortable with this line of employment."

Lizzie, my love, don't bang your head on your monitor, I swear I wasn't reckless about this! I hesitated for a moment but

it really sounded cool and intriguing, and though it sounds strange, the situation wasn't intimidating at all! And for $75 an hour!!! It's so much better than waitressing for next to nothing. Not to mention, as a waitress I'd regularly be sexually harassed by douchebags who think their cocks are the greatest thing New York's seen since the World Trade Center.

So I tell him the job's acceptable to me and we shake hands. He walks me out to his receptionist and they whisper a few words, he tells me goodbye without once looking into my eyes and disappears back into his studio. The receptionist turns to the other girls in the room and tells them the auditions are over. They pack up and go, and she has me sign a bunch of documents and details the work hours and other specifics.

I Googled his name later – Theodore Freiberg – he's quite famous around here. He's had several exhibitions in New York and Europe and is currently the talk of the town. He also appeared on various art sites in lists of top young artists, so he's probably not just some pervert who's using art as an excuse to stare at girls' pussies. I also read somewhere that he's gay.

Anyway, I've been to see him three times since then and it's by far the easiest job I've ever done in my life. I mean, it's a little boring, but he lets me read magazines and even eat during the actual session or on breaks, and I can also play on my phone and text. Yes, it's insanely weird to eat while someone's looking at your pussy but you just get used to it after a while. Jesus, it's too bad I'm not studying for SATs or something that requires some cramming! I could've made good use of this free time.

In fact, I spend most of the time just looking at him because it's interesting. He's really scared of me! He's super polite and

rarely speaks, addressing me only to make sure that I'm fine and comfortable. It's very important to him that I'm comfortable... Americans and their political fucking correctness! The first day, he mostly stared. I felt like he was trying to speak to my pussy through his eyes, as if the image was conjuring all these memories in his mind. Halfway through, he began to cry for no particular reason and it was both totally sad and weird. I asked him if he was okay and he replied, "Yes, I just need a moment." I tried to sit up and place my hand on his shoulder but he leaped back and said, "No, I'm fine. Just take a break and we'll continue in five."

While he's looking at me, he sits in front of a huge painting easel with all these electronic devices hanging from it, probably for lighting purposes. He stares at me, at the canvas, then back at me, and begins to paint. He's already begun a second painting but he wouldn't show it to me. I hope he'll chill out eventually, otherwise I'll be bored to death. Like, now I've gotten used to this bizarre situation, I just lie there.

I hope you're not freaking out about this or anything. I know it sounds slutty and maybe a little disturbing and all that, but that's New York, baby. Besides, I've already met some people here and I have friends to hang out with and stuff, but I'll tell you all about that in my next email, or on Skype, whichever comes first.

Hold on out there, alright? Just another year and eight months and it'll be over. Talk to me when you can!!! Write back soon!!! Text me, send up a flare, a smoke grenade, whatever you can.

Wish you were here.

Big hug from me, your large intestines

Subject: Who are you and what do you want from me?

Alissa? Alice??? You disgusting deviant, do you think you're Lewis fucking Carroll and I'm some girl who's about to go down your rabbit hole!?

Despite your pathetic endeavors, your letter really – I mean really – didn't make me pity you, it mostly made me nauseous. Using your writing as a feeble excuse sounds like something you pulled out of your ass. Muse??? What kind of fantasy world are you living in? I'm just a person. And not even a particularly interesting one. If you want to play catch with someone who's had everything she held dear stolen from her and rummage through my life like some filthy peeping Tom, the kind who uses a telescope to spy on neighbors who haven't drawn their curtains, just save me your poetic bullshit and cheesy metaphors. (Muse of inspiration??? You're right, if you really are a writer, your situation is, indeed, dire.)

You're twisting my arm, stealing from me, just like the scum who broke into my house, watched me sleeping in my bed, and stole my memories, so let's not sugarcoat your shit in sticky metaphors. You wretch. Seriously, don't you think you'd feel better about yourself if you just give me my stuff back and find friends in a more conventional way? I'm even willing to

continue our correspondence if it's so important to you – but please, return my laptop! I need it!!!

Fuck you.

Who are you and what do you want from me?

Liz

Subject: Your request has been denied

Dear Eliza. And I use the word 'dear' with the most sincere of intentions and not as a form of jest. I suppose you find it hard to believe, but you are dear to me. Nevertheless, your request is denied. I presented the terms of my offer and I'm postponing the deletion of your files for an additional week but only because of the affection I hold for you. This is my offer. These are the terms of my proposed deal. Write back by next week or else I will be forced to carry out my threat.

Warm regards,
Someone

Subject: Fuck you

You bastard, shithead, son of a bitch, filth, douchebag, inept, fucked up, flawed asshole. I can't believe I'm writing this but, unfortunately for me, it seems I have no choice but to succumb to your delusional blackmail. You know what? Maybe a weekly account of my miserable existence is just the punishment you deserve.

If you really want me to write to you, it's only going to happen under the following conditions: You must guarantee that after receiving 40 letters, you'll return my laptop with all my files intact. There's no way I'm promising that every letter will be 500 words long, so get over it. As proof that you haven't deleted my stuff, you must attach to your emails some of the letters you deleted from my email and other files that are saved on my laptop, you son of a bitch. You will not make use of my digital identity or log on to my accounts on Facebook, Twitter, etc. The last thing I need right now is for you to start writing creepy posts under my profiles. If you fail to comply with any of these conditions, I'll call the police. And if by chance you get tired of this disgusting game and eventually realize that corresponding with a fucked-up stranger is not the way to redeem your miserable life, I ask that you return my files and I promise not to tell anyone about this whole sordid situation.

The letters I've written so far obviously count toward my quota! This is my third letter! And, oh yeah, send me whatever it was that you claimed would serve as collateral for you not deleting my files.

It better not be sleazy or disgusting. My address: Lizzie Fine, Kibbutz Beit Katzir, Mobil Post Hacarmel, Zip Code 5283800

Fuck you! Fuck you!

And I hope you choke reading this.

Liz

Subject: Here goes nothing

Hello, scum. I've received your collateral. Your "internal organ" as you called it. Whatever...

If you insist on me describing exactly what I do all day, then I'll tell you how my mother opened the door this morning and said, "Lizzielee! Look, what a surprise, you've got a package!" in the same manner a kindergarten teacher would try to convince the unpopular kids that someone actually wants to play with them.

I was happy to discover that you sent an old notebook rather than an actual internal organ, like a liver or an appendix that you stole from another unfortunate wretch. I haven't read its contents. I don't work for you, you know. You can send your endless ramblings to your publisher or something.

You wanted me to honestly write to you about my life? So here you go. Enjoy: I woke up this morning. I currently live in Kibbutz Beit Katzir. I was born here, but if you must know, I lived in Tel-Aviv up until my computer, which you now refuse to return, was stolen. I didn't live in some luxury penthouse or anything, just a room in a shared four-room apartment that was split into tiny tin-can living spaces soaked in sodium and low in nutritional value. It wasn't the best area in town, but it was someplace you can just about manage to afford when your parents can't help you with the rent, provided you don't go out

every night or spend too much money on new shoes. That's where I lived until just recently, but once my laptop was stolen, I had to go back to my parents' house in the kibbutz. I need a computer for work and, as you already know, I can't afford a new one, so I had no choice, and now I'm working here on their ancient computer. I came back here with my tail between my legs, just like they all said I would.

So where were we? Ah, yes. I woke up this morning. I brushed my teeth. I used to brush my teeth with some kind of vigor, but lately I don't have the energy for it. I do it out of a sense of obligation. Fascinating, isn't it? Did your writer's block lift yet?

After brushing my teeth, I headed to my parents' computer. I work as an SEO (Search Engine Optimization) copywriter, which is really and thoroughly intriguing. I'll tell you all about it. I'll even send you several hundred of my articles for your reading enjoyment. Oh, shit, wait a minute... you can already read them – they're on my laptop, with you. These articles are designed to promote websites on search engines. They're not meant to interest actual readers but to appeal to Google's search bots and thus increase a website's visibility. I write measured quotas of 300-word content wherein I repeat the same phrase a specific number of times. I don't really understand the search engine's algorithms but what I do is enough to legally manipulate them.

I've already written God knows how many pointless articles on every subject you can imagine: pest extermination and floor polishing, janitorial services and estate management... I repeat a slightly different version of each keyword phrase in

every possible form. I write several dozen of these each week and increase my net worth by thirty whole shekels per article! It's a boring and comfortable job that numbs your brain (but honestly, that's what I love most about it) and, thanks to it, I can still be considered a somewhat functional person.

Let's continue with my fascinating account. So, today I wrote an article for a plumber in Haifa, and then for plumbing in Haifa. I then moved on to write about plumbers in Haifa and plumbing companies in Haifa. Got the idea? In each such article, I copiously described the misery of Haifa residents who suffer from diarrhea, which clogs their toilets, and they're then forced to use their neighbors' toilets and infect these neighbors with diarrhea, which subsequently clogs their toilets, too. My life is crazy interesting, right? Has your inspiration returned yet?

In the meantime, as you must have noticed, I checked my email and was happy to see that my disgusting stalker hasn't opened any of my mail or has at least made sure to mark them as unread. It sure is nice of you to be such a neat and considerate piece of filth, you loser.

Somewhere around lunchtime, I ate some of the food my mother brought up from the kibbutz's communal dining hall (bland boiled chicken and murdered wilted vegetables, FYI). I then sat down to study. I take psychology classes at the Open University. Or at least I try to. I tried reading the material but, after fifteen minutes, I realized I was reading the same paragraph over and over again. I tried to take a nap. I couldn't fall asleep.

My parents came home from work in the evening. They haven't been in such a good mood lately. This whole situation

with the laptop being stolen from their daughter's pitiful apartment, into which she moved alone despite their protests, has them pretty worried.

Anyway, my parents sat down for dinner so I joined them. I had no appetite. My dad wanted to watch TV while he ate and my mom objected as usual, so he turned it off. He asked questions about my studies and work and wondered whether the police had called with any new information regarding the stolen laptop. I sat with them for approximately fifteen minutes until I'd had enough. My back ached and I felt my brain about to explode so I went to sit on the couch to watch TV. My dad cleared the dishes and cleaned up while Mom wiped the table and reproached him for the way he placed the dishes on the drying rack. She sat down on the other couch and dad sat beside her.

I started watching some dumb college movie but they asked to change the channel because it was "trash." They seem to feel that I've taken over their house since I moved back in. Soon after, they began to argue about what to watch on TV. They already know they can't watch the news while I'm around so we agreed on some National Geographic special about the Bengal tiger. Within about thirty minutes, they were both fast asleep and I switched back to my dumb college movie. Once it was over, I headed back to the office that's reluctantly been turned back into my bedroom. Eventually, they woke up and got ready for bed.

At this time of night, I'd usually spend my time writing or reviewing things I've written, but as you know, I'm no longer

in possession of those materials. I also can't begin anything new here since I don't want my parents stumbling upon it and freaking out.

Ultimately, I just browsed the net and read some random crap and now I've just written to you about my day, as you requested. Next, I guess I'll just stare at the ceiling and browse the internet some more and probably fall asleep sometime around four or five in the morning.

I'm certain you found all this insanely interesting, that your life has now changed beyond recognition, and that your muse has now returned to perch on your shoulder. This was letter number four. Once you've read another thirty-six of these, I'm sure you'll feel just as great as I do. Are you now willing to give up on this silly nonsense and give me my laptop back? And with your next disgusting letter, please send me a file called "Rockin' the Galilee." Just search for "Rockin" in my documents and you'll find it.

Fuck you! Fuck you!

Liz

Subject: Rejection of your letter

Dear Liz, I thank you for your letter! I must admit that it's been quite a while since I've laughed so hard or was this saddened. I've never considered myself a sensitive person or one with an overdeveloped sense of humor, but I tend to find you both utterly amusing and heartbreaking. Nevertheless, your letter does not conform to the terms I specified under our friendly agreement and therefore will not count toward your quota. As I've stressed, you must write "candid letters in which you honestly and truly describe your experiences – your activities, observations, feelings, and thoughts." There's a reason I listed all four stipulations. I've given my request much thought. Please respect it. I have no interest in a chronological depiction of your day, nor your dental hygiene. I'm interested in reading what you're really and truly experiencing, feeling, and thinking.

I promised you questions, so here are some for you: Why does your back hurt at your young age? Why can't your parents watch the news when you're around? Why do you only fall asleep at four or five in the morning, and why can't you find another job?

I'll attach the file you requested when you properly fulfill your part of our agreement.

Warm regards,
Someone

Subject: Here's what you can do with your terms

What do you mean – it doesn't count????????? And to write about what I'm feeling and all that shit?? Who do you think you are, my fucking psychologist?! Hey, scumbag, ALL the letters count! This is my fifth fucking letter and if you don't like it, you can take my laptop stick it deep up your ass and plug it in!!! Either way, you write as if you've already got something's wedged deep inside where the sun don't shine.

Want answers to allllllll your questions? Here you go, knock yourself out: As you probably already guessed (you're just so clever, really very perceptive), my life's not so ordinary. I was involved in an accident a few years ago and things have changed for me since then. My body's like an out-of-tune piano, playing its dissonant chords under the tinkling fingers of the universe. I'll spare you, and myself, from my long list of failures. I hate being that person who always needs to explain to others why she's unable to do things, someone who has "a story" behind her. But the fact is that I can't. I can't do what most twenty-three-year-olds can, and honestly, not even what most seventy-year-olds can. It may sound overindulgent or lazy. You're probably raising a skeptical eyebrow, thinking I'm just a bum or crazy, like everyone else seems to think I am. But this is one place where I shouldn't care what others think of me. Compared to some creep who extorts recently robbed women, even I end up looking pretty decent. Good for me.

Until a few years ago, I was someone else. I had a life of my own. The whole world was in the palm of my hand and I controlled it in a way I never thought could be lost. Now, I'm just a broken version of the whole and complete person I didn't even know I was.

I used to love seeing new places and meeting different types of people but, since the accident, I feel like someone who's had their skin peeled off. Everything feels too harsh, too fast, too bright. Lights, colors, and voices all spin in my head. A moment later, I no longer know who or where I am and all I want to do is get away.

In the meantime, I patched myself an alternate route in life in which I've eliminated the chance of suddenly publicly embarrassing myself somewhere – a life where I don't need to drive, show up to work or class, I can study from home, and work my nights away.

I thought that studying psychology would help me better understand my circumstances but, so far, it's been mostly equations and simplistic rationalizations of trivial matters. Well, actually, to call it studying is a pretty wild exaggeration. I mostly stare at the texts, chase after deadlines, and can't concentrate for shit.

It's funny. In high school, I hardly needed to attend my classes. All I needed for an A was to leaf through someone else's notes and then move on to find something more interesting to do. In the army, I was an "outstanding soldier," or at least that's what they said I was. Now I work at a worthless job and can barely manage to get anything into my head.

As I've previously written, I left the kibbutz about a year ago and moved to Tel-Aviv. I tried to feel like I was actually achieving some of the things I'd planned to do before the accident. But honestly, it wasn't very successful. The move didn't mitigate my problems, it only aggravated them. I realized that no matter where I go, my problems will always follow me. The illusion I carried that something would change if I left the kibbutz shattered.

And then my apartment was broken into, my life was invaded, the computer through which I worked, studied, wrote, and communicated with the world disappeared. After the break-in, I could no longer live in that apartment alone. Every rustle, every crack would send me into a panic. So, I found another tenant to sublet the apartment and asked my dad to drive me home from Tel-Aviv, since taking the bus or the train by myself is as feasible for me as climbing Mount Everest is for most people.

On the way back to the kibbutz, I reclined across the back seat and shut my eyes like I always do. Dad just drove in silence. Dad always drives in silence, doing what needs to be done. Without a map or a compass, he resolutely navigates this warped reality in which his daughter was broken.

So, I returned to the kibbutz. I was born and raised here. There's nowhere I feel more at home or less like I belong. I know every stone, tree, and lane better than I know my own face. This place, steeped in the odors wafting from the barns and factories of the neighboring kibbutz when the wind blows from the east, smells like home. But for me, this is the most stifling place in the world. It only took a little push to get me back here.

I took a look at what you sent me... an old notebook filled with the writings of a child worried that God will kill his father. I know you're expecting me to ask about it and about who wrote it, but I'm not willing to play your creepy games.

And now for my payment: If you had to choose to hold onto just one memento from the person you cherished most in the world, what would you rather keep – a letter or a photo? I'm asking you once again to send me the "Rockin' the Galilee" file I requested.

Fuck you! Fuck you!

Who are you and what do you want from me?

Liz

Attachment: Rockin' the Galilee 1

I counted the days leading up to the Rockin' the Galilee Festival. I was sixteen, and my world was the color of eager anticipation. The night before the festival was filled with an air of adventure brought on by the tourists, revelers, and eccentric characters who flocked to the Jordan River valley every summer.

As I stepped off the bus at the station near Kibbutz Mevo Golan, Jazz greeted me with an onslaught of hugs, then smiled one of those smiles that crossed her face whenever she was up to something and said, "I have a surprise for you!"

"What is it this time?" I asked hesitantly. I've already learned to approach her ideas with caution.

"You'll see soon enough."

By the time we arrived at her kibbutz, the Golan Mountains blushed on the horizon as they basked in the glow of the setting sun. She led me to a part of the kibbutz I haven't been to before. We passed an abandoned barn and took a yellowish dirt path until we reached an old stone structure. Jazz took a large key from her pocket and unlocked a rusty metal door that creaked loudly as it opened. An overwhelming scent of mothballs and dust filled my nose and I began to cough and sneeze.

"Here it is!" Jazz switched on the light and my eyes widened at the sight of gold and crimson fabrics, crowns and wands, robes and wings. Her smile was infectious. "My grandma's now

in charge of the costume store, so here's everything we need for the festival." Her voice bubbled with excitement. "Remember how we wondered how we'd afford our trip to Eilat?" She took my hand in hers, her eyes dancing with delight. "I came up with a little idea."

"What did you have in mind?" I asked with apprehension mingled with expectation.

"Relax, my darling ovaries, I'm not suggesting we dress up like sluts and sell our bodies on the streets, although that could totally solve our predicament," she laughed. "Remember when you told me you once dreamed you were a fortune teller?"

I nodded in embarrassment. "Oh, that silly dream?"

"A genius dream!" She dismissed my self-dismissal. "What if we try to realize your dream?" Before I had a chance to reply, she continued with enthusiasm: "We'll choose our costumes, find those cards of strange drawings I have somewhere in my room, an old pot with some black coffee, glass coffee mugs, and a couple of incense burners. We'll set up a fortune-telling booth at the festival and tell people stories. People go crazy for these things! It'll be so much fun, and maybe we'll even earn a few shekels!"

I scanned the plethora of dusty costumes and glittery accessories that surrounded us, imagining us dressed up in strange clothes and sitting in an improvised booth like those we've skillfully learned to build at previous festivals we've attended. I was reminded of the preposterous tales Jazz could always invent without batting an eye, and I couldn't help but smile.

"Cool, but I'm in charge of the coffee."

Her enthusiasm was contagious. "You've got yourself a deal, babe," she cheered and hugged me. "And provided that I get to wear this!" I wrapped a red scarf studded with small mirrors around my head. "It's yours, Esmeralda!" Jazz ran her fingers through the tassels hanging from the scarf. We began trying on the various ornate costumes, bursting out laughing, dancing in front of the mirrors, and choking on the odors of puke and alcohol that dozens of kibbutz Purim parties had soaked into the fabrics. We became lords and ladies, nomads and prostitutes, a bride and a fairy, Theodore Herzl and Charlie Chaplin. We carefully selected the costumes and accessories we wanted, packed them in bags, and took them with us.

In her father's small living room, in front of the old television set that he refused to replace, we sat and made a sign for our booth: Lizzie and Jazzy's Fortunes. We told her dad it was for a school summer project. We spent the night packing and, having made sure her dad was fast asleep, blowing rings of blue cigarette smoke into the night sky as we sat on the front porch. Strange to think that uncertainty once filled me with uninhibited joy rather than horror.

The next day, we woke up at noon, heaved our bags onto our backs, and hitched a ride to the beach where the festival was being held. We found the perfect spot between some trees, spread a few mats on the grainy sand, tied some ropes between the trees, and draped them in the long pieces of fabric we'd found in the costume store. We hung up the sign we'd made, set

up a little camping stove for the tin coffee pot, and arranged a small table for the cards. We unrolled our sleeping bags in the back and I placed my guitar nearby. In less than two hours, we'd created ourselves a temporary dwelling.

"Our very own tower and stockade. At least we learned something at summer camp," Jazz giggled. We sat down and smoked a cigarette. I lit some incense and put the coffee on the camping stove, hoping the aroma would bring in our first customer.

"Jazz?" I suddenly wondered if she had something else in mind that she hadn't shared with me yet. "Are you also planning to sell people the weed we grew?"

"Only if that's what the future has in store for them," she winked at me.

Subject: Thank you kindly

Dear Eliza. I'm sorry to disappoint you but I found your letter truly fascinating. As for your question, there are not many people in the world today that I cherish enough to consider whether I'd keep a letter or photo to remind me of them. I'm not a particularly likable person and I tend not to like most people, but you, Eliza, I like. If the life of an ordinary twenty-three-year-old young woman was reflected in the writings on your computer, I would have likely spared you the dubious pleasure of our correspondence. I'm far more interested in reading about your life and your pains than being privy to banal accounts of parties, waitressing shifts, lounging on the lawn of the college campus, or whatever else you think girls your age are supposed to do.

You offered me a candid look into your life, so it's only fair that I share a little about myself. Even before I read your letter, I assumed that you lived in Tel Aviv since I live here, too, and I bought your laptop from a store in the city. My apartment is located, in all probability, in a better neighborhood than the one you lived in, within this gray metropolitan area dubbed The White City. I bought this apartment after selling my mother's apartment. I sold it to the first bidder as I could not stay there a day longer after she died.

My apartment is quiet. I don't like it when others penetrate my personal space. Whenever their voices, shades, and scents

mingle around me, I feel a strong urge to fend them off and purify the air so that I can move around freely again without stumbling upon their vestiges. Moreover, I hold no interest in mingling in other people's space. I don't often leave my home. In fact, I can count the number of times I've left the house in the past few months on one hand.

You refrained from asking me about the collateral I sent you. I'll tell you about it anyway. It is a journal I kept when I was nine years old. It remains one of the few keepsakes from my childhood. It's to be expected that I wouldn't want to keep any reminders from that time of my life, but I've often noticed that people find it hard to part with the things that hurt them most. After all, this is the mold that turned us into the extraordinary work of art we believe we are. Without it, we would just be floating in a void, lacking origin or uniqueness. Is that how you feel without your journals and letters, Eliza? You should be reassured to know that I'm treating your precious cargo with the utmost respect, even if you failed to do so. I've already acquired another laptop for my needs and I keep yours locked away in a safe when I'm not reading your writings.

I think you are neither "lazy" nor "crazy." In fact, I beg to add a sub-clause to our agreement: Please surrender your inhibitions when you write to me. Don't be afraid to be portrayed as "overindulgent," a "bum," or any other description you bestow upon yourself through the exhausting self-flagellation evident in your words. You're right. Compared to me, you'll always be considered an exemplary citizen, so set your mind at ease and allow your writing to flow freely. Your wish will inevitably

come true. I will most likely choke one of these days – we'll all eventually cease breathing, you know.

This brings me to my next request from you. Tell me about the accident and about your friend, Jazz, who stars in many of your files. And please take care of yourself.

Warm regards,
Someone

Subject: Go call your mother Eliza

Will you stop calling me Eliza? I hate that name and the last time someone called me by that name was at the doctor's office. My name is Liz, or Lizzie if you really insist. And stop calling me "dear," like I'm your friend and you really care about me or something. You don't know me and, if you really cared about me, you wouldn't be blackmailing me.

Tell me about the accident, you say. A punch in the gut. How can you ask someone to tell you about their last moments? I now realize that, in just one heartbeat, something can happen that will take away your entire life and everything you could have been... that the things that helped you survive, your reasons for existing, can be taken from you.

The accident. One moment that can never be undone. This equilibrium seems so unfair. One moment equals a whole lifetime, several lifetimes. Hers, all who loved her. Mine. It's absurd that you can't rewind the film strip of time back into the fucking camera of life, edit just one moment out, and leave it on the cutting-room floor. But that's just how things are.

The accident. Talking about it is impossible yet very simple. I don't remember any of it. Isn't that funny? The one moment where my life went up in fucking flames – literally, not just some bad metaphor – has been wiped from my memory. There are so many things about the accident that I don't know. True, there's

the highway police report with all the evidence they gathered, but I have no personal memory of it. Maybe you were involved in it? Why not, actually? Sometimes it seems that everything in my life's related to the accident, that the one moment that I couldn't cut or edit isn't over and will never be over.

It was my 20th birthday. Jazzy and I went out to have fun. We loved dancing the night away and that's just what we did. We stayed on for as long as we could until the DJ began playing music that was meant to drive away those who had yet to leave the dance floor. It was that music that we enjoyed the most. The endorphins bouncing in our brains, my eyes locked on hers, our bodies flickering like the strobe lights on the dance floor.

At around four in the morning, we left the club and headed back to my house. (Jazz had recently returned from New York after a year-long stay. She didn't have her own room at her kibbutz and I was still serving in the army, so she stayed with me at Beit Katzir.) That night I'd been drinking, so I climbed on the back of the motorcycle she bought for us with the money she'd saved and held on to her as we rode for about a quarter of an hour. At this point, we were exhausted and blissful, our bodies buzzing from the sounds, lights, and dancing. I sat behind her, clasping my arms around her waist and leaning my helmet-clad head on her shoulder. I may have fallen asleep. I've no idea.

The next thing I remember is a bright neon light and a horrible feeling. I was completely disoriented when I woke up, but my body was fully aware. From within a nauseating fog, I could hear my mom say to my dad, "Look, she's opening her eyes!" and I saw their faces hovering above me.

Apparently, a vehicle on the opposite lane swerved and hit us head-on. The roulette wheel of life says that a couple of inches to either side and we'd have been spared. They tried to hide the details from me but I insisted on hearing everything. The force of the impact flung Jazz into the air and she landed on the road. I was probably propelled for a shorter distance and "luckily" landed on some shrubs on the side of the road. Our motorcycle crumpled like a paper ball and caught fire. Jazzy died instantly. When I spoke to one of the doctors in the hospital, he swore she didn't suffer. I hope that was true and that he didn't just lie to me to spare my feelings or something. I know that, in reality, it doesn't matter anymore but it does matter in the scenario I replay in my head, rewinding and replaying, backward and forward in time.

In those moments when I can't stop dwelling on it, she's hurting again through me. I don't believe in life after death or reincarnation. She's not hurting anymore. I'm not bearing her pain, only my own. She has always been a part of me. I've known that since the day we met. Now she's gone, and I don't really exist either.

I was unconscious for several hours. I didn't suffer any serious injuries, just a few bumps and bruises and a blow to my spine that led to a herniated disc, but nothing more. One might say it was a miracle that I got out of it alive. Lucky me. But everything's changed since then.

Jazzy. Jazzy is Yasmin. Or Jazz or Jasmine, as she was called by her mother and the loser boyfriends that her mother managed to find in every hole in the US. Jazzy is a daydream, a childhood memory. She's my spirit or my soul or my nostril or my tear duct.

To me, she was a sister. We weren't born to the same parents and, if you looked at us, you wouldn't think we looked alike, but we knew. Talking about her is almost as impossible as talking about the accident. I loved her. It wasn't romantic love. It wasn't sexual. You must have wondered about that by now. It was a love shared by two people who started from the same place even if no one knew it except for them. Maybe it was similar to the kind of love shared by twin sisters. I loved her as one should love oneself, though no one I know ever succeeds in doing so, certainly not me. She was my benchmark, my self-outside-myself. She's been gone for three years, three months, and two days. And with every passing day, I feel as if I've taken a wrong turn and I'm afloat in some nightmarish, flawed, and ridiculous version of my life.

So why do I need my computer so badly? You must have already guessed: that's where all my memories of Jazz are stored. Memories of what she was and what I was – before the accident. The letters she wrote to me and I wrote to her, the journals I kept before and after, memories of Jazz that I hurried to record before they faded and got mixed up in my head. Not to mention her letters that you've deleted from my email, you son of a bitch! Good thing you have a safe. Take the best possible care of them, they're worth far more than your miserable life.

I don't have the strength to curse you anymore. I'm tired now. Send me Jazz's next letter from New York. I need to feel close to her for a bit.

Fuck you. Who are you and what do you want from me?

Liz.

Subject: What/If

Dear Liz. As requested, I'll call you Liz. As I read about your accident, I was reminded of this passage that I came across among your files:

"What if I'd been born on a different day? If you weren't such a good singer? If you'd stayed in New York? If you'd had the 'flu during that conference and we'd never met? If I'd stood in line at the armory just a few more minutes that Thursday and caught the 'flu from the soldier in front of me and told you: 'Forget it, I'm too sick to go out. Let's stay home.' If we'd chosen a different club? If the music had been bad and we'd decided to split an hour earlier? If only I'd ignored that last song. What if I'd insisted on staying for just one more song? If you'd given that long-haired dude who wanted to talk to you a chance and lingered in conversation for just a few more moments? If I'd left my coat at the club and gone back to find it? If you'd looked for your keys for five seconds longer? Just five seconds. What if I'd sneezed and looked for a tissue? If I'd drunk less and laughed less? If I hadn't stopped to look at that neon sign in the parking lot that had one burnt-out letter, giving it a whole different meaning? If our fucking motorcycle had stalled just one time? If it had rained, forcing us to borrow a car from the kibbutz? If you'd ridden just a little slower or just a bit faster? If the traffic light had turned green or if another light had turned red? These

thoughts haunt me. What if?"

If only your "what ifs" were, indeed, "ifs" and not "if onlys." I'm sorry for what happened to you, Liz, but please know that I was not involved in your accident. I wish I had answers to the questions that mar your sleep but, unfortunately, I have none. If you're worried that I'll try to toss you some words of wisdom or trite aphorisms such as "life must go on," rest assured that I've no intention of trying to offer you consolation for something that cannot be consoled.

It may upset you to read this, but I'd like you to know that I care about you. I know I have no right to, but I feel obligated to do so. I shall now return to my miserable life (if I may use your warranted description) and stop writing. My ex-wife used to say that a good friend should know when to talk and when to keep quiet. I excel in the latter. I'll revert to my silence now. I attach the letter you requested.

I have two questions for you this time: What was your life like right after the accident? And why do you loathe the name Eliza?

Warm regards,
Someone

Subject: OMG, my darling pancreas!

How's that soldier you told me about in your last letter? I hope they found a place for him to sleep on weekends and such. Maybe you can just make a little room for him in your bed? Is he hot? Is he on fire? Is he doable?

There's so much happening here. I think I no longer feel completely like an alien. I mean, I don't stand there like a weirdo with my mouth gaping open looking up at the skyscrapers every time I leave my apartment.

The biggest news is that Theo has finally shown me his work!!! Well, to be honest, he didn't exactly "show" it to me. I peeked, but that's not the point. As you know, since we began working together, I've been nudging him to show me what he's been working on at the other side of the studio. The cheeky fellow arranged his workspace in such a way that, no matter where I turned, I couldn't see his canvas. At first, I just asked if I could take a look and he always replied, "No, not yet." I eventually stopped asking, but enough is enough, man! It's been three months!

A few days ago, when he went out for a pack of cigarettes, I snuck into his side of the studio. Yes, I know what you're thinking, I also can't believe I waited so long to take a peek. Anyway, you won't believe what I saw! There wasn't even a single painting of my pussy!!! All the electronic devices and shit

SNUNIT LISS | 55

hanging from his easel weren't for lighting purposes as I first thought but sophisticated cameras and screens and mirrors, and the weirdest part – are you getting this?? – none of them were directed at me while he's working. They're all pointed at him!! On and around the easel are photos of him looking at me and monitors continuously playing videos of him looking at me as he paints. There were three huge self-portraits of him looking at my naked body. Anyhoo, all this time he wasn't even painting me, he was painting himself looking at my pussy! Can you imagine?!

I was shocked because it looked like a scene from CSI Miami. But then I suddenly realized that these paintings were really sad, like heartbreaking, sis: blue, red, and purple shadows of Theo, detached and captivated and isolated as he's staring at my fucking vagina.

I stood there naked with tears in my eyes. I was so engrossed in the paintings that I didn't even notice that he'd returned and was standing right beside me. He started shouting at me, "What are you doing? You shouldn't be here!" I swear it was the first time I've heard him utter anything other than a whisper.

I didn't know what to do. I just moved closer to him and said: "Theo, I'm so sorry about everything." And I didn't mean I was sorry I'd peeked since that's my fucking right, but for everything he'd probably gone through that made him so sad and detached. I hugged him and he didn't shrink away from me, although he didn't exactly hug me back. He started crying, too.

We stood there for a while. I'm naked and hugging and he's tall and fully dressed and not hugging, and we're both wailing

like hungry kittens. He eventually pulled away and lowered his eyes, apologized for "losing his temper" (Jesus, how I hate that shitty American politeness) and said I could go home for the day. I said there was no way I was leaving him alone in such a state, so I got dressed and forced him to come out with me.

I seriously have no idea how he even survives in this city. He's so delicate that you wouldn't notice him even in a small room. On these crazy streets, where everything just roars around you, he's completely submerged. People bump into him on the sidewalk and just keep walking through him. We walked for a while in silence until I noticed a vibrant ice cream parlor and pulled him in. At first, he protested, saying he wasn't in the mood, but I managed to convince him not to let me eat by myself.

He sampled every flavor until he decided on the one he wanted, sitting across from me like a six-foot-two-inch five-year-old licking ice cream from a gigantic cone. He looked so ridiculous, like an anorexic giant on a binge diet, that I couldn't help but burst out laughing. I was worried he'd be offended or something, but he gradually began to smile. His smile was soon replaced by a burst of laughter, desperate, sounding almost like a cough. He tried to stop but he couldn't. We both sat there, bursting our seams laughing, and the awkwardness between us melted like our ice creams. Once he composed himself, he said, "You know, it's a good thing you peeked. I wouldn't have dared to invite you to look at my work on my own."

"You're really fucked up, aren't you, Theo?" I snickered at him.

"I think it's a little something we have in common, my dear," he replied in the same coin.

That's all babe, I've got to go. Catch me on Skype when it's Friday night on your side of the world, just like we planned.

Love you.

Your darling central nervous system

Subject: Letter Number 7

Hello, scum. I decided to number my letters to ensure you don't attempt to inform me again that my letter doesn't count because it doesn't follow clause 67c of the International Stalker Treaty or something.

Not that it's any of your business, but I hate the name Eliza because it sounds like something that happens when you take too many antidepressants, like something stuck in your throat. In Hebrew, it means "joyful" and who can be joyful all the time? Certainly not me. Besides, it's a name for little old ladies with blue hair.

In case you're really interested, Eliza was my grandmother, my dad's mother. I never knew her. She died of malaria when my dad was a little kid. How can you name a child after someone who died from a disease?! But at least now I have the dubious pleasure reserved for those named after dead people: I already know what my name looks like on a tombstone. Actually, there's something comforting about that. In short, Eliza was my grandmother and I'm Liz, or if you must, Lizzie. That's all.

If you want to know what happened after the accident, you'll need to ask someone else because my memories from that time are fuzzy. The hospital, Jazz's funeral, the pain... I seem to recall it all through a fog of shock and painkillers. I remember the

details, but the figure standing in the midst of it all doesn't look or feel like me. I was hospitalized for several days, underwent various tests and the doctors recommended physical therapy. "It's imperative to gradually return to your normal life," they said. "It's imperative not to stay in bed all day." People tell you so many things in these situations.

I guess I was in some kind of shock. Jazzy died. The fact that someone could exist and then suddenly cease to exist still astounds me. You're a whole, entire world to yourself and just a grain of dust in the scheme of time and the universe. Everything you are and everything you love can end in an instant and the rest will ultimately spoil and rot away slowly. I wrestled with these insights for a little while, but I lost rather quickly.

After the shock wore off, I found myself crying on the couch at my parents' house. I couldn't bring myself to return to my apartment in the kibbutz, so I ended up moving back in with them. I cried for days, nights, weeks, months. I think I cried an entire lifetime – for Jazz and for me and for everything I still didn't know. It wasn't the discreet weeping of the noble heroines I'd read about in books, who swallowed their sobs and only allowed a solitary crystal tear to run down their cheek. It was an ugly cry brought on by rage. It was wails, contortions, bodily fluids, and teeth. I cried and kicked and fumed and envied... a terrible envy that grips me till this day, of anyone who still doesn't know that something like that could happen to them. I envied anyone who strode with ease along the lane outside the window, any character who moved with ease on TV, on an ad on my computer, or in a book. I was jealous of who I was before

the accident and of the plans for the future I'd made with Jazzy.
I envied my parents for their ability to wake up every morning,
leave the house, and head to work, because their lives, after all,
had gone on when mine came to a halt.

At that time, I could hardly move from the excruciating pain
in my lower back. I hobbled around like a bad caricature of
someone who was born with no joints. Electric currents of heat,
cold, and prickling sensations shot up my legs. Such were my
circumstances, stuck in my parents' house for months on end.
They're such gentle people, my parents. I've never heard them
shout or cry in my life. We never talk about emotions in my
house. We never fight. At most, we argue. We can laugh, but
never too loudly. And suddenly, there I was, stuck all day in the
middle of their living room like a beached whale, wetting their
couch with all its salty seawater. My parents tried to push me
back into the sea, but my sorrow was so heavy and burdensome
that it became impossible.

They crept around me on eggshells, drove me to physiotherapy
sessions, which I hated, and tried their best to comfort me. When
I was a teenager, they once attended a parenting workshop in
the hope that it would give them the tools to contend with my
teenage rebellion that swept through their tiny house like a
hurricane. They heard some silly lectures from a psychologist
who was later reported to be a pedophile. But there were no
workshops that could teach parents how to handle a situation
where their adult offspring suddenly turns back into a helpless
infant, someone who can hardly walk, can't stop crying, and lies
on their couch all day not wanting to move.

I heard them losing sleep, I saw the wrinkles on their brows deepen. We were moving backward as if we were on some strange journey through time. They recreated the best womb they could, and I nestled within it, crying and kicking. It was rather odd, but after about eight months, almost out of the blue, I ran out of tears. It didn't become easier or better, but I just knew in my heart and mind that there was no use in crying any longer. Several weeks later, I returned to my apartment in the kibbutz that waited for me like a bubble in which time had stood still. The storm had flung me onto a strange and foreign shore that was my new, crappy life.

My physical condition slowly improved. I was able to move around with more ease. I could walk and sit, but somehow the rules had changed. I can't do what I used to do and I can't be who I used to be before the accident. It's as if I'm in a nightmare – everything around me seems to have remained the same except for the fact that Jazz doesn't exist. And I don't really exist either.

Okay, I've rambled enough for one day. And if I'm already being forced to pour my heart out, I might as well earn some cheap thrills from this fucking deal. So here's a question for you: what did you mean when you wrote, "I don't often leave my home"? Like, at all? Since when? What's the deal with that? How does that work? Oh, and I hope you rot in hell.

Fuck you. Who are you and what do you want from me?

Liz

Subject: Mirror Image

Dear Liz, I'm sorry it took me longer than usual to reply. I spent the last few days trying to imagine your life, envisioning you in my mind's eye lying on your parent's couch, finding it difficult to move, living on measured rations of mobility while your thoughts and emotions don't heed your body's commands.

My life is, if you will, a mirror image of your life at that time. I bear no physical disability that prevents me from leaving my home yet, when I open my front door, I'm overcome by an overwhelming force compelling me to stay amidst my four walls, to avoid the soiling looks and scents of others and reject meaningless socializing.

I can't put my finger on the particular day I became a recluse. Through the course of the past few years, my life has undergone a certain process of dissolution. Over time, I found I had less and less strength or motivation to put on my "normal" face and play the role we're all expected to play when we interact with others.

In fact, it wasn't that long ago that I led an ostensibly fairly normal life. You already know I lived with a woman. You may find it hard to believe, but a sane, wonderful woman, to be exact, once promised to spend the rest of her life with me. It's alright – she's recanted her promise since then... or was it life that recanted its promise? The woman who was my wife and I

ultimately discovered that the promises we had made to each other were bound to those we wanted to be and not to whom we really were. I also had a "day job." You surely know that one cannot make a living from writing books these days. The realm of words, the only place I could conduct myself comfortably, also served as my livelihood. I owned an advertising agency, a small boutique firm with three employees. During my work hours, I served as a pen for hire, selling my words to the highest bidder. I had clients, budgets, meetings, and presentations. I woke up each morning, drove to the office, came back each evening, caressed my wife's neck, breathed her in. I spent my nights writing my books.

And all this time I knew I was pretending. Though I appeared to be functioning, successful even, I felt as if the disguise I had put on would eventually be shed from my body. I was right. Over time, cracks began to appear on the surface of my life. The solid infrastructure on which my daily life was built gradually fell apart. My wife left me. I didn't hold her to blame. She extended me a period of grace long after I abandoned our marital life while we still shared a home.

Leaving for the office every morning became increasingly difficult. On some mornings, I didn't show up at all, while on others I turned up drunk. I gradually lost my ability to carry on the usual mundane conversations, the trivial banter people use in an attempt to forget.

My practice dwindled, as did my patience for the daily routine. My employees quit or were let go and I no longer had

the funds or the will to pay the office rent. Today, I continue to occasionally fuse together some words for the few clients who, for some reason, remain loyal to me, and manage to earn enough to pay for the food I eat and the bills I must pay.

There was no specific day on which I decided to stop leaving my apartment. During that period when I did manage to get myself out of the house each morning, I believed that it made sense to participate in the colossal show called life taking place out there. Yet, slowly, the absurdity of it all became increasingly more vulgar. I found it unbearable to walk down the street and see people talking on their cell phones with garish loudness and greeting each other with empty tokens of politeness. Their looks felt sharp upon my skin. Perhaps I can understand something of what you are going through. Leaving my house and meeting other people began to cause me pain – not actual, physical pain, but one that I find impossible, nonetheless, to bear.

So I stopped going to the office as I no longer had an office. I stopped escorting my wife to visit her parents as I no longer had a wife. I stopped changing my clothes in the morning as I had no reason to do so and I stopped shaving as there was no one to shave for. There's something liberating about this surrender, in the recognition that you are what you are, in abandoning the aspiration to be something else, something better.

I remember the day when I noticed that I hadn't left the house for over a week. The thought did not weigh me down. I lacked for nothing. There were times where I was seized with trembles. Yet, throughout that week, I didn't experience even one such episode. So I tried to see how long I could keep it up. Another

three weeks passed before I next needed to leave my house, and then six weeks after that and two additional months after that. Fortunately, we live in an age where there's hardly a need to step out of the house in order to survive. Almost any product or service can be ordered. Almost anything can be shipped or delivered for a fee.

For special matters, I have Hanan, perhaps the only person apart from you and my clients with whom I maintain regular contact. He usually sleeps on the bench outside my building. Yes, I recognize the irony of the situation. The man who doesn't leave his house enlists the services of a homeless man in a kind of dysfunctional outsourcing.

When I need something that can't be delivered or undertaken in any other way, I simply open my door, peek out and call for Hanan. If he's around, I tell him what I need or want and he knows he'll get paid. I don't think we're very different, he and I. My mother left behind an apartment and a sum of money. His mother, it seems, did not. In another life we could, perhaps, have played opposite roles.

This is me, Liz, this is my life. This time, I won't conclude with a question but with a homework assignment: read through the hostage I sent you. It will tell you more about me than I ever could.

Warm regards,

Someone

The Diary

Dear God, please don't kill Dad. God don't kill Dad. God don't kill Dad. God don't kill Dad. God don't kill Dad. God don't kill Dad. God don't kill Dad

God don't kill Dad God don't kill Dad God don't kill Dad God
don't kill Dad God don't kill Dad God don't kill Dad God don't
kill Dad God don't kill Dad God don't kill Dad God don't kill
Dad God don't kill Dad God don't kill Dad God don't kill Dad
God don't kill Dad God don't kill Dad God don't kill Dad God
don't kill Dad God don't kill Dad God don't kill Dad God don't
kill Dad God don't kill Dad God don't kill Dad God don't kill
Dad God don't kill Dad God don't kill Dad God don't kill Dad

I'm not very good at talking, but I have Trunkelump and I have a diary that Mom bought me and said that when I'm feeling sad I can write in it so I'm writing now. Mom brought Trunkelump and the diary from America where she flew for a conference. I was scared when Mom was away. I was left alone with Dad. I was scared Dad would get mad. I was also scared he'd just not talk to me. I was mostly scared that he'd lock me in the closet all the time but he ended up locking me there just twice and then she was back and I got Trunkelump.

When Mom gave him to me, I wrote to her on my yellow notepad: What's his name?

What would you like to call him? Mom asked.

I thought about it and said: El... Eleph... Elephanti.

And Mom said: That's a rather simple name, isn't it?

I didn't really understand what she meant and Mom said: Maybe we should look for his most prominent feature. I pointed at his trunk so she said: I suggest we call him Trunkelump. So, I nodded yes with my head, though it's a name with so many letters that get stuck in my mouth.

The first day after Mom flew to America was really bad. Jonny bullied me at school. I wanted to use the bathroom during recess but he stood in my way and didn't let me through.

He said: Say you're a fat poopoo head or I won't let you use the bathroom.

I didn't answer but I started sweating behind my ears. My hands were also wet all of a sudden. I almost dropped my backpack. Jonny knows I'm not good at talking and he always bullies me. I hate talking and I hate Jonny. I hate going to school and I don't hate staying home but I do worry there. I'm scared Dad will get mad and I'm also worried about Dad. I didn't answer Jonny so he moved closer and said: The fat poopoo head doesn't wanna talk? Fat poopoo head, say you're a fat poopoo head.

I saw his face get really close to mine and I saw his cheeks turning pink and shaking like he was also a little scared even though he pretends that he's not and he's a lot bigger than me. I didn't say what he told me to say because I knew that, even if I tried, the words would get stuck in my mouth and everyone would laugh at me and he would, too. I didn't do anything. I just stood there like a fat poopoo head and felt the tears rise in my throat and press on the insides of my eyes and I thought to myself in my head: Just don't cry just don't cry and I could feel the tears starting to come out and I wanted the whole world to disappear, Jonny and the stupid school and the pee that was pushing to come out and the words that always got stuck in my mouth.

And the teacher came over and asked: What's going on here? And she told me to come with her and then turned to Jonny and all the other kids who gathered around to see what was happening and said: What is this? Go back to class! She took my hand and started walking really fast and I followed. I never walk fast enough. I really needed to go to the bathroom and I started crying even though I really didn't want to. She noticed that I was crying and stopped to think like she remembered something and

asked me: Do you need to use the restroom? I nodded yes with my head. She walked me back to the bathroom and waited for me outside. I went in and closed the door and peed and then I sat down on the toilet and cried a lot and I was afraid they could hear me outside and I thought about Mom and when she'd come home even though she just left and what would happen at home today and if Dad would get mad.

Then I washed my face and the water splashed on my shirt. I came out and the teacher stood there and the lines on her face looked so straight and her eyes slanted down like she also missed her mom a little and wanted to go home and was also kinda scared of what would happen there. She asked me to come with her and walked me to class.

When school was over, I hurried out of class and lowered my head and ran down the stairs really really fast hoping Jonny wouldn't get a chance to catch me and I went straight home as fast I could.

When I got home, I opened the door and it was dark even though I knew that Dad was there. I closed it carefully behind me and walked through the rooms looking for him. He wasn't in the living room or in the bathroom. He usually doesn't go into the kitchen and he also wasn't in my room. Finally, I found him lying in bed and there was a strange smell. I moved closer and I heard him snoring so I left quietly so he wouldn't wake up. I went to the fridge and took out a bottle of chocolate milk and watched TV.

Trunkelump has a special button that, whenever you press it, he speaks English. I don't speak English. I don't speak Hebrew very well, either. I mean, I understand Hebrew but the whole speaking thing doesn't work so well for me. When I try to speak, the words always get stuck in my mouth. When I say Dad, for example, I end up saying Da... Da... Da... Da... Da... Da... Daddddd. And the 'D' can get stuck in my mouth like even a thousand times. And then Dad gets annoyed and I give up and just sit there silent and angry at what kind of boy I am who can't speak even though I know all the words in my head.

But Trunkelump can talk with no problem. He can only say a few things and not everything he wants but what he does know he says with no problem. I know he's just a stuffed animal but it makes me feel good that Trunkelump can say things with no problem. When I hold him, I feel that I can also say things with no problem. And in English. So I take Trunkelump wherever I go. I see kids staring strangely at me at school but they stared strangely at me before, too, so it doesn't really matter. I put Trunkelump in my backpack and whenever I feel a little weird, I squeeze him and he talks. I did it in class a couple of times and the teacher said it's not allowed and took Trunkelump away. But when she took him from me, I screamed and cried and started yelling and running down the hall. I didn't plan to do it but I was scared she wouldn't return him to me and I didn't want him to be under her desk and maybe another kid would take him. The shouting and crying

didn't get stuck in my throat like words do. The teacher stopped our lesson and ran after me down the hall. She told me to stop and when she reached me, she sat down beside me and asked: What's wrong?

El... El... Elephant. You too... tookkk. You took my elephaaaaant!

Do you want me to give it back to you? she asked

I nodded yes with my head. I prefer saying what I want with my head because it saves the whole problem of the words getting stuck.

She looked at me quietly and said: If it was any other student I wouldn't return the elephant until the end of the day, but because it's you I'm willing to compromise. I'll give you the elephant, but you have to promise me that you won't press his button in the middle of our lessons because it interrupts the class. Do you promise?

I nodded yes with my head.

So we have a deal? she asked and held out her hand.

I shook her hand and we returned to class together. When we walked into the classroom, the kids were all running around, yelling and talking. She walked me back to my seat and said: The party's over, quiet please. Return to your seats, everyone. She gave me back Trunkelump and I felt all the kids staring at me and I felt an uncomfortable pinch of embarrassment in my stomach but I was also happy and I hugged Trunkelump and had to keep myself from pressing the button because I promised the teacher. And I don't press it during class anymore.

Mom bought Trunkelump in America but he's actually an elephant from Africa. That's what she told me when I asked her where he came from. Anyway, these are the things Trunkelump says:

Help me, I need you!

Thank you for coming to Africa to rescue me.

You are a great friend of the animals.

I am thirsty, do you have some water?

I will never forget what you did for me.

And sometimes he just makes the kind of noise an elephant makes.

Besides Trunkelump, I also have books as my friends. Mom says it's important to read. When we meet people we don't know, Mom often tells them that I knew all my letters when I was just two years old. When she says that she speaks more slowly and opens her mouth bigger so that they can all hear what she said and no one will miss it. I don't really understand why it matters because I don't think I knew what to do with all those letters when I was two.

Mom says that every well-bred person should read books. I'm not sure what well-bred means, maybe it means someone who comes from a large family of people who know things, that whoever belongs to that family must know secrets that are only written in books. Maybe before well-bred people accept someone into their family, they give him a secret test and ask him special questions that you can only find their answers to in books. Like only if he knows that Captain Nemo was the captain of the Nautilus from Twenty Thousand Leagues under the Sea can then he belong to that family. And then they throw a big happy party like the kind you see families have on TV and suddenly he has grandparents and aunts and uncles like some of the kids at school have and everyone loves him and they eat cake together and sing songs. And they're all well-bred together.

Mom says that whoever reads books becomes a better person. I'm not sure that's true because sometimes bad things happen in books. I love my books because, whenever I read them, I

sometimes feel like I'm really in them. Like when I'm reading Around the World in 80 Days, I can sometimes forget that I'm at home or at school and feel like I'm on a faraway train or a steamer, which is probably a really good ship, far, far away in the world, surrounded by ocean. And Jonny can't come anywhere near me and Phileas Fogg and Passepartout need my help to make it around the world on time so there's no way they'll put me in the closet.

God don't kill Dad. God don't kill Dad. God don't kill Dad. God
don't kill Dad. God don't kill Dad. God don't kill Dad God don't
kill Dad God don't kill Dad God don't kill Dad God don't kill Dad
God don't kill Dad God don't kill Dad God don't kill Dad God
don't kill Dad God don't kill Dad God don't kill Dad God don't
kill Dad God don't kill Dad God don't kill Dad God don't kill Dad
God don't kill Dad God don't kill Dad God don't kill Dad God
don't kill Dad God don't kill Dad God don't kill Dad God don't
kill Dad God don't kill Dad God don't kill Dad God don't kill Dad
God don't kill Dad God don't kill Dad God don't kill Dad God
don't kill Dad God don't kill Dad God don't kill Dad God don't
kill Dad God don't kill Dad God don't kill Dad God don't kill Dad
God don't kill Dad God don't kill Dad God don't kill Dad God
don't kill Dad God don't kill Dad God don't kill Dad God don't
kill Dad God don't kill Dad God don't kill Dad God don't kill Dad
God don't kill Dad God don't kill Dad God don't kill Dad God
don't kill Dad God don't kill Dad God don't kill Dad God don't
kill Dad God don't kill Dad God don't kill Dad God don't kill Dad
God don't kill Dad God don't kill Dad God don't kill Dad God
don't kill Dad God don't kill Dad God don't kill Dad God don't
kill Dad God don't kill Dad God don't kill Dad God don't kill Dad
God don't kill Dad God don't kill Dad God don't kill Dad God
don't kill Dad God don't kill Dad God don't kill Dad God don't
kill Dad God don't kill Dad God don't kill Dad God don't kill Dad
God don't kill Dad God don't kill Dad God don't kill Dad God

don't kill Dad God don't kill Dad God don't kill Dad God don't
kill Dad God don't kill Dad God don't kill Dad God don't kill Dad
God don't kill Dad God don't kill Dad God don't kill Dad God
don't kill Dad God don't kill Dad God don't kill Dad God don't
kill Dad God don't kill Dad God don't kill Dad God don't kill Dad

Some days are good, some days are so-so, and some days are not good. I can usually already tell by morning what kind of day it's going to be by looking at Dad, and then I try to guess how I should behave. If it's not going to be a good day, it's better that I don't try to talk at all and that Dad notices me as little as possible, because a not-so-good day can easily turn into a really bad day but sometimes, just sometimes, a not-so-good day turns into a so-so day and that's really good.

Yesterday was not a good day and I knew it from the start. Dad was cloudy. This is how not-so-good days usually begin. I can see a sort of large, gray cloud around him, turning him sort of darker and making it harder for him to see everyone else. He woke up, but not exactly. I got up, got dressed, brushed my teeth, organized my backpack, and took Trunkelump, and all this time Dad just sat on the living room couch without moving. I went outside quietly without trying to say goodbye. On the way to school I thought about Dad and if he'd be okay and if he'd eat something before I came back.

It was actually an alright day at school. I sat with Trunkelump as usual. I try not to do anything special so kids won't notice me and if there's a day when Jonny and his friends are busy or bullying someone else, then it works. I thought about Dad all day and what would happen when I came home. I was also worried about him and wanted to see if he was awake.

When I climbed up the stairs to our apartment, I already tried to feel what was going on up there. Maybe Dad's day had changed. I'm always looking for clues. Sometimes you can hear and feel things even before you actually see them. At first when I came in, everything was fine. He was sitting at the table looking like he did in the morning. I tried to be as quiet as possible. I wanted to go straight to my room but my tummy was making noises. I decided to eat first. I went to the kitchen and opened the fridge and tried to be quiet. There was cheese and bread so I decided to make a sandwich. I wanted to use the cutting board Mom slices bread on so I won't leave crumbs. I took a chair and tried to reach the cabinet where the cutting board was stored. I stood on the chair but the board was still too far away. I stretched a little more and reached out my hand to touch the cutting board. Just as I reached it, the chair toppled over and I fell with it and a couple of dishes nearby also fell and crashed to the floor making a very big noise. I was sprawled on the floor and it hurt and there were sharp pieces of broken plates all around me and I knew that now this day had turned really, really bad.

When I looked up, I saw Dad standing above me with his cloud. He yelled: What did you do? And I cried and he said: I can't deal with you today. And he grabbed my arm and I already knew what was going to happen. I knew it since I woke up that morning. He dragged me to the closet and pushed me inside so that I'd sit on the closet floor and closed the doors and locked them with the special lock and key. He looked at me through the closet door shutters and walked away. A second later, he unlocked the door, threw my backpack at me and locked the closet door again.

I cried. After I stopped crying, I looked through the shutters and tried to see what Dad was doing. Sometimes he calms down pretty quickly and opens the closet door. I knew it wouldn't happen this time but I still hoped. I heard him scooping up the broken dishes in the kitchen. I later heard him going to the living room. He didn't turn on the light but, from his shadow, I could tell that he'd picked up a bottle and started drinking.

In class the teacher told us that God always looks down at us and whoever does bad things will go to Hell when they die, that it's a really awful place where you burn and burn even when you're not even alive. Whoever does good things will also die, but at least they'll go to Heaven, which is probably a much better place to be in if you're already dead.

Dad just sat there and I was getting cold and slowly my body started shaking. I was hungry and my tummy made loud noises and again the tears started coming out. Trunkelump was out there and I wanted to hug him and squeeze him so he'd talk a bit. I wanted Dad to let me out of the closet and I felt my body shaking more and more and I was angry at him. Why was he just sitting there drinking from his bottle and leaving me in the closet? I knew he was doing something bad. I started to worry about him. When Dad does bad things and I get angry at him I start to worry about him. If he does bad things, he could die and go to Hell. I decided to stop being angry. I took out my diary and my pencil from my backpack and decided to write to God again and ask him not to kill Dad. If God looks down and sees everyone, he'll probably be able to read this. If he sees me asking

him not to kill Dad even though Dad locked me in the closet, he'll probably forgive him.

I didn't know how many times you're supposed to ask God for such things so I wrote 100 times asking him not to kill Dad. Because 100 is a really big number and if God reads that I asked 100 times for him not to kill Dad, he'll probably understand that it's serious and forgive him. After about 70 times, my hand started to hurt but I didn't give up because I needed to do this to protect Dad.

When I was done, I counted and found out that I actually only wrote it ninety-seven times so I added three more and counted again and this time there were 101 so I erased one. I don't know how much time I spent writing and counting but, when I was done, I noticed that I wasn't shaking anymore and I felt better because I was pretty sure that this would convince God so I was less worried about Dad. I was still hungry and still cold but suddenly it was easier. Sometimes it's easier for me to just be in the closet because at least when I'm in there I don't have to worry that Dad will lock me in the closet and then the thing that I'm most worried about disappears. In the closet, I also don't need to be careful about anything or try to speak.

I think I fell asleep because I woke up when Mom opened the closet door. I saw her standing above me. She didn't say anything. I was lying on the closet floor and her head hovered high above me like a balloon with really sad eyes in its middle. She held out her hand, helped me stand up and said quietly: You must be hungry. Come to the kitchen. Before I left, I grabbed

the diary because I didn't want Mom and definitely not Dad to see what I wrote there. On the way to the kitchen, I saw Dad sleeping on the couch in the living room and the bottle was still beside him but it was empty.

God don't kill Dad God

don't kill Dad God don't kill Dad

My mom and dad are both doctors but they're not physicians. They don't treat people. My mom studied linguistics, which is not the same as logistics but it's a bit similar. It's like studying the logic of words. She's an important doctor for Hebrew words, and everywhere we go people know her name even when she doesn't tell it to them and when they look at her their eyes get wider.

Mom says that it's very exciting that we're taking part in shaping a new language and that it's a family effort because Mom has to work very hard for it and Dad and I let her. Mom explained once that the Hebrew language is like a very special ancient palace and that new words want to enter it all the time. My mom is the gatekeeper of this palace, deciding if the new words will be allowed to enter or kept out. She sits with her friends at the university and they look at each word closely, turn it over and examine it just like doctors do with people. Just like a detective, my mom sometimes needs to use logic to discover where a word came from and which words are its friends and sisters. So she opens old books and uses a special phone to call other gatekeepers all over the world.

If the word fits, Mom and her friends in the place called The Academy of the Hebrew Language allow the word to enter the palace and write it down in all sorts of important places where all the Hebrew words are written and they tell everyone about it and the newspapers sometimes even write about it and repeat the things Mom said. I like reading those articles. Whenever I read

Mom's name in the newspaper, I suddenly feel bigger.

It's always important for people to speak correctly when they're next to Mom. Whenever we go somewhere and meet someone, the teachers at school for example, they all use longer words and also pat my head and smile at me. It's important to Mom that I speak well and she corrects me sometimes. For example, if she read my diary, she'd have said that you don't write whenever but instead you should use when, or the occasion. But in my case, she doesn't need to correct me a lot because I don't speak that much anyway. Mom doesn't like it when I use words like poo or shit. She said it stains the Hebrew language. I don't understand how it's possible to get a language dirty if the dirty words are also a part of that language. Maybe those words need to be erased from Mom's books, but then what words will people use when they see something dirty or when they're angry at someone or when they want to hurt him?

Dad is also a doctor but not of words. Dad is a doctor of physics, which means that he's a doctor of how the world works. Dad says that things don't just happen and that there are laws for how the universe works, that everything happens because there's a law that makes it happen that way. For example, if you drop a plate, it's because Earth pulled it down since it's strong and has gravity. Many things have gravity but, because Earth is so big, then all the things on it are pulled toward it. Even the moon, which is smaller than Earth and isn't even on it, is pulled toward it. But the sun is bigger, so Earth is pulled toward the sun, I think.

I don't really understand how it is that all things in the world happen because of these laws. There are lots of things that don't

happen exactly the same way each time, as if they don't have any
laws. For example, sometimes Dad gets mad at me for something
and sometimes he doesn't. And there are kids who have moms
who smile easily, like Roy from class, whose mom always comes
to pick him up from school at the end of the day, and kids with
moms who really need to make an effort in order to smile, like
mine. I guess there are lots of rules I don't know yet and that's
why people like my dad try to understand them.

Mom says Dad is brilliant, which doesn't mean he shines and
sparkles like a clean dish but that he's really, really smart. Mom
and Dad met at the university. She was keeping Hebrew safe
and he was examining the laws of the universe and I guess they
realized right away that they needed to form a sort of team of
detectives.

Dad once worked at the university, like Mom, and he even won
an important prize awarded to special doctors who study the laws
of the world and people gave him a special payment called a grant
so he could continue to examine the laws of the universe.

Although Dad is a brilliant physicist, there's one law of the
universe that he's been trying to prove for many years and can't
succeed. To prove something in physicists' words means that he
needs to put together all sorts of numbers and letters that are
called formulas and show everyone that the law is real and not
just something in Dad's head like his thoughts. Dad spent many
years in his office at the university and tried to write the formula
of this law but he failed and eventually they stopped giving him
the grant and he stopped going to the university and working
there.

I don't exactly understand this law that Dad knows and can't manage to write. I asked him to explain it to me a few times, so he wrote all kinds of letters in English on the board in his study and drew lines and shapes and started talking really fast. He picked up a couch cushion, threw it on the floor and picked it up again and then took another cushion and brought it closer to the other cushion and suddenly pulled them away from each other quickly. Then he looked at me and saw that I was just standing there staring at him without moving and realized that I didn't understand anything, so he stopped talking. I guess I'm not brilliant like Dad.

I think Dad feels about this law of his like I do when I can't speak, like something just stopped in his head or in his life and he can't work it out even though he knows all the parts. I see him sitting at his desk for many hours or drawing shapes and numbers on his board. I hear him talking to himself in a low voice, saying names of numbers and letters in English. Eventually he always leans his head down low between his hands and looks over the papers on his desk. He can sit like that for a very long time.

Dad says there is no God, there are just people who are too stupid or too lazy to understand the true laws of the universe. Dad says that people need to give a name and a face to things they don't understand so they invent legends about a great Father in the sky who watches over them so they can keep living their little lives. I don't know what the difference is between big lives and little lives, but that's what Dad says. I'm scared that, if Dad's wrong, then these things he says upset God even more than when he locks me in the closet. So that's why I try to protect him and

write to God for him, just in case.

If God is like a great dad in the sky and if he sometimes does bad things, I wonder if there are people trying to protect him from going to hell, too. Who do they write to?

I'm sitting under the blankets in my room holding a flashlight and writing in my diary and the door is closed. I'm trying not to listen but it's hard. I hate it when Mom and Dad fight. Hate it hate it hate it. I wish they'd stop. I wish my bed could turn into a train or a steamer that sails around the world. If that could happen, I'd never come back. Not even after eighty days.

Mom says: You must pull yourself together. I can't come home every evening to this graveyard.

Dad says: Listen to Her Majesty! I don't uphold the palace to standards you approve of?

And Mom says: Don't play dumb, you know exactly what I mean. I can't deal with this... this... darkness. You need to take care of yourself. I consulted with Rosen from the Department of Psychology and he recommended...

And Dad shouts: Rosen? That quack? How dare you speak to others about me? Especially with that loser from the Department of Charlatan Studies!

And Mom says: I had to talk to someone. We can't leave it all locked up in this house. I can't take it anymore. It's not right, it's not healthy for you, it's not healthy for the boy.

And Dad says: Look who's talking? You ran away from your responsibilities. All you do is run away. All these years you've been running, ever since I met you. It's so easy for you to collect your awards and adulations all around the world while I stay here taking care of your child.

And I think Mom starts to cry and says: Taking care? Taking care? Of my child? You... You... For heaven's sake, that's not how you take care of someone.

And Dad says: I don't see you doing any better.

And Mom says: We can't all fall apart with you. Someone must go on living. Someone needs to be the breadwinner. I can't perish here with you within these walls. You need to learn to let go. You need help. We need help.

And Dad says: Find help for yourself first before you presume to turn to incompetent fools who believe their fantasies are science so they can fix your broken husband.

And then it's quiet.

And then he says: At least I'm here with the boy. At least I'm here with him instead of running away.

And Mom says: One can run away even without leaving the house.

And now they're both quiet. And someone goes into the bedroom and slams the door shut.

I don't know why Mom and Dad even fight. They barely talk to each other even though they don't stutter. Mom comes home late from the university every night when Dad's already asleep or just staring at the TV or at the wall. He never asks her how she is or how her day was and she doesn't walk up to him to say hello like you see on TV sometimes.

Even though Mom's a doctor of words, she doesn't like to talk that much. Maybe it's because she loves the words so much that it's hard for her to use them for no special reason. It's like the fancy dishes we have stored in the cupboard that we're not

allowed to use because they're only for special occasions. But we never have a special occasion. When Mom's at home, Dad never locks me in the closet, but sometimes when it's so quiet I want to lock myself in the closet and disappear.

Today was a good day, the kind of day that begins with only a very small cloud over Dad's head. I spent the whole day at school hoping that everything would be fine when I got home and it really was. When I came home, Dad wasn't drinking from the bottle and wasn't even asleep. He was sitting in the living room drinking coffee. I walked over and carefully sat down next to him. He was watching a sitcom on TV so I watched it too and he laughed a couple of times, so I laughed, too. And when I laughed, he looked at me but not with angry eyes, but with eyes that smile together with the mouth.

When the show was over, he asked me if I wanted to solve a crossword puzzle together and I was very happy because that's what we do on the best days. I like crossword puzzles. There's no talking needed to solve them. Many times, I know the answers from books or TV shows. It's enough to know the words and then you just arrange the letters, each one in a separate box. You don't need to try to pronounce the letters together. They stay there locked up in their boxes and can't come out suddenly and cause trouble.

So I nodded yes with my head and Dad looked for the newspaper and found a crossword puzzle and brought us each a pencil. He placed the paper on the table and we sat down next to each other on the couch in front of the table. He read the clue and, if I knew the answer, I wrote it down with my pencil and didn't even have to try to say it out loud. And if I didn't know the answer

Dad would say what he thought the solution was and I would signal yes or no with my head. I always nodded yes because Dad was always right because he's brilliant.

Afterward, there were a few letter boxes left that didn't work out so we checked the answers again and if there were any mistakes we erased the letters and thought of new solutions. At the end, the crossword puzzle was full of letters that were arranged neatly in their boxes and I felt that my tummy was smiling. Dad told me that I did a good job.

And then suddenly Dad put his hand on my shoulder and looked at me in a different way than he usually does and said: I know it's not easy with me but I want you to know that it's not your fault. You know that I love you very much, right?

I didn't know what to say so I just nodded yes with my head.

A few days ago, I had a really, really bad day at school. I felt it coming. Jonny and his friends stared at me even more strangely than usual like they were checking where I was going all the time, and it made me not want to go anywhere and just stare at my knees until I turned into a boy-shaped little ball and the ball would get smaller and smaller until no one could ever see it again.

Once I couldn't hold it anymore, I went to the bathroom during recess. I walked into the stall but couldn't close the door. Suddenly I saw that Ron, who was friends with Jonny, was pushing the door and coming into the stall with me. He yelled: Come on, he's over here. And then Jonny and another friend of his, I don't know his name, came into the stall, too, and there was barely room inside for everyone and they closed the door. Jonny said here's the fat poopoo head and I felt my throat go dry and my whole body freeze.

And Jonny said, We finally caught this fat poopoo head. Fat poopoo head needs to go potty cause that's where all the poopoo goes and his friends laughed. Jonny's friend whose name I don't know lifted the toilet seat and pushed me inside and my backpack fell to the floor and Ron and Jonny laughed and then Ron said, Wait a minute you need to take off your pants before you go to the bathroom, so pick him up. Then the other friend started to pick me up and I wanted to scream at him to let me go and to kick and scratch his face and bite his nose until I tear it from his face and spit it out so he'd bleed all over the place but I couldn't move

or make a sound come out of my throat. Jonny pulled down my pants and underwear and pushed me back into the toilet and Ron said good now flush it.

There were a thousand thoughts in my head. I wished I was in the submarine Nautilus that no one even knew about, and I could just go down the drain in it and sail through the sewer until I reached the sea and, there, I'd continue to live under the water without seeing anyone else ever again and forget all about this place. Forget about this stinky bathroom with its freezing water and Jonny the jerk and Ron and their friend and this stupid school and Dad with his bottles and his clouds and Mom with the Hebrew she keeps guarding at the university and all the words that always get stuck in my mouth and about the closet.

And I wished I was a robot like in the book I, Robot so I couldn't feel anything, and I'd live in a power plant on a faraway planet and nothing around me would exist or be real and it was just me and the power plant. And I imagined I had a special weapon that can both shoot and cut things with fire and how I'd pull it out of my pocket from my pants that were now hanging soaking wet around my ankles and shoot Jonny's friend in the head and blast it off until he stops laughing and how I cut Jonny's hand off and he starts crying and begging me to stop but I don't stop and cut his other hand off too and there's lots of blood everywhere and Jonny cries and then I shoot his stupid friend Ron in the mouth and he stops laughing too and I'd leave the bathroom and run away and I'd be able to talk with no problem and nobody would laugh at me or look at me strangely ever again... but none

of that happened and Jonny told Ron to flush the toilet again as the poopoo didn't go down the drain.

And then suddenly someone opened the door and asked what was going on here and I saw that it was the teacher. I saw that she noticed me and the look on her face changed all of sudden. She was quiet for a moment and then she yelled: What are you doing? Jonny, Ron and their friend ran away. She bent over toward me and asked: Are you okay? And picked me up and saw that my pants were down and said oh dear and pulled them back up quickly. I grabbed my backpack from the floor and took out Trunkelump because I wanted to make sure he was okay. My whole body shook. And the teacher said: I'm sorry. I'm so sorry.

And I squeezed Trunkelump and he said: Thank you for coming to Africa to rescue me.

And the teacher took a deep breath.

And Trunkelump said: I will never forget what you did for me.

After a while, the teacher helped me stand up and took my hand and said: Come with me. And even though the bell had already rung, she didn't hurry to class or ask me to go in. Instead, she walked me to the principal's office. She took my hand and I followed her. My hand trembled in her hand and the air trembled inside my body.

She told me to wait for her on the chair outside the principal's office and walked in without knocking and shut it loudly behind her. I heard the teacher yelling and the principal yelling and the teacher saying: I warned you, I warned you something like this would happen. They stripped off his clothes. When I heard her say that the tears rose up my throat and in my eyes again and

suddenly I noticed that all my clothes were wet and Trunkelump was also wet from my clothes.

When the teacher walked out, the principal followed her and put her hand on my shoulder in a strange way and looked at me. I was worried she'd be mad at me. The principal told the teacher: I'll take care of the class. And she walked away with this kind of serious face. The teacher told me: You don't need to go back to class today. I'll take you home. And she took my hand again and we left the school and walked to her blue car and she opened the door and fastened the seatbelt for me in the backseat. I was worried about what Dad would do when he saw me come home early with wet clothes and a wet elephant.

The teacher drove up to my house and got out of the car with me and took my hand and my backpack and I held Trunkelump in my other hand and she walked me to the stairs. She asked: Is there anyone home at this hour? And I said: Da... Da... Da... Daddddddd. She stopped and thought for a moment and asked: Will you be alright from here? And I didn't know what to say. I didn't want to be in school so I just nodded yes with my head and she said goodbye.

I opened the door quietly and looked for Dad and saw that he was asleep in bed and I was happy because I didn't want him to ask why I was home and get angry. I went to my room and got into bed and took out my books from my bag and tried to read but I couldn't. I guess I fell asleep like that because, late that evening, Mom woke me up and asked if anything had happened at school today because the secretary of her department told her that someone from the school had called when she was in

an important meeting. I didn't answer so she said: Go take a shower.

The next day, I was really scared to go back to school and that morning I tried to get Dad mad at me so he'd lock me in the closet although he never locks me in the closet in the mornings but I tried anyway and he just yelled at me: What the hell is the matter with you? And he opened the front door and left me on the front step and handed me my backpack. I was late and walked quietly into class but the teacher wasn't mad and didn't tell me to get a tardy slip from the principal's office. She just walked over to me and placed her hand on my head. I was afraid I'd run into Jonny and Ron and that stupid friend of theirs so I didn't leave the classroom all day and even though I really needed to go I didn't use the bathroom. But I didn't see them at school that day or on any of the days after that or since then. I didn't see them at school ever again.

God don't kill Dad God don't kill Dad God don't kill Dad God
don't kill Dad God don't kill Dad God don't kill Dad God don't
kill Dad God don't kill Dad God don't kill Dad God don't kill Dad
God don't kill Dad God don't kill Dad God don't kill Dad God
don't kill Dad God don't kill Dad God don't kill Dad God don't
kill Dad God don't kill Dad God don't kill Dad God don't kill Dad
God don't kill Dad God don't kill Dad God don't kill Dad God
don't kill Dad God don't kill Dad God don't kill Dad God don't
kill Dad God don't kill Dad God don't kill Dad God don't kill Dad
God don't kill Dad God don't kill Dad God don't kill Dad God
don't kill Dad God don't kill Dad God don't kill Dad God don't
kill Dad God don't kill Dad God don't kill Dad God don't kill Dad
God don't kill Dad God don't kill Dad God don't kill Dad God
don't kill Dad God don't kill Dad God don't kill Dad God don't
kill Dad God don't kill Dad God don't kill Dad God don't kill Dad
God don't kill Dad God don't kill Dad God don't kill Dad God
don't kill Dad God don't kill Dad God don't kill Dad God don't
kill Dad God don't kill Dad God don't kill Dad God don't kill Dad
God don't kill Dad God don't kill Dad God don't kill Dad God
don't kill Dad God don't kill Dad God don't kill Dad God don't
kill Dad God don't kill Dad God don't kill Dad God don't kill Dad
God don't kill Dad God don't kill Dad God don't kill Dad God
don't kill Dad God don't kill Dad God don't kill Dad God don't
kill Dad God don't kill Dad God don't kill Dad God don't kill Dad
God don't kill Dad God don't kill Dad God don't kill Dad God

don't kill Dad God don't kill Dad God don't kill Dad God don't
kill Dad God don't kill Dad God don't kill Dad God don't kill Dad
God don't kill Dad God don't kill Dad God don't kill Dad God
don't kill Dad God don't kill Dad God don't kill Dad God don't
kill Dad God don't kill Dad God don't kill Dad God don't kill Dad

I haven't written since that happened.

I didn't go to school anymore either. I stayed home.

Mom also didn't go to work and stayed home with me. All day, lots of people that I don't know came to our house to bring lots of food and leave it on the table and sit on the couch and on the chairs and drink coffee and open the windows and the blinds and lots of sunlight came in and if Dad was here he wouldn't allow any of this to happen and would've definitely thrown everyone out and we'd finally get some quiet around here. But Dad's not here.

Grandma came. I didn't see her for a long time but the day after it happened, I heard this crumpled voice call out: Where is he? Where's the boy? I saw her and she looked just like I remembered, only her face was longer and more stretched out and she shouted: Look how much he's grown! Oh, dear what a tragedy, good Lord. And she hugged me before I had a chance to move and she had this strong scent that pinched my nose from the inside. She kissed me with a sticky kiss that I wanted to wipe away but was too embarrassed. I wanted to run away and go to my room but it wasn't polite.

Other than her, many other people that I don't know come to visit. People from Mom's work and maybe from Dad's work from a long time ago and I keep hearing words that I don't exactly understand like such a loss and tragedy and once I heard Grandma whisper to Mom in the kitchen: I knew this would

happen. And I wanted to yell at her, if you knew then why didn't you tell me? And why didn't you tell Mom that she shouldn't be spending all her time protecting Hebrew words but that she should be protecting Dad, too? And why didn't you come here to help Dad? But I didn't say anything.

All day I just want to find somewhere quiet. The air in the house smells like the breath of all these people that I don't know and it stays behind even after they leave and their voices fill the rooms and there's nowhere to sit and think and write in a diary.

Yesterday, I felt like the air just wouldn't go into my body because of all the sounds and smells of other people so I went into the closet and closed the door and tried to imagine that everything was quiet outside and that Dad was sleeping in the other room as usual but I knew that wasn't going to happen and I felt like everything that happened was rising up my throat and shaking my whole body and I squeezed Trunkelump over and over again and wondered why this world is such a poopoo head and why I was in the closet when it happened and why did Jonny put me in the toilet and why he didn't just flush me down the drain and how I couldn't save Dad and why didn't God do what I asked him to even though I wrote to him 100 times and then I remembered what Dad said about God and I felt empty inside.

And then Grandma opened the closet door and said: Oh, poor dear, what are you doing in here? And her smell came into the closet even though I didn't want it there and she started crying again and said: Ayyayai what a tragedy, ayyayai what a tragedy what a tragedy, and pulled me out and I squeezed Trunkelump who said: I am thirsty, do you have some water?

I wait all day for the people to leave our house so I can finally have some quiet at night, but when nighttime arrives and it's quiet all of a sudden and I'm lying in bed, I can't stop thinking. I think about what could have happened if I hadn't upset Dad or if the cloud over his head was smaller that day or if the lock on the closet door had broken or if God had read my diary and listened even though Dad told me in the first place that God isn't even real. I think about what a stupid kid I am that I couldn't help Dad and was just stuck in the closet when it happened. And I think about what could've happened if I'd managed to break the poopoo lock on the closet door or managed to yell loud enough so that all the neighbors in the building and in all the buildings on the street and in the whole city could hear and come to see what happened and open the door and rescue Dad and then he would have felt better and stayed alive and wouldn't have locked me in the closet again and even if he did I wouldn't care as long as he was in the living room.

And I can't stop thinking about all the things that could've happened and all the things I could've maybe done to stop what had happened. That I sat in the closet and saw Dad through the shutters sleeping on the living room couch and suddenly start to cough and throw up again and again, but not sitting up, just coughing and throwing up and shaking all over while I try to break down the closet door so I could help him stand up and give him some water without dropping and breaking any cups and I can't manage to open the closet door and I yell Daddd Daddd Daaaaddd again and again until I start losing my voice but nobody heard me. And I can't stop thinking about what I

could've done to get someone to help. Maybe I could've somehow banged on the walls or lit a fire and sent a smoke signal or tried to catch the sunlight with my glasses and signal to someone in the building across the street with Morse code even though I don't know Morse code and it's just something I read about in my books. I think and think about all the things I could've done before Mom came home and saw Dad lying there and yelled: No No No! No, just not this! Wake up! Talk to me!!! And I watched through the closet door shutters as Mom picked up the phone and I heard her yelling: It's my husband, he's not breathing. She turned and leaned over and slapped his face and kept yelling for him to wake up. After a while there was a knock on the door and Mom opened it and lots of people in strange uniforms and a kind of bed on wheels came in and Mom told them: Hurry he's over here help him!!! And they bent over him and said all sorts of things like: Male in his forties... alcohol poisoning... vomit aspiration... no pulse. And I heard Mom yelling: No! No! And someone asked her: Ma'am, is there anybody else in the house? And suddenly she started screaming. And I heard her running through the house and moving closer to the closet. She unlocked the closet door and I ran to Dad and saw him lying on the couch with throw-up on and all around him. Lots of dirty throw-up. And he looked like he was sleeping in a sort of broken way.

Subject: Letter Number 8

I read the "hostage" you sent me and once again I find myself in a rather strange situation, unsure if this is real or not. After all, if you are truly a writer, as you say you are, you'd be able to make such things up. Or maybe you just stole a diary from the neighbors' kid or something; you're probably capable of something like that as well.

But the yellowing paper and the childish handwriting look too authentic. Somehow, I have a feeling this is something even you'd find difficult to fake. And honestly, I read it all in one breath.

So, assuming this diary is real and is yours, what am I supposed to do with it? Am I supposed to feel sorry for you now? To keep in mind that in every one of your words there's a little, stuttering boy locked in the closet?

Like, what? You want me to be the friend you never had as a child? Someone you can exact your revenge on for the abuse you endured? If all this really happened to you, then I'm truly sorry but it doesn't give you the right to be shitty. Clearly, there wasn't anyone to teach you that this is not the way to make new friends.

If you so desperately want a sincere correspondence, I'm not going to write about myself after I read all that shit. I'll do what a normal person does in a normal conversation when they

SNUNIT LISS | 107

hear something so abnormal, and I'll ask you to elaborate. Tell
me – without your flowery descriptions, sarcastic expressions,
threats, extortion, and petty metaphors – is this thing for real?
Did you write it? When? Did your dad really abuse you and lock
you in the closet and all that? Did he really die with you looking
on? (If so, then I'm sorry.) And what happened afterward?
Fuck you.

Liz

Subject: A People Person

Dear Liz, as you've already gathered, I'm not a people person. However, I believe that you are, at your core, and thus I shall accept your remarks concerning the normative manner of interpersonal communication, and I shall answer your questions.

Yes. The diary is, indeed, real. As noted in it, I kept it as a journal when I was nine years old after my mother bought it for me on one of her frequent business trips and until my father's death. Yes – everything occurred as described, and the details are real, or at least reflect my point of view at the time.

You are correct. Sending you this kind of diary was a manipulative tactic. I knew that, after reading it, you'd be compelled to lower some of your defenses and I believe I was right, but that wasn't my only motive. Since I'm now in possession of so many parts of your life, it seems only fair that you hold on to a significant, perhaps the most significant, part of mine. You haven't backed up your files, and my diary also has no backup. You were right when you claimed I was flawed and, if I can engage in a moment of dime-store psychology, I presume the roots of that defect are described in the journal I sent you.

I stopped writing after my father's death. I was angry with the diary, my writing, and myself. I was angry for placing my

trust and hope in it, believing it could save my father. I had no father, I had no God, I had no words. At some point, my mother found the journal in a drawer in my room. I assume she read it. Over the years, I wondered where it had gone. I found it at her house after she suffered a stroke. I stumbled upon it while I was gathering some of her things to bring to the hospital. It was carefully wrapped inside an old shoebox in one of the drawers of her bedside table. You're the second person (besides the woman who was my wife) with whom I've shared this.

Practice what you preach. As I expect you to reply to my questions, I shall now reply to yours. Yes, my father used to lock me in the closet. He was a genius in the field of theoretical physics but, as you likely understood, much like his son, he had little talent in the field of interpersonal relationships.

My father did not abuse me, Liz. He instilled his doctrine in me, the teachings reflected in the distorting mirror that perpetually surrounds me. He bequeathed me with the mark of Cain, leaving me detached, removed, and protected from the hustle and bustle of the world. He provided me with the one place where I felt calm and worry-free, where I was not expected to be immersed in the world and the world could not be immersed in me. He took that place from me when he died and, to some extent, I've longed to go back there ever since, into the dark closet, illuminated by the streaks of light filtering in through the wooden shutters.

My father's sin was not the closet but his failure to understand the laws of the universe. I don't mean the universe he tried to decipher in his anguish-laden study, rather his own private

universe and his inability to detach himself from his professional failures and his theory, to which he clung stubbornly despite being unable to prove it till his last day. He failed to attach himself to what was present and real in his world: my mother and me. He took a mistress passed down from father to son in our family – alcohol – and plunged into a nightmarish vortex of failures until he drowned.

From my writings, it may be inferred that my father was a violent man but, in fact, there wasn't a soul in this world that understood me as he did. When my father looked at me, I knew he saw me as I was. I thought I felt the same with my ex-wife but, eventually, I was able to deceive her as well. I could never have deceived my father. I never tried; he was the root of deceit within me.

Though the renowned genius managed to choke on his own vomit before I reached the age of ten, he managed to pass his doctrine on to me. When I look in the mirror these days, it's as though I'm seeing him.

I hope I've answered your questions and am willing to answer any further queries you may have. I attach the second part of "Rockin' the Galilee" from your computer files. I'm worried about you and ask that you write about yourself again. Please would you share with me what happened when you attempted to live on your own after the accident?

Warm regards,

Someone

Attachment: Rockin' the Galilee 2

Asaf Avidan took the stage and we were feeling thirsty. Jazz needed the restroom, so we agreed that I'd buy us drinks and we'd meet back at the far-right corner of the last row. I went to the nearest stand, basking in the thick festival scents of sweat, cigarette and weed smoke, fast food, and cheap aftershave. I bought a couple of beers and headed to our arranged meeting point. Jazz wasn't there. I waited fifteen minutes, a half-hour, forty minutes. She didn't answer her cell. I began searching for her; maybe she arrived before me and decided to move up toward the stage?

I made my way through the sea of sweaty bodies as they moved as one living organism to the rhythm of the music, singing in unison:

"Now that you're leaving
It's got me thinking
Maybe I'll do a little leaving too..."

Asaf crooned on stage and I threaded my way through, sending one arm forward, one foot forward, another arm, another foot, then again, edging slowly through the swarming crowd, exchanging glances with curious guys and hopeful girls, whipping back around with every hand that mistakenly grazed me as they danced.

"Everybody's slowing down
Everybody's slowing down but us..."
Jazz was nowhere to be seen. I extracted myself from the crowd and kept searching for her. I passed by the mobile toilets and knocked on the doors one by one.

"Jazz, are you in there?" She wasn't. I wandered between the concession stands and the vendors' tables, spinning from the whiff of grilled hot dogs to the hot steam of corn on the cob. I walked between the colorful clothing racks, among the hangers of sarongs and tables of ornate jewelry, asking the vendors if they'd seen a thin, pale, beautiful girl with long hair, and they all shook their heads and shrugged. I called her cell over and over again and only reached her voicemail. Where are you, Jazz?

I headed over to our stand. Maybe she went back there? I found Mikey sprawled on the mat, playing his guitar.

"Did Jazz stop by?" I asked him in the calmest voice I could muster.

"No, isn't she with you?" He stopped playing.

"She was, but I went to get us drinks and haven't seen her since. I called but she's not picking up."

"Dizzy Lizzie, what am I gonna do with you and that crazy sister of mine? Let's go look for her together." He sighed, grabbed his backpack, and stood up. "Did she say where she was going?"

"To the restrooms, but I already searched there."

"Let's try looking there again." Once again, we walked together through the stalls and the stands. When we came up empty, we headed back toward the stage, where Yuppies with Jeeps were performing their set. "Let's look for her in the audience. Maybe

she's just high on the music and can't hear her phone." He took my hand so we wouldn't lose each other and easily cleared a path for us through the crowd. His large body tore through the human web that bonded back together after we passed through it and he tightened his grip on my hand.

"The dean's daughter enjoys sado and cocaine in ideal conditions..." the soloist was singing, and Mikey rubbed the back of his neck in deliberation, drew my arm toward him, and pulled me out of the crowd.

"Could she have gone to the beach, that crazy-assed girl?" he asked with obviously growing concern.

"Maybe," I shrugged helplessly. We walked toward the shoreline where partially dressed teens were scattered all along the beach. Couples lay on towels facing the dark water, their bodies wet from their skinny-dipping escapades. The moonlight reflecting off their moist skins made them seem like slithering sea creatures.

"You've got reception, right?" Mikey asked, taking out his phone, calling my number, and making sure we heard it ring.

"You head north and I'll head south, we'll circle the beach until we meet at the other end, and if you find her, slap some sense into her, and you better call me, Dizzy Lizzie," he belted out commands in a tone he'd mastered in his army infantry unit.

We split up and I walked along the dark shoreline. I used my phone light to illuminate my path and the faces of the teens lying on the beach, blinding couples and interrupting kisses as I went, until I saw shadows moving near an old, abandoned shed at the edge of the water. I drew nearer and discovered a middle-aged

man, his back leaning against the mold-covered shed, his legs spread and bent at the knees, with Jazz sitting between them. Her back was pressed against him, her body limp and her head slumped sideways. His hands moved across her body, glided over her breasts, and stroked her legs. His hand slid under her shirt and cupped her breast, and he began kissing the back of her neck.

"Lizzzzzzzzie!" she called out with a drunken grin as she noticed me, staring with a pair of huge, dilated pupils that gleamed through the half-veiled eyes of an alcohol-induced and God-knows-what-else stupor. A loud burp escaped her lips and she giggled. "This is Lizzie, my sister," she told the stranger who seemed extremely displeased at my unwelcome arrival. Suddenly, she bent over and puked on his knee. Half-digested pieces of the hot dogs we'd eaten earlier splattered all over his jeans.

"Ugh, you're disgusting!" he shouted, shoving her away from him as he stood up and shook off some of the vomit.

"She's disgusting?! You're disgusting, you dirtbag! Can't you see she's barely conscious? Why are you touching her, you pedophile?! Get away from here before I call someone!" I screamed.

"Whatever. Who needs your disgusting friend, anyway?" he snorted at me and walked away. I sat down beside her and cradled her close to me.

"Such love, Lizzie, such lovvvvve," she slurred, her lips sluggish from alcohol.

"You flake! Do you know how worried I was about you?!" I scolded her.

"Calm down, my darling brain, we're having fun," she giggled. "This is fun? You screwball! I've been looking for you for hours. Your brother's freaking-out worried." I tried to be mad at her, but my anger was eclipsed by how glad I was to find her and how I dreaded the thought of what might have happened if I'd arrived just fifteen minutes later. She was grinning and calm, enveloped in her inebriation, indifferent and helpless and unaware of her condition. I pulled my phone from my pocket and called Mikey.

Once I hung up, she puked again. I gathered her long hair and held it back for her, wrapped my other arm around her waist, and felt her body tremble against me.

"Why do you always have to take things a step too far, Jazz?" I sighed.

"Lizzie, Lizzie, Lizzie..." she murmured, "Life should be enjoyed."

"I'm not really enjoying myself tonight," I stroked her clammy forehead.

"Lizzie... You want me to read your future? I'm a professional fortune-teller."

"Go ahead, tell me about it," I grinned.

"You'll graduate with ho-nors, and then you'll be an out-standing soldier. After you serve your term, you'll travel the world with me for a little while, but you'll soon realize that you're wasting your time and go to co-llege to study something like really important, and you'll graduate there with ho-nors, too. Finally, you'll meet some genius and marry him, and I'll be your odd little friend, Jazz, that inflamed appendix who doesn't

go to school, and doesn't really work and never manages to stay in one place or commit to anything real... your weirdo friend that your guy will have no choice but tolerate."

"Geez, shut up already, you screwball." I planted a kiss on her head, which reeked of vomit. "Some fortune teller you are. If you know so much about the future, why don't you ever know when it's time to stop drinking?"

"Cause it's not fun to stop drinking, my darling liver!"

Mikey appeared and found us hugging, laughing our heads off. "Great, Tweedledee and Tweedledum are back together again," he hissed.

Subject: Letter Number 9

As for lowering my defenses, I'll tell you again to go fuck yourself. Listen, I'm sorry you were a little boy who was locked up in a closet and I'm sorry your dad was a son-of-a-bitch sociopath who managed to sire another son-of-a-bitch sociopath who's resolved to prey on my life because he has no life of his own. But no matter what kind of kid you once were, you're now nothing but a miserable bully who enjoys threatening me, and that damned diary of yours that broke my heart won't change that! So – fuck you. My defenses are exactly where they should be.

If what interests you is what happened to me after I went back to living on my own, I'll tell you about it. Actually, the feeling I had back then is quite similar to the way I feel when I'm corresponding with you now, as if someone's playing a joke on me. It was so horrible and surreal that I almost expected someone to jump out and tell me that it was all a hoax, maybe the failed pilot of some bad reality show that was archived and never aired on TV.

But it wasn't a hoax, it was my new reality, and it was a broken and ridiculous version of my life. Jazzy wasn't there, and Jazzy was my connection to everything. All those crazy associations spinning through my head that no one ever understood, all those strange thoughts that made the rest of the world look at me funny – she thought of them herself before we even met. It

was as if we shared a language only we could understand.

We called ourselves "soul sisters" and we were a religion with just two worshippers. We were always first for one another, before family, before boyfriends, before our other friends. When I thought of the world, I thought of it together with her. Every moment I was misunderstood or unwanted, every bad thing I went through was less terrible because she was there, she understood and accepted me.

And then, suddenly, I was alone against the world. It felt like trying to think with just one brain lobe, walking with one leg, breathing with one lung. I didn't know how to exist without her. All my plans for the rest of my life, for after the army, rested with her. I thought that, after my physical pain subsided, I could go back to being myself, but I realized that I'd changed. Every time I closed my eyes, the "what if" thoughts resurfaced. I don't remember the accident, but thoughts about it – about the day before it happened, the week, the months before it happened – linger in my mind. Thoughts about every little thing I could have done differently, that if only I had done differently, the accident wouldn't have occurred. One degree clockwise or counterclockwise on the fucking compass of life, and that car would've missed us.

Once I eventually fall asleep, my dreams are like a honey trap. I dream that Jazzy's alive and real. I dream of her in moments that really happened or in moments that should've happened, but every dream ends the same way with intense flames engulfing me and someone screaming and choking. Jazz is swallowed up within it all and I wake up drenched in sweat, my heart beating

as though I have wild horses galloping on my chest, and again having to open my eyes and again having to acknowledge, like a crowbar landing on my head, that it really happened. It wasn't just a dream.

You son-of-a-bitch. I hate that you're making me write about all this!!! I hate being that weirdo, that poor girl who can't do anything. You don't understand! This isn't me!!! I was always the strong one, the one who encouraged everyone else, the one who seemed to have all the answers and stayed cool in any situation.

After the accident, I decided I wasn't going to let this one shitty event take away who I was or change me in any way. I resolved to be a normal person again, not some kind of lazy bum who couldn't move her ass. I no longer fantasized about an epic trip around the world. I just wanted a normal life: to get up in the morning, see the sun, go somewhere, do something useful, and go back home at the end of the day to watch TV, not to think too much, to just be. I called the kibbutz work forewoman who cautiously mentioned that they needed help in the kitchen. I set my alarm clock. Do you even realize how great it is to be a person who needs an alarm clock? It means you've got something to wake up for and that your slumber's so peaceful that it couldn't possibly end of its own accord!

On my first day of kitchen duty, I woke up early and cursed and tore myself out of bed. My thoughts of what had happened to Jazz slightly dissipated in light of what needed to be done. It felt so foreign and pleasant to be useful again, to do something that had nothing to do with what I'd lost or what used to be.

The kitchen supervisor welcomed me warmly and assigned me to slicing roasted eggplants and emptying them. Dozens of eggplants roasted on metal trays in a large industrial oven. She showed me to my workstation and explained my task. I sat down and started to work, took an eggplant, and held it in my palm. Its hot flesh dripped between my fingers. I emptied it and grabbed another eggplant and then another... thick, hot flesh with burnt crisp edges and the pulp dripping between my fingers. The aroma of roasted eggplant flesh began to spread through the air in time for lunch.

Suddenly, my heart began racing with the same palpitations that wake me every morning and I felt like the end of the world had commenced in my stomach. An intolerable nausea rose in my throat. I felt like I couldn't be or breathe and couldn't stay there another moment. I didn't understand what was happening to me. I just ran away from there like a stupid little girl. I couldn't bring myself to call the kitchen supervisor and apologize. What could I say? That the eggplants had made me hysterical?

But I wanted to work. Every member of the kibbutz works. It isn't acceptable to not get up in the morning and contribute your share.

It was enough that I stayed home for a year and lived at the expense of others like a parasite. I didn't want to be the one who didn't follow the path like everyone else. I called the work forewoman again and said that I didn't know what had happened to me. I asked her to apologize on my behalf to the kitchen supervisor and asked if she might have another job for me. She mumbled something and called me back an hour later

saying that they needed help in the garment warehouse. That night, I apprehensively set my alarm. I couldn't stop thinking about what had happened in the kitchen and was anxious about the next morning. As usual, I didn't fall asleep until about five in the morning. When the alarm rang at six, I cursed it and tore myself out of bed.

Folding clothes for 700 kibbutz members wasn't the pinnacle of self-fulfillment but I hoped I could manage this job. No smells of anything burning or touching strange textures, nothing too noisy, just sitting and folding one piece of clothing, and then another and then another, concentrating on the next shirt without thinking of anything else... It would be meditation by virtue of the "Kibbutz Ha'Artzi" Movement. But there too, I ultimately caused a scene because I freaked out at some sudden noise and ran away like some screw-up. As I ran, I collided with the warehouse manager, a 60-year-old woman. Good for me. Once again, I wanted to bury myself from the humiliation.

Okay, I think you've had enough fun from me for now. Send me Jazz's next letter from New York.

Fuck you.

Liz

Attachment: OMG, my darling guts!

I tried to catch you on Skype yesterday but then I heard your message that you're confined to base for the weekend! I can't believe you're losing another Saturday because of this fucked-up nonsense. It's not like you were caught selling drugs at the base or something. Confinement just for walking around with an iPod and headphones at the Ashkelon Central Bus Station?! I hope the music you were listening to was at least worth it. I told Theo about it but he's just incapable of grasping the whole military concept. It seems so exotic to him. He imagined you riding a camel like some kind of Amazonian wrapped in an Israeli flag with a short-barreled M16 (and an iPod, yes?), until I explained that it wasn't exactly like that.

As for me, I had a pretty odd situation with Jeff this week. I think I'm going to keep my distance from him from now on. A few days ago, we went out to some club, we did some UP, which is the hottest drug in the city right now and, at first, we were having an amazing night. I felt like we were melding into each other, that the strobe lights were entering my body and painting me from the inside.

Later, we went over to his place and fucked, and suddenly it became weird. He was all intense, kept holding me, and giving me these serious looks. I wanted to leave but, out of the blue, he asked me how come I never spend the night? I told him to

forget about it, that it wasn't for me, then he blurted out: "You know you're fucked up, right?"

"Said the guy who just fucked me," I tried to blow him off.

"Stop laughing. Why are you so afraid to belong to someone?" He tried to grab the tights I was putting on and snatch them away so I wouldn't get dressed. I pulled them back from him and replied that I wasn't afraid, I just didn't want to, so he started lecturing me. "Come on, girl, just look at your job. You let some fuck look at your vagina all day. Does that seem normal to you?"

"And if it was my leg he looked at, would it be okay? What's so dangerous about my fucking pussy that it shouldn't be looked at? What, is it the sun?!" I was really pissed off, grabbed my clothes, slammed his apartment door on my way out, and finished dressing in the hallway while his elderly neighbor stared at me from behind the door chain.

So, basically, he's sexy and everything and we had some pretty intense moments together, but it was becoming more serious than I intended. I can't stand another guy trying to educate me. I've had enough of that you know. I'm only here for a few more months and I really can't bother with men who think they're knights in shining fucking armor and I should swoon when I see their white, erect horse.

Hope you're not too depressed out there. Write to me about how you're passing the time this weekend.

From me, your shameless crotch.

Subject: Morning at the Garment Warehouse

Dear Liz, your last letter struck me with a feeling of déjà vu. I reviewed the files on your laptop and came across this piece again, a short story you wrote to yourself about yourself in the third person. I copy/pasted it here:

Every morning at exactly a quarter-to-six, Nitza, the garment warehouse supervisor, passes by Tzipi, the laundry room supervisor, who smiles heartily at her. The two exchange greetings and, as Nitza continues toward the warehouse, Tzipi scowls. After all, she began her day at five. Quarter-to-six, in her book, was practically noon.

Inside the warehouse, Nitza switches on the bluish neon lights and the old air-conditioner that does its best to fill the large space with fresh air, slides open the wide doors, and steps out into the yard between the laundry room and the warehouse where Tzipi has already left the clean laundry carts for her. She wheels the carts into the large warehouse paved with crooked, grainy tiles. She turns on the radio to the IDF station to catch up on current events. If the broadcaster says something not to her liking, which happens quite often with this wise guy, she shouts at the radio and tells him exactly what she thinks of his comments so that he wouldn't dare think otherwise.

At half-past-six, she is joined by Ayala, a woman in her forties who has been working alongside her in the warehouse since the

floristry business she launched failed to take off. Ayala heads to the kitchenette and lingers by the kettle for a few moments too long, in Nitza's opinion. She then picks up her coffee cup, places it down in the usual spot at the corner of the table, faces Nitza, and the two begin folding the dining hall tablecloths together: two corners for one woman and two corners for the other, meeting each other halfway, picking up the two lower corners and repeating once again, like a remarkably purposeful dance routine.

At exactly six-forty-five, they're joined by Henia and Dina, who have been working in the warehouse for years. "Still rattling on with his nonsense today?" Henia points to the radio.

"You have no idea," Nitza replies.

"Have you seen the shorts she's wearing today?" Dina asks as Ayala steps out to wheel in another cart of fresh laundry from the yard.

"Very sexy!" Nitza concludes in an amused tone.

"Not at her age!" Dina decrees and the three of them fall silent as Ayala comes back inside with news of what's happening in the yard.

"Not as sharp as she used to be," Ayala says of Dina, who steps out five minutes later to fetch another cart of clean laundry, and points at the kitchen towels arranged in a pile, their corners failing to overlap. Nitza and Henia nod in agreement and immediately fall silent as Dina returns.

"Girls, we have a guest today," Nitza says as if she's whispering a secret.

"Who is it?" they probe curiously, accustomed to nomads without a regular work assignment being allocated to the place.

"Liz Fine," Nitza pronounces the name with a cautious distinction that can be recognized even from behind the closed doors, beyond which Liz is standing, trying to catch her breath. "You don't say? She's finally back to work?"

"I heard she behaved very peculiarly in the kitchen."

"How long has it been since her accident? A year? We haven't seen her around since then."

"Something like that. It was such a miracle. The girl she was with died at the scene, didn't she?"

Liz hears their voices echoing through the thin doors and grabs the door handle in an attempt to find the right moment to walk in, just as the doors open toward her. "Oh, Liz, hello, you're here!" Nitza greets her with a smile as she wheels in another cart of clean laundry and shoots silencing glances at her friends. Nitza leads Liz to a table beside an enormous cart full of short-sleeved shirts. This is her task for the next hour: folding the shirts into small, neat squares.

She begins: smooth out the shirt, right sleeve in, left sleeve in, fold the top half over the bottom half, turn, lift, and add to the appropriate pile according to the color of the numbered slip of paper.

How much do they know about the accident? What else did they say about her when they talked among themselves? The questions start to float around in Liz's mind. She places an imaginary hand on top of them, pushes them down, and they begin to sink, only to float back up again. She's unable to drown them. One shirt and then another, and she wonders if she's supposed to join in their conversation. What does she possibly

SNUNIT LISS | 127

have to add about the latest kibbutz gossip or the agricultural conditions? Another shirt and then another. Deep breaths. Laundry meditation. Just fold, don't think, she repeats to herself. Suddenly, a deafening roar reverberates through the room. Liz's body tenses at once and without realizing what's happening, a scream escapes her mouth. She leaps, ducks, and tucks into a ball, almost like she did in her grenade training.

"Liz?!" Nitza calls out in bewilderment and searches for her. Liz hears Nitza's flat, stiff heels clacking around the warehouse until Nitza finds her crouched under a table in one of the back rooms, panting, her body clenched, trembling uncontrollably, unable to speak.

"Lizzie, sweetheart, are you okay?" Nitza tries to place a soothing hand on her shoulder.

Liz instinctively pushes Nitza away, sending her tumbling backward, an expression of shock and chagrin on her face. Liz crawls out from under the table, bursts into tears, and mumbles, "Sorry... I'm so sorry," and quickly runs away.

The steam boiler that heats the water for the laundry machines runs for a few minutes every hour and sounds like a loud, bellowing train horn, Liz's mother explains, having rushed to her room after the work forewoman called her. She finds Liz, her teeth chattering, sitting wordlessly in her darkened, shadowy room.

What happened next, Liz? Tell me. Please tell.

Warm regards,

Someone

Subject: Letter Number 10

Yes, genius. It's something I wrote about what happened in the warehouse that day. Well done, you're a truly talented detective for insignificant matters. Maybe you should tell me what happened next? You must have already found some clues in my other writings. Sounds like you know my life better than I do. Don't you think?

When a glass falls and shatters, everyone takes a step back to avoid being injured by the shards. I felt like something like that was happening to me back then. I was broken and people withdrew so they wouldn't accidentally step on a piece of me and cut themselves. I reminded them of what could happen to them, so they preferred to keep a safe distance and look at me from the sidelines with pity and wonder.

I slowly drifted further away from my friends. They went on with their lives, working, traveling. Every time we met, everything that had happened to me and not to them stood between us like a huge shadow in the middle of the room. I couldn't tell them what I was going through. They wouldn't have understood, and they didn't dare tell me about their lives, nor did I want to hear. Every social gathering felt like a complete sham. The truth is that I hated them because none of them were Jazz, and none of them ever dealt with thoughts of death or the inability to do even the simplest things.

And I felt like everyone was talking about me whenever I left the dining hall. The talk around the kibbutz was that something not right was happening to Liz. That she's always been a little weird and now she's also incapable of getting over the accident. And okay, her friend died, but she needs to buck up, go see a shrink or something and get over it because she's only twenty-something, and true, what she went through wasn't easy, but she should count her blessings that she wasn't killed and move on with her life. In the meantime, it's our work that pays for her apartment and her expenses. We see her standing and walking and she looks perfectly fine so she should stop being spoiled and feeling sorry for herself.

Did you ever hear the song "Poor Boy" by Nick Drake? I became the village oddity. Every time I left my apartment, I felt their looks. An angled look, I call it, and think of Jazzy, who would've understood exactly what I mean.

It's impossible to approach each of those 700 kibbutz members and tell them: Listen, I want to move on with my life, I really do. I wish I could do everything I used to do. It's insanely hard to live without Jazzy but even harder to live without myself! This is not me! After all, everyone wants their freedom. No one wants to be tied down like this.

You can't come out and say all this to the hundreds of people who live around you and see you failing every day, stumbling and falling over your life like a drunken clown.

I began to feel like I was forgetting who I was before all this, the capable and joyful me, the one who never really worried, who thought nothing could scare her, and believed that a guy

who didn't call or a weekend being confined to base were actual problems.

And worst of all, I started to forget her – Jazz. I remember the panic that overtook me when I first tried to imagine her face, the sound of her voice – and found that I couldn't. I tried to remember the first time we met and suddenly I wasn't sure about a certain detail. I realized that I could also lose what little I had left of her that exists only in my mind.

I came to realize that soon, in another six months, or a year, and certainly in another five or ten years, I'll no longer remember exactly how and what we were. And no one would know how she talked and danced and sang and drove and laughed and kept quiet and did her hair and couldn't hold her liquor. I'll be the only one who knows that she was worth more than anything in this fucking place, but I won't remember why.

So I decided that this would be my job: to write about her and us and myself before the accident, so I won't forget everything we once were. To contend against all this death. So I wrote and wrote and wrote and didn't give a fuck about the kibbutz or the people outside my door.

And now you hold everything I wrote and it makes me sick to think that all my memories are there, in your hands, a part of some fucked-up and incomprehensible game.

Fuck you, and send me another of her letters.

Liz

Subject: A One-Way Mirror

Dear Liz, your naiveté surprises me. People don't want their freedom, they fear it. People want to believe they are free, while, all along, they are voluntarily imprisoned. In lieu of sending you the letter you requested, allow me to impart something:

The lobby of my apartment building features one glass wall whose exterior is coated with a reflective, mirror-like material. From inside the building, the wall is transparent and one can see through to the street, yet anyone looking in from the street merely sees their reflection while anything else on the other side of the glass is obscured from their sight. My building is located near a busy street and many people pass by it every morning on their way to their daily toil. On days when I wake early, I tend to step out of my apartment, take the elevator down, sit on one of the chairs in the lobby and watch the passers-by who are unaware of my presence, as I would a random street performance. They pause in front of the mirror-like window, observing their image, unaware that just a couple of feet from them, sits a man watching them.

Men check their teeth for any breakfast leftovers and try to wipe coffee stains from their clothes. Women fix their makeup, perfect their appearance, and adjust their breasts inside their shirts.

That is how I would frequently observe one woman who walked past my building every morning. Her skin was white, makeup-free, her clothes faded. Pale. Something about her was gentler than the pedestrian traffic that bustled around her. Every morning, she would stop and stare at her reflection, not rearranging a thing, not lifting, or tightening – just gazing at her image, and unknowingly, at me, for a long moment. I don't know her name, and she knows nothing of my existence, but I calculated and found that if I added up the minutes from each day, I've spent twenty-five hours of my life watching her, more than an entire day.

Last winter, I noticed that she seemed thinner than she used to be. Later, dark circles appeared under her eyes. Every morning, I felt she was overwhelmed with sorrow as she gazed at her reflection. I wanted to ask her what had happened, but I couldn't gather the courage to cross over to the other side of the glass. It has been a long while since she last passed my building and I wonder if she died, moved, or maybe just lost her job.

I read your depictions carefully, Liz. I have also repeatedly reviewed the narratives on your computer. I am not a big proponent of psychological therapy but I wonder, nevertheless, if you sought any such counseling after the accident. You said you study psychology. Did you not notice that the symptoms you describe are quite typical of post-traumatic stress disorder?

Warm regards,

Someone

Subject: Letter Number 11

Hello, scum. It's nice to know that you're a habitual stalker and I'm not the only one you're preying on. Does it get any more pathetic than staring at people through the windows of your building? Say, don't you ever feel like picking yourself up and trying to live your own life, one that doesn't belong to someone else?

It's quite impressive how His Royal Weirdness can diagnose me so well. Post-traumatic stress disorder, huh? You don't say? Wait a second, I'll just call Dr. House and let him know we've found his replacement. Congratulations on such a challenging diagnosis! Next time I sneeze, I'll consult with you so you can steal my tissue and immediately wonder with concern if I have a cold.

Yes, you worrisome bastard, I probably have post-traumatic stress disorder, or PTSD if you really want to sound sophisticated like I know you do. And now that we know how to neatly define the professional diagnosis, how does that help me? Did I try to seek counseling? Yes, kind of, and those treatments, like your declarations of concern, are worth shit.

But if you really must know... even before I moved to Tel Aviv, as my behavior around the kibbutz became more conspicuous, my parents began to worry. One evening, when I came over for dinner, my mother ambushed me with the following speech:

"You know, Lizzielee, we're glad you're feeling better and back in your own apartment. But we have a feeling that maybe

something isn't right." She squirmed in one of the dining room chairs that my parents haven't replaced since they were married. "After all, it can't have been easy to go through what you did, and you might as well get some professional help."

"What kind of professional help exactly, Mom? If you know a therapist who can help bring back Jazz it would be nice, but it might be a little difficult, considering her condition," I answered with sarcasm.

My father tried to persist: "I talked to Talia from the Health Committee. She consulted with the kibbutz social worker and got the details of a support group in our area. We think you should talk to other people who have undergone similar circumstances. It may help you see that it's not the end of the world."

"But it is the end of the world," I said.

"There's a whole world out there besides Yasmin, Lizzie. We just want to help you see that."

"Do you think I don't know that? I see that world, I'm dying to be a part of it, but it's like I'm... I'm somewhere else."

My mother continued. "Liz, we feel like this is out of our depth. You're dealing with something we don't understand and can't help you with, so we think you need professional help."

"So, I'm a welfare case now? The crazy one in the family?!" I felt my head heating up and my hands began to shake with anger. I stood up, walked out, and slammed the door behind me.

However, a few days later I went with my dad to the support group meeting because I also didn't know what to do anymore

and I wanted the noises inside my head to stop and for everything to return to normal, even though Jazz was no longer with me. After the accident, I stopped driving. Needless to say, I haven't even touched a motorcycle but I also tried to avoid cars as much as possible. Every time the car accelerates and the road starts whizzing by me, those wild horses begin galloping in my chest, my breathing becomes short and shallow and my head begins to spin.

When I was in high school, I crisscrossed the country on buses. Even when terrorist bus-bombing was rampant, I didn't stop. Jazz called it "Israeli roulette." We took the bus in every direction, from anywhere to everywhere, and didn't care what happened. Today, when I need to go someplace, I ask my parents to reserve a car (not everyone has a car in the kibbutz but there's a fleet of vehicles that all kibbutz members share) and drive me. I'm like an eight-year-old girl being chauffeured to her after school activities. I never sit in the front seat – it feels too close to the road. I sit in the back, tighten my seatbelt, close my eyes, and take deep breaths. If it becomes too hard, I lie down and sometimes ask my dad to stop the car so I can shamefully throw up or just catch my breath on the side of the road.

Anyway, my dad drove me to the support group that met in the afternoons at some elementary school in Hadera and walked me into the session. I hate these situations. My dad, a stooped, sixty-something, not a young man anymore, accompanied his daughter to therapy, hoping they could fix his little girl.

He walked beside me quietly until we found the right classroom, bade me goodbye, and said he would wait for me outside.

I paused at the door, inhaling, exhaling, inhaling, and exhaling. Finally, I went in. The session was already in progress. The tables were pushed up against the wall and the center of the room was occupied by small, green, plastic school chairs arranged in a circle. A quick glance at the group participants told me that none of them slept particularly well at night. The contrast between the pastel colors of the walls and the grayness of their faces sent a shiver down my spine.

"We have a new member joining us today!" The counselor greeted me. She was a full-figured woman, dressed in a flowing, loose-fitting flowery dress whose bright colors made me nauseous. "Welcome," she said and introduced herself. "Liz, right?" she confirmed. I nodded. "Take a seat," she pointed at one of the empty chairs in the circle. "I'll just sum up in a few words that this is a completely accepting environment, anything can be said and any experience can be shared, we don't judge and we don't criticize, and we also don't share anything said in this room with anyone outside this group. I also ask that we all arrive on time to avoid interrupting the session. Now, let's get back to Gadi who also joined us for the first time today and was just telling us about himself. Go ahead, Gadi."

"He lost his marbles in Gaza," an elderly man sitting beside me whispered, nodding his head toward the thin twenty-year-old who picked up from where he left off:

"So we broke down the door and moved down the hall. I went in first, followed by Atedgi, Sirota, and Cohen in the rear. Sirota and Cohen searched the two front rooms while Atedgi and I continued to advance down the hall. We heard noises coming

from inside the house and kept advancing further, me in the lead and Atedgi close behind me. Sirota and Cohen stayed behind to secure the perimeter. I walked into a large room. Suddenly I heard a tremendous explosion behind me and heard Atedgi screaming. I didn't hear Sirota and Cohen. I'd been flung forward, so I got up and picked up my weapon, then saw a boy, around twelve years old, standing in the corner of the room looking at me. He was very thin and about a foot shorter than me, exactly my little brother's height, but the explosion didn't even graze him. It was really strange. How did he escape it?! He stood there in front of me, pointing an old Uzi to my head and he had this look in his eyes, a combination of hatred and fear, a look I was used to seeing in most kids on the Strip.

"I told him in Arabic: 'Put down your weapon or I'll shoot!' Atedgi kept screaming behind me and I wondered if Cohen and Sirota were helping him or what? Why can't I hear them? The kid cocked his gun. His eyes glared deep into mine and he started saying 'Allahu Akbar.' I fired at his head before he could finish his words. There was blood everywhere and his body fell.

"I followed the screaming and found Atedgi. He had a big hole where his stomach used to be. I put my arm around him, lifted him onto my right shoulder, and moved on to look for Cohen and Sirota. The place was in ruins. I saw blood and what looked like pieces of flesh on some bricks with some smoke and dust rising from them. I reported our position on my radio and decided to get Atedgi out of there and then go back for Cohen and Sirota. I ran out with Atedgi through the doorway that no longer had a door or a hallway.

"After a few seconds, I heard a huge explosion behind us and I shielded Atedgi with my body. I heard him whisper in my ear, 'Bro, I think I'm going to die,' and I replied, 'No way, dude, it's just a scratch. Tomorrow you'll clobber me at ping-pong again.' I lay there on top of him for a few minutes and felt his body heat and I said to him, 'Bro, I think you'll get a weekend pass. I bet Anat will take good care of you at home tomorrow.'

"And he asked, 'Do you think she'll finally agree to go down on me?' Two minutes later, I lifted him onto my shoulder again and talked to him but he didn't answer and before I continued running, I looked back and saw a mushroom of smoke where the house we'd just run from had been. When we finally saw Abergil and Shasha, I realized that I was wounded, too.

"Some government official came to my hospital room to shake my hand. Honestly, I couldn't remember if he was a Member of Knesset or a minister or whatever, they just told me who he was after he left. I heard him being interviewed outside my room, 'We came here to give these injured soldiers strength but, ultimately, we came out strengthened,' and I thought of Atedgi, who'll never get that blow job from Anat.

"On the whole, I'm okay. I wasn't seriously wounded and I'm lucky to be alive. But the look in that kid's eyes has haunted me ever since. All these years, wherever I go, I see those eyes. I sit down for something to eat and suddenly I see those eyes. After the incident, I wanted to return to combat duty but they wouldn't let me because of the shrapnel injuries. They assigned me to the unit training division but, there too, I'd see his eyes everywhere. I'd be talking to a friend and suddenly he'd have

his eyes, with that glare of hatred mixed with fear. I go to sleep and see those eyes again. Eventually, I was discharged. At first, my little brother didn't understand why I couldn't look at him. He hasn't tried to talk to me for a while now. Actually, he'll be enlisting soon."

I felt the wild horses begin galloping across my chest, and once again the end of the world was spreading in my stomach. "I'm sorry," I mumbled, and just took off. I slammed the door behind me and again I was running, rushing past my dad who chased after me until we reached the car and stood next to me uncomfortably as I bent over, choking, and crying.

After I managed to regulate my breathing, I asked him to take me home, I went into my apartment, turned off the lights, switched on my laptop, and continued transcribing everything I could remember before it disappeared. Since then, my parents didn't have the nerve to suggest any more therapy, except for the physiotherapy they persistently drove me to twice a week until I left the kibbutz.

So, really – thanks for the diagnosis, Dr. Freud. It helped me a lot. Now stop fucking with my mind and send me another of Jazz's letters already. I'm not interested in reading another pseudo-prosaic description of your messed-up life, so please spare me the trouble.

Fuck you.

Liz

Dr. Jekyll and Mr. House

Dear Liz, you made me laugh again! I do enjoy your bitter sense of humor. I'm not an expert on the subject, nor did I assume that an interim diagnosis on my part would alleviate your pain. The description of your experience in the support group sounds disturbing, and yet I have to wonder – is there no other method of treatment that might help ease your suffering? I don't mean to be condescending, Liz, but you're so young! What you have experienced is certainly not easy, but I presume there are other tools that can help you cope. From our correspondence and from poring over your writing, I have the impression that you are blinded by despair. Do not let it consume you. Remember that what you have been through so far does not envelop all; it is only a short chapter in your life. As an indication of that and instead of the letter you requested, I attach a passage that you wrote to yourself, I believe, which describes, if I'm not mistaken, a completely different experience.

However, I must admit that I don't have the capacity to understand what you've lost. A relationship like the one you describe with Yasmin is foreign to me. I suppose I can understand the pain of loss, but not the symbiosis. Not the bond of kinship. I understand that your kibbutz was quite far from hers and that Yasmin lived in the United States intermittently. Tell me, how did the two of you first meet?

Warm regards,

Someone

Attachment: Itzik

"Welfareoccifer, Welfareoccifer, I need to talk to you, Occifer!" Itzik called out to me when I was first introduced to his platoon. That evening he showed up in my office, which was a tiny concrete cubicle strategically located between the showers and the latrines into which sixty cadets would storm after a long, sweaty day – just in time for the Welfare Office opening hours. With his less than average height, spiked-up hair covered in hair gel, and devious eyes, he declared: "Occifer, you've got to help me! What exactly do they want to repossess? My dad's wheelchair?!" He leaned over my green Formica table and handed me a Collection Notice he'd received after failing to repay a small debt to his cellular provider.

I promised to see what I could do and continued to follow up on him. He soon became the star of his platoon, walked around the base like a kid at summer camp, and turned any order or reprimand into a joke. Yet when the entire platoon was confined to base for a weekend, he was livid and locked himself in one of the rooms. "I've gotta take care of my dad! He barely makes it through the week without me, but now the weekend, too?" he explained through his tears when he finally agreed to unlock the heavy iron door and let me in.

I conducted a home visit. He lived in a tiny, neglected public housing apartment in Ashkelon. Slumped in the wheelchair Itzik had mentioned, his father looked much older than his

fifty years. Itzik's late mother's sister showed me in and told me that, before his illness, Itzik's father used to regularly beat his wife and four children. The mother died of cancer when Itzik was a child and, a few years later, the father was diagnosed with multiple sclerosis. His three eldest sons, remembering his abusive behavior, refused to help him. Only Itzik, the youngest son, remained to live at home and care for him.

I submitted every possible application to the Army Welfare Service and requested help for Itzik and his dad. Personally, I didn't believe he'd last out for more than a few months but I hoped that the military would give him some solace from the harsh reality awaiting him at home.

Two weeks before the months-long basic training period came to an end, I heard strange clinking noises from the latrines while I was working in my office.

"Is everything okay in there?" I shouted as I approached the doorway. There was no answer. "Is anyone in there?!" I debated whether I should enter or not. I didn't want to catch one of the cadets with his pants down. I stepped inside cautiously and saw Itzik with his back to me, lifting the lid off one of the toilet tanks. Two gleaming and promising bottles of vodka peeked up at me from within the cool toilet tank water.

"Can I help you with anything, Itzik?"

"Welfareoccifer!" He turned to me in a panic.

"Is that what I think it is?" I pointed at the bottles.

"Would you believe me if I told you it was water?" he tried.

I walked over to each of the other toilets and lifted the loose-fitting lids off the tanks. Inside each of the water-filled tanks

sparkled two or three clear bottles of vodka or arak.

"Are you mental?" I asked after lifting the last lid.

"Don't be such a pill, Occifer. I just opened a little speakeasy. That's all. I sell to anyone who needs a drink, supplementing my income. I need to make a living."

"Do you know what will happen to you if they find out? You'll be detained for much more than just a weekend. You could go to military jail for this. For a long time. Who'll take care of your dad then?"

"Jail? What?" He paled at my words. "It's just some booze. It's business. I swear it's legit."

"Not in the army!" I yelled. I closed the toilet seat lid and sat down. "What am I going to do with you, Itzik?" I ran the scenarios in my head as he stood by my side, confused and silent.

"Okay, listen," I said after a few minutes. "I'm willing to keep this to myself and not tell anyone, since jail's the last thing you need right now but only if you promise me that this matter is over and done with! Do you understand? It's not that I care if you drink, but we use live ammunition here. Someone could die because of this."

"Geez, I didn't think of that..." he muttered awkwardly.

"You know that if anyone finds out about this, I'll go to jail, too, right?"

"You? In jail?!" he chuckled.

"Yes! You still don't get where you are, do you, Itzik?"

"Okay, there's no way you're going to jail because of me, Occifer!"

"We're getting rid of all this alcohol and don't you even think of doing it again! No alcohol, drugs, super glue, Freon gas... You're not allowed to sell any of that here. Not even a Diet Coke. Do you get it?"

He looked down dejectedly and nodded. I picked up a bottle, twisted the cap open, and poured its contents down the toilet. He did the same with evident heartache. When we reached the last bottle, he opened it and said: "You know, where I come from, we always seal a deal with a drink. Will you have the last drink with me?"

There was nothing I craved more at that moment than a chilled shot of vodka, but I swallowed hard and said, "Pour it away, Itzik. Pour it away."

Subject: Letter Number 12

Wow! Itzik... I haven't thought of him in such a long time. I remember when I wrote that. I was so terrified of forgetting those parts of myself that I recounted every last detail. It seems like these stories no longer have anything to do with me, as though someone else's memory just happens to be in my head.

Anyway, I almost started looking for a Celine Dion song to play as the soundtrack for your pathetic motivational speech. It's nice to hear such an encouraging manifesto from some creep who decided that the best way to manage his own life was to never leave the house again. Your optimism really inspires me with hope, Ahitophel.

But what do I care? I'm already on letter number 12. Almost a third of this atomic mind-fuck is now behind me and I'll soon be rid of you meddling in my stinking life.

You want me to tell you how I met Jazz, which is funny because I've already written about this in detail. If you really did read everything that's stored on my laptop, you probably know it already. Maybe you just want to mess with my head? Fuck it. I'm not going to reproach you for not attaching the letter I asked for or bargain with you for it. I'll just write and get you off my back.

I met Jazz at the Kibbutz Children's Choir. It's a sort of inter-regional choir conference where kids from different kibbutz

choirs get together to sing several times a year, each time in a different kibbutz – a kind of summer camp where you learn classical pieces of music and sing them for about twelve hours a day, several days in a row. On the last day, we would perform for the hosting kibbutz as the kibbutz veterans dozed off in their chairs in keeping with tradition.

We met at this camp when we were both fourteen years old during the summer vacation between ninth and tenth grade. I was there with some girls from my kibbutz; she came along with kids from her kibbutz. She wasn't there to sing. She was just taking the opportunity to get away from her house for a few days.

I often think about our first encounter. Time and time again, I'm amazed to discover how much of it I don't actually remember. I don't really know why she approached me at that first rehearsal. It wouldn't have mattered either way, yet it's a shame that I never asked her. Who could know that my time to ask all those questions would be limited? I wish I could link all those memories together into a chain that would take on a life of its own and never disappear. I guess that's what I tried to create when I wrote down that sea of memories on my laptop that you insist on keeping.

I think she marked me. I think she was looking for someone with whom she could turn this confining choir conference into a little youthful expedition. We both sang soprano, and she stood next to me when we were divided into groups to learn the arrangement for Pergolesi's "Stabat Mater." Your Royal Conceitedness is probably familiar with the piece. Amid her

wretched attempts at scales, she began making light snorting sounds in my ear. I burst out laughing in surprise and she snorted again.

"Hey, I'm Yasmin," she whispered after a moment and I thought I recognized a hint of a foreign accent in her voice. "I'm Eliza," I replied. "Eliza??!" She looked at me in wonder and fired back: "And I thought my parents were sadists!" We both laughed and the conductor scowled at us.

After a few more stanzas, she muttered, "How boring. Like, Jesus has been dead for about 2000 years. If he heard us now, he'd be begging to be put back on the cross."

I didn't understand what she meant. Only years later did I learn that the piece we were singing depicts Mary's suffering at the crucifixion of her son. Fifteen minutes later, she whispered in my ear, "Just go along with it."

Before I could reply, she dropped, hit the floor, and lay there, her body limp. I leaned over her and started yelling, "Yasmin fainted!" and asked if anyone had some water. The entire room filled with commotion, the kids crowded around her and the conductor pushed everyone back. Suddenly, without anyone else noticing, I spotted her eyes open for a flash, searching for me and giving me a tiny, almost imperceptible wink, then immediately returning to her impressive dramatic performance. The conductor wet her cheeks with some water and she pretended to come around hazily, sat down, and mumbled something about not eating breakfast that morning. She declined all the anxious suggestions, saying that it happened to her sometimes and that there was no need to call her dad, she just needed to go see the nurse.

"Eliza will come with me!" She pointed at me. "We'll find the infirmary on our own, we'll ask around." She stood up, took my hand, and walked out of the room with me trailing behind her, flabbergasted.

I had never seen anyone behave like that. I never saw anyone so easily conceive something in an attempt to shape the reality around them, and she did it so naturally without so much as batting an eye.

"Problem solved!" she cheered as we left the auditorium. "Now they'll let us off for the day and won't bother us because they'll be worried I'll faint on them again. And I'll say that you must stay and look after me! Well, I wasn't really lying or anything, a few more minutes in there and I really would've fainted from mind-numbing boredom," she added, and I looked at her in amazement. She was so strange and charismatic. I was also feeling bored and suffocated in that rehearsal room, but I would never have dared to do what she did. I would never have thought it possible.

We didn't go to the infirmary. There was no need. We just wandered around that kibbutz and talked all day. I don't know how she knew – I have no idea how she recognized it in me – but I felt like I was talking with a sharper version of myself. We told each other about our kibbutz, our schools, our families, music, movies, boys, and TV and discovered that we experienced things on a very similar level as though a thin thread connected us.

We each felt alienated in our kibbutz and we both had good friends that we felt didn't really understand or know us. We

both felt surrounded by a world that didn't truly appreciate us or understand what we thought about all day or what we dreamed about. And here, suddenly, in this random situation, away from home, we meet a person who understands and sees us for what we are. Something mystical about our acquaintance was reinforced every time we met, even after we hadn't seen each other for months and when we shared an apartment before she was killed.

We didn't share a similar background. We were both from a kibbutz, but my parents had been married for thirty years, while she was born in the United States to a father who lived on a kibbutz and an American mother who once volunteered there. Her parents had divorced when she was young and, ever since, she had traveled between her mom in the States and her dad, who remained on the kibbutz, until one summer at her mother's, after which she never returned.

We didn't express ourselves in the same manner, but something in the way we experienced the world and ourselves, how we looked at the people around us, was identical. We were kindred spirits.

I found myself telling her thoughts I've never shared with anyone else. Unlike others, she didn't laugh or make me feel like the dumbest creature in the world. On the contrary, she completed my sentences, deciphered my feelings, and shared similar mindsets with me. We discovered that we held parallel memories from events we had each experienced separately. We both remembered the first time we heard Pink Floyd and stretched out on the carpet at our parents' house, each on a

different continent, thinking how that was it – that was exactly what music should sound like. We had both fallen from a tree at the age of seven and broken our left legs in the very same place, though in different parts of the country. We both gloomily recalled the isolation we felt during the long recovery period with our legs in a cast.

By that evening, we already felt like we'd known each other forever. "Move into my room!" She invited me and I abandoned the girls from my kibbutz without a second thought, took my mattress, and moved it to the foot of her bed. When she came out of the shower and I saw her brushing her long hair, I thought to myself that she was the most beautiful thing I'd ever seen. I didn't lust after her; it wasn't a sexual desire. It was a childhood infatuation, two girls seeing the beauty in each other that the rest of the world failed to see. I wanted her madness and charm to continue painting my life in bright colors and for her to continue to accept, reflect, and differentiate me from the rest of the world. Suddenly, I was no longer alone.

We never returned to the auditorium throughout that conference. She "wasn't feeling so well" and I needed to "watch over her." The next day we hitched a ride to the nearby city, Afula, and walked around town all day talking. We ate falafel and watched the passersby. We sat on street corners on the sidewalks, smoking cheap cigarettes and drinking cans of peach nectar. We invented in-jokes for ourselves. She told me about her mother, an alternative healer who moved around the United States in pursuit of whatever boyfriend she was dating at the time. That year, she was in Texas with some disgusting

fellow that Jazz hated. I told her about my parents, about their relationship that seemed so tedious and boring to me, and about how everyone around me seemed like they were sleepwalking through their lives. When we passed a liquor store, Jazz pulled me inside. "My mom asked me to buy her some cooking sherry," she told the saleslady with an innocent smile and took out a fifty-shekel bill from her pocket. The saleslady didn't question her request. As we hitched a ride back to the kibbutz, we slumped in the back seat and she opened her bag to show me the various bottles she'd swiped while the saleslady was searching for the sherry.

At night, we walked around the kibbutz and gulped down the fine liquor Jazz had hidden in her bag. We talked and talked, lying on the grass holding hands and staring at the starless sky. It was the first time I got drunk. "I always wanted a sister, but I didn't know there was one waiting for me out there all this time," she said to me, and I replied, "Yeah, I didn't know I was waiting for one. But I was." She was six months older than me but we decided I'd be her big sister, we promised each other we'd always take care of one another.

Upon my return home, life suddenly seemed dreary. My friendships seemed trivial and childish, the kibbutz bland and disheartening. It was a lackluster world in which I was the responsible, sensible girl who would always do what was expected of her. I felt like everyone around me was just going through the motions. I knew each of the kids in my group (that's what a kibbutz class is called) like the back of my hand. I felt like yelling: Hey, there's so much more than this! There's

a whole world out there, beyond this place! And Jazz was this whole world, embodied in just one girl.

I started living my life from one weekend to another. We'd chat every day on Messenger. We talked about everything, from songs we'd heard to an annoying kid in class, planning our next meeting. On the weekends, we preferred to meet at her place. She lived with her father, who had far less energy to check up on us than my parents did. Her kibbutz, on the shores of the Sea of Galilee, had a different vibe from my rigid kibbutz. It bore an air of eternal summer, of adventures just waiting to begin. Almost every Friday, right after school, I'd hop on a bus and ride over to see her. Her friends knew me only as I was when she was near me: wild, careless, funny, and maybe even beautiful. I liked the image of myself that I projected when I was with her.

I gave her the name Jazz, which eventually became Jazzy, and was so becoming of her - a beautiful improvisation on the monotonous tune everyone around me was playing. She called me Lizzie and together we were Jazzy and Lizzie. We were known that way everywhere. People asked if we were sisters, or wondered if we were lovers. We had a very physical relationship, always holding hands and embracing. Men would catcall us in the street: "Can I get in between you?" But for us it had nothing to do with sex, it just felt natural and right and safe to be connected.

My parents raised a disapproving eyebrow. They didn't understand this strange bond I'd formed. One day they sat me down for a talk and asked if I didn't think this relationship was "a little odd." They probably wondered if we were lesbians and

just didn't know how to ask. They said they thought I spent too much time with her, that I should see her less often and spend less time on the computer chatting with her. They wanted me to spend more time with my friends here at our kibbutz. In response, I started screaming in protest! Me, who had never quarreled with them or raised my voice before! Yet I suddenly felt the walls of the room and the kibbutz fences closing in on me so much that if I couldn't see Jazz, I wouldn't be able to breathe. I threatened my parents that if they wouldn't agree to let me see her, I'd run away from home. They fell silent, capitulated, and didn't discuss the issue again. My parents always respond to an uproar with silence.

I don't know who Jazz would have been if she were alive today. There were many things we didn't agree on, especially her frivolous attitude toward life and her well-being but I know I would have loved her just as much. Every time I saw her, even after many months apart, I felt as if I was meeting a part of myself that existed outside my body. I was her little-big-real-adopted sister and I wasn't able to protect her.

That's it for today, you leach. Now, how about you open up and tell me something about your fucking self? I deserve some cheap thrills, too. While you're giving me speeches about hope, peace, and love, tell me: how did you manage to convince a (sane?) woman to marry you? What did you steal from her to coerce her into it? How did you meet her?

Fuck you.

Liz

Subject: The Longest 20 Questions Game in History

Dear Liz, I'm sorry you lost Yasmin for all that she meant to you. I was pleased to obtain a sense of her character through your words and I enjoy feeling her as I read her letters. I find her to be an extraordinary person. Indeed, I read the description of your first encounter that you wrote and saved on your laptop with all the rewrites, comments, and question marks you added. I saw that you were determined to verify what piece of music you were rehearsing when she first approached you and read the results of your research and your detailed conclusions, all organized with academic diligence.

As I review your files, I feel as if I am walking through a museum, looking at artifacts discovered in an archeological dig, painstakingly restored and kept behind a thick glass partition with an admonishing sign above them reading "Do Not Touch." Yet, I'm not interested in cold, technical descriptions. I seek to experience these events with you, to walk beside you along memory lane, inhale the scents, see the night sky swirling through your drunken eyes. Hence, I asked you to describe the occurrences to me again.

You may be surprised to discover that Ella, the woman who shared her life with me, is a rather sane woman. In fact, she is one of the most sensible and stable people I have ever known. How did I manage to convince her to be with me? I suppose that her

decision can be attributed to her excessive, perhaps desperate, kindheartedness and her steadfast belief in the overall good, a belief that I, most likely, managed to undermine.

You wrote that, with Yasmin, you felt you could finally be "who you really were." I believe that Ella, my ex-partner, perceived me as the best version of myself. She saw me not as I am, but as I could have been if I were not so flawed. As someone who fixes people professionally, I suppose that she truly believed that our relationship, the life we would build together, could divert me from being the person my life had led me to become. As we both found out, she was wrong.

Don't worry, I won't deprive you of your share of "cheap thrills." We'll start from the beginning: I didn't steal anything from Ella other than her momentary judgment. I met her at the hospital where my mother was hospitalized after suffering a stroke.

One morning, my mother lost all sensation in the right side of her face. She tried to ignore it. She tended to try to prove her superiority over sickness and struggles by simply denying their existence. The proprietor of her neighborhood grocery store rushed my mother to the emergency room after she began to speak irrationally and staggering in front of the produce section. "Sorry I am," she said repeatedly to the cucumbers. Later that day, she lost the ability to move the right side of her body but, even more detrimental, was the loss of her ability to speak.

She wasn't physically unable to speak. Her mouth could pronounce the words but her brain no longer had the capacity to instruct her lips to form them. The area in her brain responsible

for speech was severely affected by the stroke and thus, over the next few hours, her ability to produce words diminished. When she arrived at the hospital all she could say to the doctors was, "Sorry I am," and a couple of hours later the "I am" also disappeared. Of all my mother's extensive vocabulary, the precious Hebrew language she nurtured with such care, the thousands of beloved words she cherished and was intimately familiar with as if they were a part of her family, some of which she even conceived into this world, only "Sorry" remained. Her ability to understand language, however, was not impaired in any way. It was heartbreaking, like a one-sided breakup from an ever-faithful spouse.

A conversation with someone who can only utter the word "Sorry" is a very strange experience, all the more so when that someone happens to owe you an apology or two. When she was hungry, she'd say, "Sorry." When she was thirsty, she asked for, "Sorry." When she was depressed, she whimpered, saliva dripping from her mouth, "Sorry. Sorry Sorrrrrry." When she was angry that I didn't visit often enough she'd reprimand me with, "Sorry!"

"I don't forgive you. I do not forgivvvvvvvvvvvve," I whispered to her once when it was only the two of us in that hospital room. *Fine, okay, I'll forgive you. Just shut up already,* I'd think to myself most of the time. And she'd say, "Sorry."

It was impossible to ignore the irony; the most verbal woman imaginable could only express one word. From someone rigid and pedantic, she suddenly turned into a wasted human being. After about two weeks in the neurology ward, she was

transferred to the rehabilitation unit. Ella was the rehabilitation psychologist assigned to her case.

I was in my early thirties at the time. Outwardly, I was already a completely different person from the child you read about in my journal. I abandoned that journal, yet, like my mother, I soon discovered the power of words to deceive and protect. I learned that when I write, I have power. My words can help me create a reality in which I invent myself as I wish. I found that I could become a verbal chameleon, assuming and slipping out of character. I stopped stuttering and began deceiving.

In those days, I was a senior copywriter with one of the largest advertising agencies in the country. I used words to create illusions as my trade and my livelihood. With their help, I established a lavish setting for my life. I was a peacock. Meticulously dressed and putting on an air of condescension, I appeared more handsome than I was. Most of the women around me – young copywriters, account executives and graphic designers, waitresses at the bars I frequented most nights – believed this illusion and were captivated by it.

I found it very easy to attract women with words. I recognized their recurrent hopes, desires, and fears, most of them quite predictable. I could whisper the most banal emotions in their ear and weave a fleeting reality around them to lead them on. I would flirt, ask them out to meals and drinks, caress their thighs, walk beside them, and sleep with them. I would make them believe that I understood them, mount them, and come inside them.

I would never promise anything. I maintained a calculated ambiguity, one that would leave no room for true intimacy. If

I encountered such an expectation, I'd walk away. The objects of my pursuits were familiar with the rules of the game. Most asked no questions and responded with their own distance. On those rare occasions when an explanation was demanded, I would engage in boorish behavioral tactics that would make the woman feel lucky she had escaped the relationship, or resort to a simple and rather honest explanation: I'm not interested in intimacy, I'm not built for it. I never promised anything. I'll never change.

From the moment I first saw Ella in my mother's room on the rehabilitation ward, I was triggered with a burning rage. Thin, short, and pale, she stood there wearing an oversized white coat, a name tag hanging carelessly from its pocket. Her brown, disheveled hair was gathered at the nape of her neck and framed her symmetrical features, almost ethereal in their delicacy, from which she gazed at me with huge, brown, examining eyes. The well-groomed women I knew were experts in painting their faces. I would lie on their sheets and watch them draw on new facial features before I left their beds to which I had no plans to return. Ella did not wear any makeup; she had no interest in disguising her facial features or trying to convince the world that they were any different from reality. The women I had come to know would often lower their eyes under my scrutinizing gaze. Ella never lowered her eyes. Everything about her made it clear to me that she had no interest in illusions and that she did not fall for mine. She did not look at me with coyness or desire, but with a gleam of compassion that sent a ripple of terror through me.

My mother was sitting in a wheelchair with Ella beside her. I stood in front of them, a strange triangle with my mother at its center, her body and face tilted oddly to the right as if gravity affected only one side of her body. She sent me a look full of plea and hope and said, "Sorry."

"Hello, Mom," I replied.

"Sorry," she said again with a disappointed look, apparently attempting to ask, "Where have you been?" and noting, "Look who's here."

"With whom do I have the pleasure?" I asked the woman sitting on the edge of her chair beside my mother.

"Sorry," my mother said.

"Ella. I'm a rehabilitation psychologist here at the ward. I understand that you're the son."

"Sorry," my mother confirmed.

"Yes," I replied.

"So, what exactly does a rehabilitation psychologist do when their patient can only say one word?" I asked Ella. "I suppose it simplifies the therapy sessions," I added.

"Sorry!" my mother reproached.

"There are other ways to communicate besides speech," Ella said. "We'll try to become familiar with these together with your mother, along with the verbal rehabilitation that the speech therapist will work on with her. I understand that she's very attached to language and all its aspects, but since this instrument has been damaged, we'll try to find new ways for your mother to express herself and adapt to the changes she's undergone."

"Sorry..." my mother said skeptically and I let out a chuckle of my own.

When I left the room, Ella swiftly followed in an attempt to catch up with me.

"Sorry?!" she called after me.

"I see that it's becoming contagious," I replied. My sarcastic humor didn't impress her. She sent me an inquisitive and poignant look and asked, "Can we talk for a few minutes? I'd like some information about your mother."

I overtly glanced at my watch. This woman made me terribly uncomfortable and there was nothing in the world I wanted less than to discuss my relationship with my mother with some self-proclaimed Mother Theresa.

"I've already provided all the relevant information to the Neurology Department. Have you looked at her file?" I asked impatiently.

"Of course," she replied, not allowing my questioning her professionalism to bother her, "but the Neurology Department doesn't focus on rehabilitative psychology so there are details that don't appear in the file. Since your mother has difficulty expressing herself and you're her only relative, I'll need you to provide me with these details."

"This isn't a good time," I muttered. "I'm late for a meeting."

"I ask that you make time for this. It's essential for her treatment," she pressed me.

And what did she want me to say? That my mother was an anal bitch who loved words more than she loved people, that she had devoted her entire life to the Hebrew language and

abandoned the people who unfortunately needed her, until, ironically enough, her precious language abandoned her?

At the time of her stroke, my mother was a world-renowned professor. Her colleagues and students who made a pilgrimage to her bedside during those first weeks found it difficult to see her drooling, depleted of her eloquence and articulate astuteness. Gradually, the parade of visitors dwindled. She was left alone in the hospital room with her eternal apology. The bouquets wilted and were never replaced by others.

Our roles had been reversed. She was now imprisoned in a room without the ability to express herself, while I discovered that I was just as incompetent as she was in dealing with distress and took on the role of the deserter. I couldn't stand to be near her. There was no one to frown at my absence or share my burden, so I kept my visits to a minimum, providing her and myself with a variety of excuses of deadlines and long nights at the office. I showed up days after I promised to visit and spent only an hour of my time at her bedside instead of an entire afternoon. After all, my mother had shown both my father and me the same consideration when each of us needed her attention. These were the small acts of vengeance only the two of us could discern, until – much to my displeasure – Ella appeared.

The second time I saw my mother on the rehabilitation ward, she was sitting in her wheelchair with her body still tilted to the right, yet something about her looked less flaccid. Ella sat to her left and held her left palm.

"Hello, Mom. Ella," I nodded at them.

"Sorry," my mother greeted me.

"Your mother and I are talking," Ella said as if it were the most natural thing in the world.

I regarded her in bewilderment. None of the doctors had foreseen that my mother would regain her speech so quickly.

"Through her hand," Ella explained when she noticed the confusion on my face.

"Sorry," my mother added, directing her gaze to the point of contact between them.

"I ask your mother yes or no questions and she replies by squeezing my hand. Once for yes and twice for no. Not all patients are able to use this technique, but your mother's doing great!" Ella cheerfully described the meager channel of communication she was able to provide for my mother.

"Here, have a go!" she commanded, and before I could respond, she stood up, guided me to her seat, and placed my mother's hand in mine. "Ask her something."

I looked at my mother, my mother looked at me and we both knew this was the closest physical contact we had shared in a very long time. We didn't tend to touch each other; we never talked about my personal life and certainly not of hers. About once a month, I would meet her for lunch at a restaurant. She never cooked or entertained and preferred to spend as little time as possible in her apartment. She would tell me about her work, the new reference book she was writing, the next conference she would attend, and I would tell her about my work and bear her disappointed frowns. She considered my occupation as sacrilege because I made cheap use of her beloved language. At

best, the physical contact between us amounted to a brisk pat on the back as we said our goodbyes.

"It's okay, you don't have to talk. It's just as important to recognize the value of touch as a means of communication. Our bodies can express a great deal about us even without words. This is also a way for the two of you to communicate," Ella tried to bridge the silence between us.

I wanted to strangle her and my mother said, "Sorry."

Ella was the most professionally invested person I had ever met besides my mother. There seemed to be no separation between her occupation and her personality. At work, as in her life, she relentlessly tried to push life onto a more auspicious path, seeking the strengths in situations and people that could lead to recovery and looking for detours around the impossible not out of naivety, but out of defiance in the face of the ephemerality of life.

Ella and my mother played the longest 20 Questions game in history sitting side-by-side for hours on end, my mother's left hand on Ella's. The tiny figure swamped by a white coat, always a few sizes too large, was often to be found beside my mother's slowly desiccating body.

I would walk into my mother's room and find them sitting like this, and strangely felt as if I was interrupting a flowing conversation between two old friends.

"And that's when you began your Master's degree?"

Two squeezes.

"Oh, that was later?"

One squeeze.

"And you knew right away what your thesis would be?"

One squeeze.

"Sorry."

"I'm reading her books. She's a fascinating woman," Ella turned to me before she left the room.

"Yes. A fascinating woman, indeed," I replied.

"Sorry," my mother added.

One day when I went to visit my mother, I was walking down the hall on my way to her room when I heard Ella calling my name. I turned to see her running after me. She was pale.

"You didn't pick up your phone."

I took out my cell from my pocket and found twelve missed calls. I had left it on silent mode. "What happened?" I asked, though I had already guessed the answer.

She took my hand in hers and said, "I'm sorry. We tried to reach you. Your mother passed away this morning."

I pulled my hand away and headed to my mother's room. Her bed was empty.

One of the blood vessels in her brain had ruptured and she bled into her head. She suffered severe nerve damage and was rushed into surgery. My mother died on the operating table.

I heard the details from the attending doctor, signed the documents, informed my colleagues that I could not attend the meetings scheduled for that evening, and made the necessary arrangements at the hospital. Ella followed and watched my actions from afar.

After several long hours of draining bureaucracy, as I stood in front of the elevators holding a used, medium-sized plastic

bag containing all the belongings that had served my mother in the last weeks of her life, Ella appeared behind me and touched my shoulder.

"How are you?" she asked.

"Great." I tried to distance myself from her.

"Can I help you in any way?"

"No, thanks," I hurried into the elevator that mercifully saved me.

"You'll have to deal with it eventually, you know," I heard her say behind the closing elevator door.

I stood there and felt the blood begin to boil in my veins. "You'll have to deal with it eventually?" Where did she get the nerve, this self-righteous, presumptuous know-it-all? What could she possibly know about my mother? She was just another one of those people who thought they knew her just because they'd read her books. How dare she tell me what I'd have to deal with? How did she have the audacity to give me a look that implied she could see under my skin! I'd show her exactly what I had to deal with!

That evening, I searched for Ella's home address on my computer. It took me about twenty minutes to locate her. She lived in the southern part of the city. I picked up the journal I had written as a child, wrapped it in a paper bag, and left my house.

I walked and walked. I didn't want to talk to anyone, I just wanted to yell at Ella. I couldn't handle holding a conversation with a cab driver or being on a bus or a service shuttle with strangers. All the way over to her home, I thought about what

I'd say to her, how I'd tell her that she only thought she knew my mother and that it was very easy to accept someone when all you do is hold her hand and the only thing she can say is, "Sorry," and when that someone can't run away from you, and that it must feel pretty damn good to act like a savior and observe the families in her ward and believe she could detect all their short circuits like some sort of MRI for the soul and that a few years of education in her ivory tower didn't give her the right to judge or the capacity to mend.

About an hour later, I arrived at her apartment building. I thought about what to say when I pressed the intercom buzzer but her building didn't have a front gate. I checked to see which apartment she lived in by the names on the mailboxes and started up the stairs. The stairwell smelled of urine and I quickly realized that Princess Ella lived in a rather shabby neighborhood. There was no doorbell or sign on her front door, just a rusty apartment number. There was no response when I knocked. I knocked again. It was already late in the evening. I began to wonder if I'd come to the right place or if she may still be at work when I suddenly heard the lock turn and then another lock and I saw her peek out from behind a security chain.

She opened the door wearing frayed boxer shorts and an old T-shirt. Her eyes were red and swollen and she clutched a handkerchief in her hand.

I stood on the doorstep and held out my paper-bag-wrapped journal to her. All those words I had planned to shout at her hung suspended on the tip of my tongue.

"What are you doing here?" she wondered.

"I..." I began to speak and stopped myself. "Why are you crying?"

"Because your mother died," she blew her nose loudly, "and also, I broke a glass." She turned and retreated into her apartment, shuffling in her flip-flops through shards of glass scattered along the narrow corridor between the front door and the kitchen. She picked up a broom. I followed her in, the broken glass crunching under my shoes. Wordlessly, she placed a dustpan in my hands. I bent down and lowered the dustpan to the floor as she swept the tiny shards toward it. Three huge cats padded around her on their soft paws, navigating with perfect balance between the pieces of glass as they rubbed their tails against her.

"Ouch!" She suddenly groaned in pain. As she lifted her right foot, I saw blood dripping from it. I came closer to her so that she could lean on me and led her to the tattered sofa in the living room. She sat down and began digging into her foot, searching for the shard of glass that had found its way into her skin through the flip-flop. "Can you get me some tweezers from the bathroom? Down the hallway to your right." I silently did as she asked.

"Look inside the drawer on the right!" she called out from the living room.

When I returned, I found her weeping again. I sat down beside her.

"Let me try," I examined her foot, which was almost as tiny as a child's foot, and extracted a thin, elongated shard of glass

from it. All the while, the cats climbed all over her and stepped on me, wriggling between us. She wiped the tears from her eyes.

"Did it hurt that much?" I asked.

"I'm not crying from the glass," she explained dryly.

I sat there in silence and then stood up and continued to sweep the floor. "It's everywhere," I muttered as I discovered more and more shards of glass in hidden corners.

"Yeah, some cups are made from thick glass, and even when they smash on the floor, they hardly break. But a thin glass, just a slight drop's enough to shatter it into tiny pieces."

"I think it's all gone now." I examined the floor again after I was done.

"Thank you," she said.

I sat down on the couch beside her again and asked, "It's not too deep, is it? Do you need stitches or anything?"

"I'll survive." She grinned. I was surprised to hear a note of cynicism in her voice.

"Why did you come here?" she asked. All the words I wanted to shout at her had gone into the bin along with the shards of glass.

"I... It doesn't matter. Read this." I placed the diary in her lap

I knew I should just stand up and leave but I didn't want to. I wanted to stay there beside her and revel in that peaceful silence, disturbed only by the enthusiastic purring of her three cats, ensuring that she was okay in that tiny apartment with mold on the ceiling, drawers missing from the cabinets, and no bolt on the front door to separate her apartment building from

the rest of the world. I suddenly realized that this was the first time I had seen Ella without her white coat.

I saw her again the next day at my mother's funeral. This time, she wore jeans and a plain black T-shirt and maintained a stoic expression behind her dark sunglasses. Just as she observed me from afar at the ward the other day, I now observed her. The condolences, the handshakes, the strange procession to the burial plot, saying the *Kaddish* – it all transpired around me as I searched for Ella with my eyes. I was worried I'd lose sight of her among the throngs of my mother's academic colleagues, students, and Ministry of Education officials who had absented themselves from her sickbed but returned to pay their last respects.

As my mother was laid in her final resting place, Ella didn't stand among the gathering crowd but watched the proceedings from a distance. As the crowd dispersed, she drew near, stood facing me, lifted her sunglasses, and looked into my eyes without saying a word.

"Will I see you again?" I heard myself asking her. She took my left hand in hers and squeezed it once.

And from that moment on, there was Ella, no longer my mother's psychologist. She was the rehab for the way I'd dealt with my life thus far but also a new and much more powerful drug. She was the smartest, funniest, and most calming woman I have ever met. Yes, calming. When I was with her, the perpetual anguish perched on my shoulders seemed to dissipate. There was no need for pretense around her. She saw who I was and accepted me against all odds. For reasons I could

not comprehend, she even appreciated me and desired me.

All I wanted was to be with her. Beside her. But in her company, I couldn't maintain the behavior I'd adopted for myself. There was no point in smiling that arrogant half-smile I would consciously use to evoke a sense of inferiority among my colleagues. There was no reason to dress to impress as designer clothes had no effect on Ella. There was no need to use lofty expressions since I couldn't patronize her.

My nightly bar crawls through trendy hotspots were replaced with evenings on her tattered sofa as she caressed my hair and told me about her childhood in Leningrad. I felt I didn't want anything else. I didn't need anything else.

I think you've met your fair share of cheap thrills for today. And what about you? Your texts are so focused on Yasmin (by the way, why did she stop visiting her mother?) and on yourself. Men are practically absent from your narrative. Does Lady Love ever frequent your sheets?

Warm regards,

Someone

Subject: She really does sound special

So why did you end up separating? Does it have anything to do with the fact that you speak (and write) like a pretentious prick? I swear you're so full of yourself.

Liz

Subject: Indeed she is

Dear Liz, you didn't number your letter so I assume you understand that it will not count as part of your quota.

Perhaps, one day, I'll tell you why we separated.

You didn't answer my questions. Is there no romance in your life? And why did Yasmin stop visiting her mother in the United States?

Warm regards,

Someone

Subject: I heard you the first time

If you must know, Jazz stopped visiting her mom because one of mommy dearest's creepy boyfriends put his hands all over her and it took her mom about two years to believe that it had happened.

And as for me? I'm just a guy magnet, right? Strange that you're even asking. I don't believe that I can attract someone. I don't feel like I could please someone. Don't feel anything much, actually. I don't think anyone can really understand or want to bring all my shit into their world. Why would anyone want a girl who can't go anywhere, a girl who, instead of thinking about vacations and school and parties, spends her days ruminating about death and wakes up every night from nightmares like a little kid? Yes, there were a few, some even said how special I was and promised not to freak out. So they said, but they freaked and ran back to their normal, sane lives. And it's fine because I didn't really want any of them anyway. In any case, they were just an attempt at distraction, destined for failure.

Liz

Subject: That's unfortunate

I was sorry to read about what Yasmin went through at her mother's. Nevertheless, I do believe that everyone has a chance at love, Liz, even you – a greater chance than you think, I imagine. There's much to gain from it.

Warm regards,

Someone

Subject: And this coming from someone who never leaves the house?

When was the last time you made love with someone other than your hand?

Liz

Subject: At least I tried

Warm regards,

Someone

Subject: Oh well

I guess it's just too late for me. And it really doesn't matter, I won't be here soon anyway.

Liz

Subject: Better late

What did you mean when you wrote, "It's just too late for me," and, "I won't be here soon"? Why do you deny yourself the chance to love or be loved? Where will you not be?

    Warm regards,

Someone

Subject: Never mind

Forget it. Just a slip of the keyboard.

Liz

Subject: Was it really?

Dear Liz, are you "blowing me off"? Your words did not seem so casual. What did you mean when you wrote that you, "won't be here soon," and that, "it's too late" for you?

Warm regards,

Someone

Subject: Enough already

Okay, why are you making such a big deal about it? I just typed some things without giving them too much thought! Isn't it enough that you steal my past and force me to dwell on it? Now you're trying to interpret every line I write?! Geez, just let it go!

Liz

Subject: Liz's fortune-telling

Dear Liz, I will not "let it go"! You've written some very disturbing words. Tell me what you meant by, "I guess it's just too late for me. And it really doesn't matter, I won't be here soon anyway."

Warm regards,

Someone

Subject: Liz?

Dear Liz, I have read over our recent correspondence again and again, and your replies leave me rather uncomfortable in light of your general state of mind. I can't help but ask you: are you thinking of harming yourself in some way?

Warm regards,

Someone

Subject: First Warning

Dear Liz, you haven't answered my question. I see that you've logged in to your Gmail account and so I know that you're out there. Respond immediately, or else... I shall delete a substantial number of your precious letters. Are you planning to harm yourself?

Warm regards,

Someone

Subject: Oh, come on

Enough is enough!!! Who do you think you are??? Florence fucking Nightingale's evil twin? Who are you to judge and interrogate me??? What do you care, anyway?! Do you think the fact that you've forced me to become your freaking pen pal gives you the right to act like you're my best friend or shrink? Get out of my life and stop pretending to know me or care about me. Keep reading the stinking letters I write to you, jerk off on them for all I care, use them to squeeze out your next novel or whatevz, just leave me alone and stop trying to pseudo-solve my problems!

Fuck you. Who you are and what do you want from me?

Liz

Subject: Second Warning

Dear Liz, and I use the word "dear" sincerely and not just as lip or keyboard service. You are, indeed, dear to me. I'm afraid I'm beginning to understand your intentions. Are you planning to kill yourself, leaving your journals behind as some kind of ineffectual monument to Yasmin or the devil knows who else? Could the real purpose of your writing be to create a keepsake not for yourself but of yourself, after you are gone?

If that's not the case, please convince me otherwise, but if my assumption is correct, know that I do not intend to cooperate with your morbid game. I would love nothing more than to be the wedge in the wheels of your foolish plan.

Let me make this perfectly clear: if you kill yourself, all traces of Yasmin's letters, your records of her, and your friendship, will be lost along with you. I must further clarify that if you fail to convince me that you do not intend to harm yourself, I will do everything in my power to stand in your way. I refuse to play a supporting role in your final act.

I offer you my friendship, Liz, and my impatience. If this is indeed your intention, I will not allow you to slip away through the fingers of the world.

Warm regards,

Someone

Subject: Letter Number 13

Once again you threaten me with the only tool in your possession. I'm tired of your threats. I'm tired of everything. What if I have surrendered to everything I couldn't be? And what if this helplessness has triumphed too many times?

If you can't move around and be happy, or be anything that others your age and others in general are supposed to be, or be what you're meant to be, how long before you're just gone? If you're unable to hope, unable to heal, how long will it take until you disappear?

And what if you're right and I can no longer be that "person who can't"? I can't go on living among my memories. The life I used to have seems to mock the person I've become. I can't live with a human-sized wound. Who's going to take it away from me? You?

You know what? You're right, Sherlock. You finally perceived something that wasn't written in my letters. I've drifted so far away from the person I once was that I don't see a way or a time for me to return. I look ahead and I see more despair, atrophy, and misery – more of this creature that I've become, who I despise, and I can take no more.

This nothingness is ever-present in my life. It stalks me like a wounded, starving animal. At night, I can see its glassy eyes glaring at me through the darkness. During the day, I feel it

wandering around the room, moving among things like a ghost, soundlessly, ready to pounce. And I'm tired. I don't think it's going anywhere, and I don't want to try to run from it anymore. All the books I wanted to read, all the things I wanted to learn and become... I can't reach them from here.

I once believed that there's a thin thread of goodness that moves through our lives like some kind of invisible seamstress sewing things together. Today, I know that's bullshit; it's all random and only people who have never faced real problems still believe that the universe will sort things out for them. And I hate the defilement that this loss of faith brings with it, the intimate acquaintance I've formed with the cruelty of the world.

Honestly? For the past three years or so, I've been waking up every morning and asking myself, "To be or not to be?" not as a metaphor, but pragmatically, just as you'd decide between wearing the green shirt or the yellow one. Day after day, I've chosen "to be" but the disparity between the person I once was and the person I am today is growing, while I'm slowly shrinking.

The truth is: death is the only thing I seek. Every high rooftop seems like a chance for redemption and every name in the obituaries is someone to envy. I don't want to be like this anymore. After so many things that I couldn't choose, I finally feel like I have a choice in the matter. I'm allowed to choose at least one thing in this life, even if the choice I make is to end it! For far too long now, I've been a source of shame and sorrow to anyone who's ever known me. I don't see how this is ever going to change and don't want to take on that role anymore. I'll pass, thanks.

And as for all those anti-suicide advocates who post their shit on the internet, let's see how they feel after losing everything they loved in this world: the person they loved most, their hopes, and their dreams. Let's see how they'd go on living without losing themselves.

While you shut yourself up in your swanky Tel Aviv apartment, choosing to escape from your personal hell, I have no such option. I can't escape my nightmare – I live it in my thoughts, irrational fears, unbearable bouts of anxiety that I just can't find a way to stop. So, fuck you, with your double standards and your self-righteous threats and your bogus concern. Get out of my miserable life and go back to fiddling with yours!

Liz

"Hello?"

"Hello. Mrs. Fine?"

"Yes, who's calling?"

"Keep an eye on your daughter."

"What? Who is this?"

"You don't know me, but I know Liz and I'm calling to let you know that you should keep an eye on your daughter. She's planning to harm herself."

"What?! Who is this?!"

"Liz is planning to kill herself, Mrs. Fine. Look after her."

"Hello? Hello?"

Subject: A Wedge

Dear Liz,

In case you needed proof that I'm a man of my word, you just received such. The rules have now changed:

1. Your laptop will not be returned to you until I am convinced that you have no intention of taking your own life.

2. Whenever I do not hear from you or fear that you are planning to harm yourself, I will call, and the next phone call will not be to your parents but to the kibbutz offices, the police, or the mental health services. As I've made clear, I do not intend to stand by while you plan your demise.

3. Every time you ignore my request, I will delete one of your files. Remember the email in which Yasmin wrote to you about buying the motorcycle you two chose together? You can wave that email goodbye. Permanently.

4. From time to time, I shall send you a task. If you fail to complete it, I will erase more memories or call the relevant authorities who will ensure your well-being in even less pleasant methods than the ones I'm taking. You can surely imagine what those methods could be.

5. Your first task, Liz, is to send me a list of things worth staying for. That is to say, staying here for, in this world,

alive. I don't care what you think of my request. Send me a list of things that make life worthwhile. And no, I'm not interested in knowing how absurd this task sounds to you.

Warm regards,

Someone

Subject: Letter Number 14

Listening to Radiohead's Kid A for the first time. Sitting in front of someone and feeling with utter certainty that everything is in its right place. The inexhaustible possibility that it could happen again with people I have yet to meet. The first sip of a good cup of coffee after a caffeine-crave that has screamed in my veins and crawled down my arms. The first sip of a cup of coffee spiked with whiskey. The first sip of a shot of whiskey without the coffee, rolling it around slowly in your mouth as if it were a secret or the essence of all your good memories that no longer hurt to remember. The same with a glass of Merlot. A kiss cocktail (half Merlot, half vodka). A first kiss with someone I wanted to kiss. Saturday morning newspapers. Sappy romantic comedies. Cafés, smoky bars, steam, the color red, rain outside my window. Cats. Cozy slippers. Summer, sun, bikini, feeling pretty, anything related to water. Floating on your back facing the sun, in the middle of a pool or at sea, at two in the afternoon or two in the morning. Sunlight flickering on the water at all hours of the day. The moon. Night swimming. Being naked. The feeling of a large, cradling hand. Music enveloping your body, *Ágætis byrjun*, talking with the world. Discovering a new album. Listening to an album I managed to forget and realizing why I loved it at the age of nine or thirteen or seventeen. Pat Metheny, Bright Size Life, Coltrane on a rainy

day while cooking pasta. Friday afternoon gliding into Saturday. Listening to the Beatles and remembering cravings from when I was ten years old. Listening to Pink Floyd and being so awed, when I first heard them, that someone had made music that was everything I thought music should be. Meeting a person who inspires the same kind of awe in me. The possibility that someone like that exists. Reading poetry by Yehuda Amichai: "Open Close Open," "Six Poems for Tamar." When sex turns into slow dancing. Hugging shirtless for the first time. Breathing each other in for what seems like hours, hours that seem like moments. Approaching the light at the end of all tunnels. When he holds my hand. The torment on the way. The white flash at the end of total physical exertion. The possibility that I could be someone's mom, and that I'd be a really good mom. Singing. A good conversation that turns into a dance. A rainy day and a colorful crowd in Tel Aviv. Jerusalem at dusk. Milky, white light on stone walls. A crowded street, infinite possibilities, my dreams, my hopes, New York, and all the places I haven't visited yet. Effortless calm.

And what's on your list, you loser?

Fuck You.

Liz

Subject: Good Girl

I must confess that I didn't understand some of the entries on your list. I was often compelled to refer to my search engine for consultation. I continue to monitor your virtual presence to ensure you're still there and look forward to receiving your next letter within a week at most.

My list is quite short: You.

Warm regards,

Someone

Subject: Letter Number 15

"You." How typical of you to write that. Such laconic, passive-aggressive pompousness. I'm the reason your life is worth living?! Really? Why me? How come?

Do you want to know what I think? I think it's easier for you to focus on me instead of on your own life, a life that you somehow managed to fuck up entirely. It's convenient for you to tell me and yourself that you actually care about me, that with my help you'll be able to write your next fucking novel. Along the way, you'll also manage to save my life and we'll both experience a form of fucking catharsis and Google the sunset together.

But life is not an artificial backdrop made up of words. You don't know me, care about me, or want contact with any other creature in the world. I'm just trapped in my own head and pathetic enough to make you think you can have the best of both worlds by communicating with someone and even helping them without having to see them – *really* see them, not through some one-way mirror.

I was so angry at you for making that damned phone call to my mother. I'm still angry. But do you want to hear something sad? I can't hold it against you. At the end of the day, I guess I'd have done the same if I found out that someone was planning to off themselves. I'd do everything I could to stop them.

The truth is that wanting to die, planning to die, has served

as my only safe haven in recent years. It was a thought that gave me total peace, something that depended solely on my own decision. But it was also the loneliest place, a place no one else could be allowed to enter because, once they did, my safe space would dissolve.

If you really want to die, you don't make idle threats and you don't share your desire with anyone else for fear of losing the opportunity. You don't make failed attempts, either, because you only get one shot. If you fail, your only escape route will disappear and you'll forever bear the mark of Cain on your forehead. You'll always be the one who tried, who came too close to the edge.

And then you came along and fucking-well thrust yourself into this dark place of mine and flung open the door and tried to let my family in, too. It was quite elegant on your part to scare to death a couple of sixty-something-year-olds.

In the meantime, I did some damage control and managed to distract them from that horrible phone call of yours, but I must admit that the very fact that you know brings me some comfort in a twisted sort of way. At least now there's one person with whom I don't need to pretend, someone who knows what I really think about all day, who knows that I want – truly want – to die.

Maybe you're surprised at this sudden confession. I admit to being a little surprised, too, but I'm tired of being mad at you. You wanted this role? You got it! You've now become the person I can talk to about these things precisely because you're the most messed up person I've ever known, yet I have no idea

who you really are; you read all my stuff without me asking you to, and you're not my friend, and we don't care about each other in a conventional manner.

If you really care about me as you claim you do, prove it. Come on and be my real friend. Not a friend with threats, ultimatums, and penalties. Be a friend who deals with my shit. Be here with me in this place where I've existed ever since death, much like you did, forced its way into my life and my head. Live with me through that question that plagues me every morning: to be or not to be? Choose the green or yellow shirt. Help me understand why I should go on living because, with all due respect to what I wrote in my list, great music is not a good enough reason, not when you're suffering through almost every single moment and feel that you're no longer yourself. I want to find a way to stay, I just don't know how. Help me understand why I shouldn't leave. There's no one else I can turn to.

Lots of things happened here this week. I'll write all about it in my next letter.

Liz

Subject: A kick in the underbelly

Dear Liz, I am indeed surprised by your words. I must admit that this wasn't the response I expected. After all, you are very familiar with the fact that I have no friends and that transparency – how shall I say it – is not my forte. And yet you place these two terms, friendship and sincerity, as necessary provisions for your survival. And yes, you're right, I've placed myself in this position. No one asked me to be here.

I humbly accept the challenge you've laid out before me. I will try to "be here with you," as you put it, but this agreement does not replace or supersede my suspicion or my previous demands. Remember, Liz, I'm the son of a suicidal father and I know that those who are addicted to thoughts of their demise may, much like alcoholics, do their best to appear clean just so they can once again turn to the object of their addiction.

You are correct. I've no right to present you with demands or lecture you, but I feel I have a duty to do so. I don't intend to sit idly by once more as a person dies before my eyes. Therefore, our friendship is one thing and my demands are another: don't give me a reason to suspect that you're planning to end your life, or else – you know the drill.

You've piqued my curiosity. What else happened last week?

Warm regards,

Someone

Subject: Letter Number 16

Okay, okay, give it a rest, will you? Terms and demands... Jeez, you're exhausting. It's quite ironic though, the fact that I'm going to tell *you*, of all people, what happened here.

Okay. So you probably remember the night you called my parents and scared my mom half to death. So that evening, another really strange thing happened. I went out of my parents' house for a short walk. I do that sometimes. Unlike you, I'm not agoraphobic or anything. In Tel Aviv, I'd go out for walks every once in a while. I liked feeling invisible. One of the best things about living in a big city, especially for those from a kibbutz, is that no one knows who you are. You can look around without anyone looking back at you. You can't experience that in the kibbutz, where, every time you leave the house, you're surrounded by people who know who you are, whose kid you are, whose grandchild, and what your story is – at least, in their opinion. It stresses me out. I cringe when I see those, "there's that weird Liz" looks. So, I don't leave the house here too often. But in the early evening, when the sun begins to set, I stroll along the lanes that lead off the sidewalk near my parents' house. The kibbutz nursing home is close to my parents' place. At night, you can hear the residents shout sometimes, haunted by nightmares or memories.

Anyway, while you were almost giving my mom a heart attack, I was strolling near the nursing home and one of the kibbutz veterans that I didn't know drove his mobility scooter toward me. Suddenly he stopped and looked at me like he was seeing a ghost. His shriveled body was transfixed in the soft pleather seat and his fair skin turned even paler. "Is everything okay?" I was worried he was having some kind of seizure there and then in front of me.

"Eliza? Eliza Fine..." he muttered to himself.

"Yes," I replied cautiously, surprised he knew my name.

"You can't be Eliza Fine!" he claimed decisively.

"But... it is me!" I countered, embarrassed and angry. What did he mean – I couldn't be who I am? Maybe the gossip about me leaving the kibbutz had reached the nursing home as well?

"*Zol zayn a lign, abi s'shaynt.* You're not really here!" he scolded me, and then murmured in wonder: "But you look just like her, a spitting image." He rose from his scooter and shuffled, hunched over, toward me. He had a prominent hunchback. His whole body seemed as if it sought to look down at the ground, while only his head rebelled against it and jutted upward. His gaping eyes stared up at me. He placed his hands on my shoulders and then felt my face gently. "Eliza... Eliza..." he whispered and continued to examine my face as if I was an archeological exhibit. His fingers, as wrinkled as if they'd been soaked in water for a long time, inched up toward my eyes, shaded my eyelids like curtains, pressed against the bridge of my nose, slid down, and lingered on my neck.

"*Zol zayn a lign, abi s'shaynt*," he muttered again and decided, "No, you're definitely not Eliza. But you look so much alike! Poor Eliza."

I began to understand what was going on here. He must have known my grandmother, Eliza. It wasn't the first time I've been told how much I resemble her.

"My grandmother lived here many years ago. Her name was Eliza Fine. Did you know her? My name's Eliza, too. I mean, Lizzie. I'm Tzvi and Rachel's daughter," I explained while his hands were still resting on my skin.

"Ah! Yes, of course! Oy, a broch. What a fool I've made of myself. What do you youngsters say? Fail!" The wonder in his eyes was replaced with curiosity. "Oh, you're clearly Eliza's granddaughter! A carbon copy!" He continued to examine my face, fascinated. "Of course I knew Eliza. I worked with her in the chicken coops. Poor Eliza. Such a dear woman. I'll never forget the day I found her hanging from that rope. And despite the rope, we buried her inside the fence. I'm sorry for my blunder, *maideleh*. At my age, well, you know, the shelves upstairs are no longer very organized," he apologized, turned, waddled back to his scooter, switched it on, and rode off toward the dining hall.

I stood there, dumbfounded. His words resonated in my ears. What did he mean, "I found her hanging from that rope"? And what was the deal with the fence? After all, Grandma Eliza died of malaria. Didn't she?

I went back to my parents' house feeling utterly confused and found them in the living room. Something in the way they were

standing there, both of them together, seemed odd.

"Listen, something really weird just happened to me." I wanted them to clarify the things I had heard.

"Liz, we want you to sit down," my mother said firmly.

"What?" I didn't understand what she wanted from me. "You're not going to believe what just happened to me. I have to ask you something."

"Sit down, Liz. We need to talk to you!" my mother commanded in a very uncharacteristic tone. I sat down on the two-seater couch. They hesitated for a moment and then sat down in unison on the other couch facing me.

"Are you planning... to do something to yourself, Liz?" My mother searched for the right words. "Do you have thoughts of... harming yourself?"

My father sat beside her, his head bowed, twiddling his fingers, and staring down at them with a stern look.

"What?!" I blurted in bewilderment.

"Liz, if you're considering self-harm, you must tell us!"

"Where did this question even come from?!" I confronted them and began to realize what you had done.

"Some man called the house and told us you were planning to hurt yourself."

"What do you mean, some man?" I tried to distract her.

"We don't know, he didn't introduce himself but he claimed to know you. It was a very frightening conversation, Lizzie."

I began to feel the rage surging through my body, heating my shoulders, pulsating through my arms.

"That makes no sense at all! You're asking me questions about suicide? Why are you so afraid of it? Because of Grandma Eliza?"

They both looked up in perfect sync as if someone had coordinated their movements and exchanged a meaningful look. I didn't need any further confirmation.

"What do you mean, because of Grandma Eliza?" my father asked slowly, his voice low.

"Some old man I just ran into outside told me I look like her and that he found her hanging from a rope. Is there anything you want to tell me?" I challenged them. They both fell silent.

"That's not the issue right now, Liz. Grandma Eliza isn't here. You are."

"So, you don't deny it?!" I felt my skull going up in flames. "Some idiot crank called you and now you're all wound up? Answer the question!"

"Who'd call and say such a thing, Liz? Why would anyone make up something like that?" my mother persisted.

"How should I know?" I lied. "And that's exactly what I'm asking. Why would anyone make up something like this?" I yelled. "And what about you, don't you have anything to say?" I confronted my father and suddenly realized that he was looking at me in horror. I remembered his expression when I woke up after the accident, and during the time where I was lying down on their couch, and when I ran out of the support group meeting in tears. This look was different, more anxious than ever before.

I wanted to get the hell away from there, but I knew that my racing heartbeat would soon overwhelm me and I didn't want to contend with the prying eyes of the kibbutz members I'd surely encounter along the lanes. So, I ran to the room I've appropriated for myself in their house and slammed the door behind me.

Liz

Subject: "It may be a lie, but it's beautiful"

Dear Liz, the subject line of this email is the translation of the Yiddish saying the old man muttered when he saw you.

I feel almost obligated to apologize for causing such a commotion in your life, but in all honesty, I feel no remorse. Think back to the horror you saw in your father's eyes. Have you given it any consideration? Your parents would certainly not have chosen me as their advocate yet they allow me to serve as such. It is your parents' right to know that you're planning to harm yourself.

I believe you are a brilliant young woman, in some ways very mature for your age, and nonetheless, in other ways, it seems that you are completely blind to your surroundings. You cannot imagine how your suicide will affect your parents. If you are determined to take your life in your hands, you must "be there," as you demanded of me, to approach the matter with eyes wide open and acknowledge the consequences of your choices. Who better than you knows the destruction strewn in the wake of the death of someone close?

If you simply miss the days when you had control over your life, take control of what you have right now. Acknowledge the fact that you have a problem that can be managed, treated, and lived with – through gritted teeth, perhaps, through struggle and pain, but all these are preferable over nothingness. Lean

on your parents. Believe me, they would rather grit their teeth along with you than do so after you're gone.

I enclose another email from Yasmin written to you from New York. I couldn't help but recall it in light of recent events.

I gather that you think your parents' reaction confirms your grandmother's suicide. Nevertheless, this story could just be the hallucinations of a dementia-stricken senior citizen. It sounds like something you should explore.

Warm regards,

Someone

Attachment: What's up, my darling wisdom tooth?

Hi, Babe. Sorry I couldn't catch you on your cell yesterday. You won't believe what's been going on here this weekend! Remember Jane, my roommate? So, she hasn't been doing too well lately. She got another rejection from a record label and her boyfriend had enough of her (not that I blame him, the girl has a super talent for pissing people off). Anyway, since it happened, she hasn't moved much, she just lies in bed all day like some zombie. It doesn't bother me too much. We're definitely not BFFs and she's not the first girl to get depressed cos her boyfriend dumped her, but it's dragged her right down.

The other day, I walked into the apartment and heard a strange noise coming from her bedroom. I opened the door and caught a glimpse of her sitting on the floor and cutting her leg, slash-by-slash, with one of our fucking kitchen knives! She screamed at me to get out but I snatched the knife away from her hand. She started chasing me and tried to grab the knife back. It wasn't particularly hard to dodge her as she was bleeding all over the floor. I opened the kitchen drawers, took out all the knives, shoved them into a paper bag, and told her I was tossing them in the trash. She yelled at me, "Fuck you, I hate you!" and ran to the bathroom. So, I found her cellphone, called a few of her friends whose names I remembered her mentioning on several occasions, and told them what she did. All the while,

I was making sure she wasn't checking out on me with some razor blade in the bathroom, right?

Obviously, she was crazy mad at me and all that shit but, yesterday, various friends of hers started showing up here. Now she hates me and isn't talking to me, like we're in the fourth grade or something. But at least there are people here who know her properly.

For sure, it's going to be super weird in the apartment in the coming weeks. I'll need to keep a trillion eyes on her, but it's better than scraping blood off the floor and trying to tell her parents in the Midwest what happened to their precious daughter.

I'll definitely be online tonight, so talk to me when you can.

From me, your darling vascular system.

Subject: Letter Number 17

Seriously? Not that I wasn't glad to receive it, but still – using one of Jazz's letters as an argument against me? Do you have it in anything more transparent?

I need to think about all those things you wrote. That is, as soon as I stop laughing at the absurdity of *you* telling me that I need to be more honest.

I'd like to keep arguing with you about that but there have been things more important than that bullshit happening around here in the past few days. After that phone call, my parents' house was like a minefield with no warning signs posted around its perimeter. I locked myself in my room for the next few days. On my brief outings, they both stared at me with concern and averted their eyes when I stared back. My mom tried to talk to me several times, but I pushed her away. I ignored her. I scowled.

I felt imprisoned. My cards were revealed, my secret death wish exposed. I managed to suppress their questions with questions of my own that went unanswered. All the things left unspoken hovered around us like a bad stench that no one dared to mention.

Meanwhile, I couldn't stop thinking about that conversation with the old man near the nursing home. So many questions arose in my mind. Did my grandmother commit suicide? The

thought haunted me. I gazed at my computer screen, reading the same paragraph over and over again. The other day, I found myself staring at the textbooks lying open on my bed at the same page as the day before, and I realized I couldn't go on like this. I had to know.

I headed to the kibbutz nursing home. The supervisor greeted me with surprise. "Liz, what are you doing here?"

"I'm looking for a person, I think he lives here. I don't know his name. He's not tall. He has... he's a bit hunched over." I was uncomfortable using the word "hunchback."

"Eliza, the granddaughter of Eliza!" I heard him approaching along the hallway, waddling as fast as he could, leaning on a walker whose front two legs were encased in split tennis balls. "Have you come to visit me?"

"Ah... actually, yes," I confirmed, surprised at myself.

"Nahum, I didn't know you were acquainted with Rachel's daughter," the supervisor marveled.

"Well, of course, we're old friends. After all, I knew her grandmother."

"Nach'che, you're always full of surprises!" She spoke to him like he was a child.

So his name is Nahum. Nach'che.

"Shall we sit in my room? I have tea and cookies!" He cheered and began to advance slowly down the hall.

"Ah... sure." I pulled myself together and joined him.

"So, Eliza, the granddaughter of Eliza..." he paused and stared at me when we reached his small room.

"Liz," I corrected awkwardly.

"Yes. Liz. You'll have to forgive me, it's just, well, God help me. I've already told you. You're the spitting image of your grandmother." He gazed at me for a long moment before he composed himself and asked, "Tea? Coffee? I don't have any milk, but they'll probably have some in the kitchen. Do you like chocolate chip cookies? Maybe some wafers? I've got some here for the grandchildren when they visit. They haven't been for a while. Oh well, they must have more interesting things to do than listen to their *altelach* grandfather rattling away with his stories. Pretzels?"

"Sit down. I'll do it," I suggested.

"*Oy*, well, don't put me out to pasture too soon, these old poles can still do some work," he protested but had a hard time opening the kettle and filling it with water. I helped him while he picked out two old plastic plates from the small dish rack and opened a cupboard from which dozens of sealed snack bags in a variety of colors peeked out, crammed against one another between the small shelves. He brought out five of them, struggled as he opened each one, and carefully arranged small piles of snacks on the plates. "I hope they're still fresh. I don't get many visitors and I'm not allowed to eat these things," he apologized.

He placed the plates on a small dresser that stood in the center of the room and invited me to sit on a lonely chair that stood facing it. He sank into his armchair, made himself comfortable, sighed, and surveyed me again. "So, to what do I owe this honor, Eliza? Um, Liza, you call yourself?"

"Liz," I corrected. "I... I wanted to hear more from you about

my grandmother." I didn't know how to better phrase my question.

"*Oy*, Eliza, may she rest in peace," he sighed. "A broch, what we went through with her. And your father. He was just a *yingele* when it happened. Some members of the kibbutz blamed her, but no one was really surprised. After all, we saw things. Well, in those days, what did we know about mental health? Social support? We just knew we needed to work to survive. No one ever talked about such matters back then."

"So, she didn't die of natural causes?" I tried to steer him in the right direction. He responded with a burst of disheartened laughter.

"Natural causes? *Oy*, Liza. When you reach my age, you'll come to know that every living creature is fated to die, but death is never natural."

"So, what exactly happened to her?"

"Well, no wonder you came to see me. Your grandmother could never let things go, either. Look..." He searched for the right words, cleared his throat, and continued. "I heard that in the agricultural training farms in Poland your grandmother was called "Smiling Eliza," but when I met her here, at the kibbutz, she rarely smiled. You know, Liza, at the kibbutz, we valued uniformity. We thought everyone should be the same, think the same, feel the same. And if we couldn't feel it, then at least we should say the same and do the same. But your grandmother... Well, she wasn't the same. Especially not after what happened to your grandfather. You must know about that."

"He died in prison."

"Yes," Nahum confirmed. "Look. Your grandfather, he was, as they say, a head above the rest. Here in the kibbutz, we had laborers, we also had intellectuals, but your grandfather – he was both. Well, he had a personality, the kind of man who always knew what to say, a mediator. He was the kibbutz secretary and was arrested in the wake of the Hebrew Resistance Movement. You must have learned about it at school. The British suspected that members of the movement against the British Mandate were hiding here, in the kibbutz. They searched everywhere and *gornisht*. They interrogated your grandfather and, of course, he didn't disclose a thing. Well, as far as I know, there was nothing to disclose. So, they arrested him, took him to the prison in Acre and he never returned from there. He sent letters for a while, but then there was an outbreak of some disease among the prisoners and the letters stopped coming. Agents of the movement received notice of his death." He paused, lost in reflection.

"And your grandmother, she... well, drifted further away from us. If she rarely smiled before, once your grandfather passed away, she also rarely spoke. I worked with her in the chicken coops. Oh, how she hated that job, but that's what the kibbutz needed. And she worked with dogged determination, cleaning fervently even when it was already clean, more and more. We held fascinating conversations; she had such a sharp wit! But after your grandfather passed, well, it became more challenging to get the words out of her."

I looked at him intently, alert, and he continued.

"At that time, more and more survivors arrived, you know, and with them the news. We began to understand a little about

what had happened there in Europe, in Poland. Gradually, we realized that there was nothing left. I always thought to myself that this was what broke your grandmother – not the story with your grandfather, but maybe all of it together. How she loved her sisters and her father! She would tell me about them and their house in Warsaw with a sparkle in her eyes.

"Here at the kibbutz, we loathed that kind of European bourgeoisie, but when we talked in the chicken coop, Eliza would delve into stories of her youth. I could sense that she missed the beautiful clothes, the culture, the Warsaw of her childhood, and, most of all, her family. She hoped one of her sisters had survived. Every time an envoy from the kibbutz headed to Europe, she gathered the strength to show him the photographs, direct his search, and question him upon his return. In time, she realized that nothing was left and I think it was too much for her. She had lost far too many things.

"She stopped showing up to work at the chicken coop. She stayed in bed all day. And then the kibbutz started talking. How could this be? A kibbutz member who isn't sick and isn't working? We would always say: 'From each according to his ability, to each according to his needs.' So, please, you have the ability! Go out into the sunshine! Get up and work! It will do you good. No one understood exactly what was happening to her. What did we know about things like depression? We didn't believe in depression, we believed in laziness! We had to be strong, healthy, active. We knew what happened to the weak or the ailing. They would be sent to the left during the selection process!

"Anyway, one morning I arrived at the chicken coop and found her. Well, no need to get into the details. She was hanging from a rope, the kind used to tie the chicken feed sacks, her head drooping down. I ran to her, lifted her legs, and held her up like that for a while, shouting for her to wake up. Despite all the mess up here on the shelves," he pointed to his head, "I will never forget that day. Her body was stiff. I tried to shake her, wake her up. I was alone there. I ran to get a knife and a chair. I cut the rope and tried my best to resuscitate her, but *shoin*, nothing could be done.

"You know, according to the Halakha, we were supposed to bury her outside the fence, and even though the kibbutz cemetery isn't religious, we were afraid of any repercussions. She didn't deserve to be buried outside alone. Your father certainly didn't deserve that. No father, no mother, and outside the fence? So we didn't talk about what happened to her. We buried her and kept quiet.

"Among themselves, some were angry. What a thing to do! A person needs to pick themselves up. It's tough here for all of us, but we need to roll up our sleeves, buckle down, work, and build. If we all stop to look back, we'll end up frozen, a pillar of salt like Lot's wife. And then what will become of this place?

"Nowadays, we know that we're not all the same, Liza. The kibbutz isn't what it used to be. Oy, look how long I've been talking." He stopped and sighed, looking at me and assessing my reaction.

"Is it possible that she didn't do that to herself?" I asked. "Maybe someone hung her? Could it have been a murder or something?"

"Look, Liza. We thought about that. After all, it wasn't too long after the War of Independence. We looked for evidence, but there were no footprints other than her own and no fingerprints. No one had a motive. We just didn't realize how much she had struggled to cope, to conform. Oh, well, *az der vorem zitst in khreyn, meynt er az es iz keyn zisers nito*. We didn't know any better. We believed that the best way to help someone was to force them to stand up on their own two feet, and she could not stand."

"And you? Like, you just kept working in that chicken coop after you found her there like that?" I wondered.

"What else could I do? Someone had to feed the chickens. I kept going. It was just another obstacle among many to overcome. But I never forgot her. Well, you saw how she popped into my head the minute I saw you."

I needed to process all the things Nahum had told me so I turned the conversation to his life, his family, his grandchildren. While he was talking about them, the details of his story raced through my head. I tried to imagine what had happened in that chicken coop, which today is nothing but a crumbling, abandoned structure tucked away in the fields of the kibbutz.

I didn't know how to thank him for this talk. This elderly man, completely unrelated to my life, had revealed a story that the people closest to me never shared.

When I stood up to leave, he faced me and placed his hand on my cheek. "Take care of yourself, huh, *maideleh*? And come talk with me again. There are so many stories from those years. Sometimes you need to pick up a book from these old shelves

and read from it before it becomes too muddled in there to find anything," he said with poignant humor and pointed at his head.

On my way out, the supervisor looked up from her desk and called me over. "Lizzie, look, I don't know what Nach'che told you. He's very nice, a smart man, there's no doubt about that, and he also has a sense of humor. It's quite something! But anything he says should be taken with a grain of salt, because he's... as they say, not altogether with us. You know, loneliness can play games with people's minds."

"But his grandchildren, they visit sometimes, don't they?"

"Nach'che has no grandchildren. His wife died of cancer twenty years ago. I'm not sure you'd have her, Malka. They had no children."

I came out of there more confused than when I went in.

There was much more after that, but I've rambled enough for today.

Liz

Subject: When a worm sits in horseradish, it thinks it's sugar

Dear Liz, I turned to my search engine to look up the meaning of the Yiddish expression Nahum mentioned: *az der vorem zitst in khreyn, meynt er az es iz keyn zisers nito.* The subject line of this letter is its translation.

So much is happening, Liz. I'm curious to read the rest of your exploits! You previously wrote that you miss adventures, parties, festivals, or the devil knows what. You lamented about trips and journeys that never transpired. What's the purpose of all those escapades if not to experience yourself in extreme situations and push yourself to the edge? And who do you think has gone through a more far-reaching "journey into self" (to borrow this New Age term, which I can't tolerate) – you, or some twenty-something hipster doing drugs in a loud, crowded, artificially-lit club?

Who do you think has stretched to their extreme? All those young people dancing at parties, flying to the ends of the earth, taking drugs to gain some absurd social validation, or drinking themselves senseless in clubs? They don't challenge themselves as much as you do. The person who remains with himself, alone between four walls, without the bustle of humanity, with no

chemical substances or distractions, hour after hour, day by day, comes far closer to the edge than all those masked clowns at clubs and parties. Believe me.

It seems that your life has seen more traffic than usual lately. What happened after your ambiguous visit to the nursing home? I look forward to hearing from you.

Warm regards,

Someone

Subject: Letter Number 18

Listen, I'm not sure about what you wrote. I don't think people can push themselves to just one extreme. You can get to know yourself in countless extreme situations. The ones I've undergone are not something I would experience if I had a choice. If we're talking about despair or fear, I guess I did go further than most people. But if we're talking about things I've seen or tried, or learned about different cultures and places, then I'm just an infant. What can I possibly know about these things? Everything I managed to experience occurred before the accident. At least I accomplished a few things before it happened.

It's kind of ridiculous that you rant about all sorts of fucked-up rationalizations in an attempt to convince me that my life's not that crappy. I don't see you battling against your misery like that, against your childhood, your wife dumping you, or whatever happened between you two. I don't see you trying to convince yourself that these were valuable, enriching experiences in order to extract yourself from the stinking swamp that is now your life. Not leaving the house is your idea of pushing yourself to the edge? Is that your excuse?

Forget it. These rhetorical discussions are exhausting. I'd rather just tell you what's happening in the here and now. After my conversation with Nahum, I was completely dismayed. Why can't anything be simple? I had no idea if what he told me was

true or if he was just a poor old man imagining things. On the one hand, he spoke with absolute conviction about grandchildren who don't even exist, and on the other hand, the things he told me about my grandfather were true as far as I know, and also about my grandmother and her work in the chicken coop. But then again, the man was sure I was my grandmother. I no longer know what to think. I'm tired of secrets, tired of not knowing, tired of things that are better left unsaid. I figured that, if my grandmother did kill herself, there must be some evidence of the fact in my parents' house.

So I've been into their bedroom where they keep all their documents and paperwork and looked through binders and folders. They're very well organized, my parents. Neat, efficient, everything in its place. I found bank printouts, medical records, and my school report cards – fourth grade, fifth grade, sixth grade, everything filed in perfect order. Army recruitment and discharge papers. Store receipts, warranty certificates. Two binders related to my accident. There were my hospital discharge documents, doctors' letters, and dozens of receipts from the physiotherapy clinic. Photos, photos, and more photos. My childhood photographs, all of us smiling by some lake on a sunny day. I think I remember that holiday. I was about four years old.

I emptied more drawers and scattered the papers across my parents' bed... documents, more and more documents. I moved to the desk in the room that was once mine and upturned the desk drawers to examine every carefully arranged plastic protector sleeve. In one drawer, I found several photos of my

mother's parents. They also lived on the kibbutz and I knew them as a child, but I still couldn't find anything related to my father's parents. I went back into their bedroom and kept on opening binders, scattering documents and pictures until I reached my father's nightstand. In the bottom drawer, under the medals and awards from his army unit, I found a bunch of yellowing stationery filled with cramped handwriting, and each sheet was signed: "Yours, Eliza."

I gently ran my hand over the old paper. It was so thin that I was afraid it would crumble between my fingers. I breathed in the aging pages, scrutinized the tiny handwriting, and tried to distinguish the imprint the ink made on the paper to see if it was weak or strong.

The letter read as follows:

Dear Shlomo,

For some time now, it seems that the dam separating my past and my present has burst. My former life has returned to haunt my mind. Now and then, as I wake at dawn, I can taste my mother's apple pastries in my mouth. Fifteen years have passed since I last bit into one. It tastes fermented and rotten in my mouth. One morning, I imagined that I awoke to the sun's rays coming in through my father's study window at my parents' house in Warsaw. I remembered how the sun illuminated his wrinkled brow as he pondered over his books and, for a moment, it seemed that all those ancient books he used to read opened before me and simultaneously uttered all the things he knew and had yet to teach me – a cacophony of words and information, hustling to and fro.

Just like a digested meal regurgitating back up one's throat, my old acquaintances resurface in my mind as if they are flesh and blood. The humble shopkeeper from the street corner. What has become of him? And Gittel, the seamstress? Despite my attempts, I cannot banish them from my thoughts. In the middle of the day, I suddenly remember the Muranów quarter before it was imprisoned within brick walls. I feel as though I am walking through its streets, enveloped in the images of haberdashery shops, the calls of vendors selling their wares, and the sound of children reveling on the sidewalks as they return from school. Sometimes, unexpectedly, I feel as though the whole city has resurrected in my mind with all its streets and people and sidewalks and buildings that were once there and are now no more. I wish to persist with my work yet find it difficult to uphold my routine when an entire dead city exists in my mind.

Yours, Eliza.

Dear Shlomo,
Last night, Brunia came to me in my dream. She was so very thin, her skin pale, her clothes frayed. The ground around her was burnt, barren, smoke rising from the ashes. She staggered a little, turned to the left, and stood there. I asked her to make herself heard but she did not reply. She gazed at me in silence. We stood facing each other as strangers.

Yours, Eliza.

Dear Shlomo,

Zalman Weinfeld, who was sent to Europe as an envoy on behalf of the movement, returned from his mission. I went to meet him and asked him if he had come across Yonah, Perla, Brunia, or my parents, whose photographs I had shown him before his voyage. He replied that he had not seen any of them. I asked him if he had seen my parents' house and he replied in the same tone. No house. No opera, no museums. No ghetto, either. Only the Vistula River remained.

Yours, Eliza

Dear Shlomo,

Yesterday, on my way to work in the chicken coop, I looked up at a flock of migratory birds flying across the sky. They flew in perfect formation and suddenly one bird fluttered away from the flock, dived, and dropped to the ground. I wondered how all these birds were able to effortlessly circumvent the forces of gravity, while this lone bird could not.

Yours, Eliza

Dear Shlomo,

I look at Tzvi and see you in him. All the good in the world is wrapped up in this child. When he walks up to me with his intelligent smile, my heart aches that I am not able to return his smile. As he returns from the children's house to our little unit, eyes blazing with excitement and mouth full of tales of adventure, the room remains dark and cheerless and I cannot bring myself to rejoice with him. The nectar of life seems to be infused in his blood

while the life force within me grows dimmer. Every morning, I vow to greet him at the door today with a smile and behave as I should, but I am not as I was. I regret that you were taken from him while I remained. How greatly he would have benefited from a father such as you, whereas I bestow upon him nothing but sorrow and shame.

    Yours, Eliza

Dear Shlomo,

Last night, I saw Brunia in my dream once again, even thinner now, her hair sparse and brittle, her body withered as if she was only a shell of her former image. This time, she spoke, but it was not her voice emitting from her lips, it was yours. In your voice, she said that she had found you and that you were not well. When I awoke, I felt that all the things that are gone beckon me to join them.

    Yours, Eliza

And then my dad came home. I'll tell you the rest next time. Copying all these letters has exhausted me.

    Liz

Subject: One Edge, Many Extremes

As to the first part of your letter: be it one edge or many extremes, there is only one truth. What has happened cannot be undone; you will never have another past. Nor can you have another present. Your future, on the other hand, could change, or at least so I believe, if you confront your present instead of giving up on your life altogether.

I'm amazed by those letters you transcribed! It seems they shed real light on a piece of your past. The stage is yours now, Liz. If you insist, I'll tell you more anecdotes from my dreary life, but the subject matter you have recounted is far too important for me to divert the discussion. What happened when your father came home after you found the letters? Tell me.

Warm regards,

Someone

Subject: Letter Number 19

You keep writing about the power I have to control my life's path. You're such a sworn optimist. It's so easy to stand on the sidelines and talk about someone else's life. If you're such a believer, why don't you go to therapy and learn how to get out of your own asshole? Why didn't you try to resolve matters with your ex? It's so obvious you still love her. I'm pouring my heart out here and you haven't even told me why your wife dumped you.

Anyway, when my dad came into the bedroom, he found all the open binders, the upturned drawers, the scattered photographs – and me, sitting on the floor by the nightstand in the middle of all this chaos, holding his mother's old letters. Sure enough, his face turned pale.

"What happened to her?" I demanded to know.

He stood there, wordless.

"Tell me! What happened to her?"

He approached and sat down beside me in silence, reached out and touched the letters cautiously as if worried his touch would disintegrate them – and still didn't say a word.

"I went to the nursing home, Dad. I talked to Nahum. He told me he found her hanging in the chicken coop. And all these letters! Tell me!" I raised my voice.

"Come on." He got to his feet and reached out his hand to help me up from the floor. I laid the letters on the bed, took

his hand, stood up, and we left the house. We didn't speak but I knew where we were heading. We passed the houses with their moss-covered red rooftops at the far end of the kibbutz, crossed the narrow stream on the dilapidated iron bridge, and passed the long wooden structures of the nearby school until we reached the tall grove of eucalyptus trees enclosed by a rusty fence, near the orange groves, and entered the cemetery.

We walked along the rows of graves. There aren't so many here, maybe 300. I don't know if you've ever been to a kibbutz cemetery before. They're not like those in the city. There's no way they'll start erecting high-rise, vertical cemeteries here any time soon. Kibbutz graveyards are more like a holiday resort for the dead.

We passed the rows of newer graves and turned west toward the older ones. The older the gravestone, the smaller it was. I can never locate her grave with ease. It's hidden among several other flat and sunken stones that all look alike, but my father knew exactly where to find it. We stood in front of the familiar gravestone engraved with my name.

"Look around, Lizzie," Dad spoke for the second time since he entered the house. "Notice how all the stones are inscribed with an epitaph in memory of the deceased?"

I've never really noticed it. I looked around the nearby graves: "Loved the land of Israel and its people," "Our friend," "Man is but the imprint of his native landscape."

Eliza's grave had no epitaph, just numbers: year of birth, year of death.

"She was a very special woman," he continued. "Myetek – do you know who that is? Gal's grandfather from the Alon group?

He was with her in training. He took me aside one day and told me that she was smart as a whip. Beautiful, too. All the boys had a crush on her. She was a loving mother. I don't think she was sad when I was very young, but once my father died, she changed. You must understand, Lizzie, I was just a child when it all happened. I can only tell you what I saw as a boy. At first, she would clean our unit obsessively and fume if I made a mess. Later, she stopped cleaning altogether. Gradually she stopped going outside. When I came back from the children's house in the afternoon, she'd be in bed. I tried to cheer her up, but I never could, so I went to play outside so as to not disturb her. In the evenings, I'd return to the children's house alone. 'Mother needs to rest,' she'd tell me. I once brought her some food from the dining hall and she was furious. 'You don't need to take care of me!'

"One day, Esther'ke Kaplan – do you know who that is? She was the kibbutz nurse at the time. She came to the children's house and took me aside. She told me that my mother had died at work. Please understand, Lizzie, they didn't tell me anything, either. It wasn't something people talked about openly like they do today. They didn't go into too much detail, just said there was an accident at the coop. There was a small funeral, different from most funerals in the kibbutz. Not too many words were spoken, no praise of the deceased.

"I'm not sure exactly how I learned what really happened to her, but I knew. There was talk. One day, Hilik from my group told me that my mother had hung herself above the chickens.

"Before I married your mother, we sat down with Esther'ke

to ask what had actually happened and she told us that your grandmother had hung herself. You already know that Nahum found her. He tried to revive her, but she had already been dead for several hours. She probably went there in the middle of the night so that no one would find her in time. Esther'ke said they called the county doctor, who determined the cause of death and helped them sweep the details under the rug so they could bury her inside the cemetery. She said they even investigated whether it was a murder, but no, no one else did it. She did it to herself."

"Why didn't you ever tell me anything about this?"

"Lizzie," he paused, swallowed, and continued. "Look. How shall I say this? I wasn't enough for her. And I didn't want you to feel... didn't want you to ever think that you were not enough. I wasn't able to save her and I didn't want you to think that you needed to save me."

"I don't think you weren't enough for her. I think that she believed she wasn't good enough for you."

We fell silent for a while and then I asked, "But... how did you turn out so normal? With your degrees and the commando unit and everything? After both your parents died like that?"

"You have to understand that, back then, it wasn't so unusual to be an orphan. All the kids in the kibbutz slept in the children's house and spent only a few hours a day with their parents. There were lots of migrant kids. That's what we called the Holocaust survivors. What I went through was nothing compared to their stories from over there – war, diseases. Death wasn't an occasional guest as it is today; it was a part of

the family. And in any case, the kids in my age group played a role no less important than that of parents. We slept together, studied together, ate together, and after high school was over, I guess my army unit became my family, and later your mom and I became a couple."

We continued to stand there looking down at the gravestone that bears my name, and I wondered if sadness is hereditary, like a savings bond issued in my name, without my knowledge, even before I was born and inherited her name. A legacy of despondency... and when the time came to inherit that despondency, I received a registered mail from my DNA: the sorrow, the grieving, it's all there, flowing in the blood. It can be diluted for a generation or two but it will resurface again for your daughter or granddaughter when life takes them just a step too far. Was the self-destruct button always there, lying in wait within me, waiting to be pressed?

Liz

Subject: Thanatos

Dear Liz, you wrote about an inherent self-destruct button. Could such a mechanism inherently exist not only within people but also within relationships? My relationship with Ella was one such case. As soon as I first laid eyes upon her, a stopwatch that neither of us was aware of began counting down the days to our inevitable demise. And perhaps we both knew it but preferred to ignore the ticking timer.

As Ella and I became closer, I made it clear that I would never be a father. She was familiar with my childhood traumas. She knew what kind of parents I had, whilst I knew that if I ever became a parent myself, I couldn't help but relive those experiences. I couldn't imagine myself showing physical affection to a child of my own. To properly raise a child, flesh of your flesh, you must utterly and completely dedicate yourself. I knew I had no capacity for such dedication. Every time I imagined a child between us, I saw myself withdrawing further away, seeping into alcohol. I knew I could never put my predictions to the test when a helpless infant was involved.

For her part, Ella understood the role alcohol had played in my genes and knew that if I began to drink, I'd revert to my alienating self. Thus, our agreement was as follows: she would give up on having children and I would give up alcohol. And perhaps that's how the self-destruct button was activated.

"Are you certain?" I asked her one evening.

"Yes." She was resolute.

"And you won't regret not having a baby? You'll be willing to live without a child of your own?"

"I want you. You'll be my child and I'll be yours, you'll be my father and I'll be your mother. That's enough for me."

She believed she could do it, and for a while we did. The distorting mirror between us seemed to melt away. For a few precious years, I was her father and her son, I sheltered her with compassion and was enfolded within her. Together, we raised a private world of our own where we didn't need to pretend or shield ourselves from each other. Through the course of those years, I left the big advertising agency and set up my own small firm. I'd spend my evenings writing my novel and Ella, my first reader, would approach every new chapter like a girl unwrapping a present, and delve into my world. We would walk for hours through the city streets, our arms around each other, gazing at the city lights as if we were window shopping. We would sit outside quaint little cafés, her hair blowing through the steam rising from the strong, black Russian tea she always ordered, talking about everything and nothing or poring over our work, me on my book and Ella on her patients' files.

And it was enough for a while. For several years, I had everything I needed and I wanted to believe that she felt the same way. Yet, as the years passed, I began sensing something else. Ella was not herself. A limpness enveloped her. Since I had always been wary of her regretting her promise to me, I followed the signs and saw them emerging: her eyes would fix on baby

strollers in the street and follow them longingly. For a while, she insisted on entertaining only friends with small children and later refused to invite such friends at all. She would become invested in her patients' children or grandchildren, taking an almost intrusive interest in them.

One night, she began crying over a book she was reading in bed. I embraced her.

"You're sure, right? That you don't want a child," she asked, though she already knew the answer.

"Yes."

"And that can't change? Despite everything?"

I shook my head.

"But things are different for you now that we're together."

"I'm not capable, Ellie," I apologized and kissed her shoulder.

"You're not going to end up like him, you know, or like her. You are your own person."

"I'm sorry, Ellie." I knew then what she still could not bring herself to believe – that everything we'd been through together, all the goodness we had sown in each other, was not enough to expunge the inheritance bestowed upon me.

"He would be so beautiful, our child," she said through her tears.

"That's true, he would." My tears mixed with hers. I brushed her hair away from her face, ran my fingers over her chin, across her cheek, and kissed her neck. "You can have a child without me. I'll understand,"

"Stop it!" she protested.

"It's a possibility, Ellie. It exists, you can't deny it," my voice cracked.

"Not leaving you." She doubled over as if I had kicked her in the stomach with the very idea. "Forget it, I'm not leaving you." She hugged me. Her tears ran down my chest while my tears moistened her hair.

But another kind of child was conceived in our home that night: a distance, a transparent balloon that grew and swelled between us. We embraced it from both ends and, as we attempted to draw closer to each other, it pressed against us like a kids' party game.

Ella's unrequited passion for a child transferred to stray animals. Time and time again, she would return home later than expected, disheveled from a rescue mission amidst some bushes or from under a car, holding a neglected kitten, an abandoned puppy, or an injured bird. More and more lost and wounded animals joined our three cats and she devotedly cared for each. As our conversations dwindled, the number of animals in our apartment grew. They scurried around us, whimpering, barking, chirping, and fighting instead of the things we dared not say to each other again: "I long to be a mother," and "I cannot be a father."

Instead of talking about ourselves, we began talking about the animals. "The bird's wing is healing nicely," "The cat threw up today," or, "The dogs need to be walked." In the evenings, we found ourselves sitting silently in front of the television with creatures of all kinds sitting in our laps, on the floor, in the rooms, and in the cages along the hallway.

My Ella. I saw her fading away and knew that it wouldn't be long before she would be unable to bring the child her entire being yearned for into this world. And I knew she would never

break the promise she'd made me. After all, I was the largest stray animal she had ever rescued. I realized that it was up to me to drive her away since she would never willingly let me go but would languish if she stayed. But I couldn't leave her. I had, therefore, no choice but to make her leave me.

It didn't happen overnight, and in one sense it was the most challenging thing I ever did. I felt as if I was killing something. In another sense, there was nothing easier. I just needed to revert to my old self: leave, relapse, and let myself be who I really was, the person she forced me to improve through her very existence: the selfish, weak-willed, phony, coward I was before.

Gradually, I ceased doing the big things and the little things. I stopped shaving, I stopped asking her about her day when she came home, I stopped listening when she spoke and I stopped speaking to her. I stopped making an effort to wake up with her in the morning or go to bed with her at night. I stopped watching what I ate, clearing the dishes, or taking out the trash. I stopped looking at her when she talked to me or when she made love to me. I stopped making love to her and sleeping with her. Later, I stopped going to the office or leaving the house. I would manage my employees through scowling emails and stay home in my underwear, spending my days in front of the computer, browsing the internet, and flipping the screen closed whenever she entered the room. Some days, I would sleep until evening as the animals constantly trod on my body as if to check I was still alive. She would come home from work and look at me in wonder. "You didn't leave the house all day?"

"No."

"What's going on with you?"

"Leave me alone. I'm tired." I'd turn my back to her, switch on the TV, light a cigarette in bed even though I knew she hated it, and stare at the screen.

The animals would flock to her like a band of avid fans. A cloud of fur, purrs, and barks would envelop her, necks and tails would wrap around her, and she would speak tenderly to them – "My cutie," "You're so beautiful," "Are you purring, my sweet?" – drawing the love I withheld from her beloved animals. She would spend her evenings engrossed in forums and Facebook groups for animal lovers, looking for a foster home for another cat or dog she had rescued from the street while I'd watch TV, sleep, or soak in endless baths.

Soon after, I began to disappear. I'd leave the house in the evenings before she returned from work and come back hours later.

"Where were you?"

"Around."

"Is something wrong?"

"No, I just needed some air."

"Well, you didn't leave the house all week."

"So you're counting the times I leave the house now?"

"I'm worried about you. I don't understand what's happening to you."

"Stop worrying about me. You keep worrying about your cats and dogs and birds and insects and the mentally incapacitated. Ella the Savior. I'm not one of your patients, okay? Get off my back."

She sighed and went to the other room, a trail of cats and dogs in her wake. I heard her crying through the closed door. We went on like that for another year, and she didn't leave. At times, I heard her mumbling something about wanting us to go to couples' therapy, and I'd dismiss her and go back to staring at one of my screens.

Until I started drinking. I don't even know if I did it in order to completely negate the last pledge between us, or simply because I wanted to. Dammit, I wanted to drink and for this sainted martyr to stop pinning her hopes on me and sacrificing herself for my sake. I wanted her to leave! I didn't do it flagrantly; I didn't crack open a bottle of vodka in the middle of the living room or sip the wondrous nectar directly from the bottle in front of her eyes, but I didn't try to hide it, either.

One night, I returned from my wanderings, wobbling and inebriated, holding a bottle of cheap whiskey that I'd bought from a corner store. It was three or four in the morning. I walked into our apartment, switched on the dim light in the hallway, and saw her, awake, sitting on the living room couch. I sat beside her, a stench rising from the clothes I hadn't bothered to change in several days, my face covered with three-week-old bristles. I was buzzed with alcohol, worried that she'd start sobbing but she didn't cry. She just sat facing me with wide, expressionless eyes.

"There's no point in asking where you've been, right?"

"Oh, no, don't start now, just not right now." I grabbed my spinning head.

"What's going on with you?"

"What's going on is that this is who I am. This is the man you chose, okay?"

"That's not true, this isn't you! Something's going on. There's something you're not telling me. I just don't understand. There's something I'm not able to see. You're not letting me."

"There's something you're not telling me, there's something you're not telling me," I mockingly imitated her voice. "Here she is, Saint Ella, the great savior. Poor thing, there's someone you can't rescue?" I continued with vicious sarcasm. "What's going on with me is that I'm not one of your Rehab Ward patients and I'm not some case study for your next paper. This is me, sweetheart; this stinking drunk is your man. Sorry if that ruins your fucking redemption statistics." I brought my face closer to her beautiful face, my lips to hers. I knew she could smell my breath. I tried to reach for her breast and cup it.

She recoiled with a look of disbelief: "I don't understand what you're talking about. It was never like this between us. It was just you and me. There's something I'm just unable to see in this whole picture. I can't seem to reach you and there's no point in trying when you're like this, not letting me. You idiot. It's not about a baby, or that you've stopped going in to work, or that you don't shower, or that you eat junk all day, or that you're clearly battling an undiagnosed depression. It's not even that you disappear at all hours of the night and it's not even about this –" She took the bottle from my hand, brought it to her lips, and took a swig. "It's that you're not here, not with me, and I don't know where you are. You're working so hard to build a wall between us and I don't know why, but you've succeeded.

I can't fight to be with you anymore. I was willing to give up everything to be with you, but you gave up a long time ago. So, fine, you won. I'll look for another apartment." She took the whiskey with her and went to the other room.

A few days later, she – along with all her belongings, her cats, her dogs, the bandaged pigeon in its cage – was gone. We were never legally married as we had exchanged our vows privately, so there was no need for any official uncoupling. I did that on my own, months ago.

If you feel any anger or contempt for me as a result of this account, surely you'll take comfort in knowing that Ella is now loved by someone else, someone worthy and more deserving of her than I ever was. He was in her class at university. I knew he was in love with her. He consoled her after our separation. Unlike us, they were properly married and now she's carrying his child. She's due in about three months if I'm not mistaken. She didn't miss the train. Maybe she'll even be able to bring another little one into the world if she wishes, and I suppose she'll want that very much. And that's more or less the answer to your question about why my wife dumped me.

Warm regards,

Someone

Subject: Coward

You're a pathetic coward, you know that? Why didn't you let her make her own choices? Do you think she loves him, her new husband? As much as she loved you?

Liz

Subject: Rest your mind at ease

Oh, hello there! Look who just burst in with her curt, opinionated declaration! Yes, I know. Pathetic coward is a title I've rightly earned. But, before you brand me with my pathetic wretchedness, allow me to ask you a question: if you had a little brother or a nephew, would you let me babysit him even for a brief hour? And there's your answer. I did let Ella choose, but she repeatedly chose me, instead of choosing herself. I had to make the right choice for her. No, I don't suppose she loves her husband as much as she loved me but you mustn't feel bad about that. I think she's better off with him. And who'd have guessed that there's a hopeless romantic in you longing for a happy ending? It's a pleasure to make your acquaintance.

Warm regards,

Someone

Subject: Letter Number 20

Hello, dear stalker. Before I start scattering pieces of my soul around in the way I know you love, let's linger on the exciting milestone we've reached here. This is the twentieth stinking letter I've sent you! Happy anniversary to us! You know what's funny? All this time I've been writing to you, I've poured out quite a few memories. In fact, the more I write to you, the less I need you and that damned laptop. Maybe by the time you agree to release it, I won't even need it anymore. Okay, relax, we're not there yet. I still want what's mine back.

As for your last letter, I don't understand how you can be so sensitive and such a thickheaded piece of shit at the same time, but there's nothing new about that; I'm familiar with both these sides of yours. Anyway, don't worry, I'm not here to analyze you with dime-store psychobabble, but I can tell you all about it. Psychobabble for a great many dimes, to be exact. That's what I went through this week.

After visiting the cemetery, I wanted to end the cycle. I think my grandmother died because of secrets, you know? Because she had no one to talk to, or because she didn't want to talk to anyone about what she was going through until she decided to save the world from herself and vice versa. As we stood there by the grave, I realized that I can't do what she did. I saw my dad standing there, hunched over, and suddenly he looked so

small, as if he'd shrunk when he told me what had happened to her. I knew I couldn't preserve this tradition of keeping all our problems bottled up and living or dying with them alone. After we walked home in silence, I locked myself in my room and heard my parents talking through the thin walls. My father said: "I told her," and, "It's okay." And, "No... I don't think she's angry."

The next evening, as my parents sat on the couch watching TV, I told them I wanted to talk. They gave me that look again, apprehension mingled with concern.

"You're right. I'm not really okay," I said. And I told them. Not everything, but most of it. About the anxiety attacks and how every time I try to do something I'm consumed by such a wave of fear that I can't help but run, and that I miss Jazz terribly. And that it doesn't fade, only intensifies. And how I miss who I was before, and that they know that I wasn't like this once.

"And... about that call you received. Look... I... I don't want to die, but... I also don't know how I can go on. It's like I try and try, and end up failing each time, and I'm tired of trying. Maybe I really do need help because I've tried to cope on my own but I just can't."

"Who was that man who called, Lizzielee?"

"Just someone I know from Tel Aviv. I guess he's been worried about me since I moved back here," I told a half-truth. Tears welled in their eyes as I spoke. My father sat down beside me and wrapped his arm around my shoulders.

"I'm glad you talked to us. We'll... we'll seek some advice. We'll think about what's best to do," my mother said.

Early the next morning, I woke up and found her sleeping on a mattress at the foot of my bed. I sat down on the floor beside her and gently stroked her light brown hair with hints of white sprinkled throughout it. It wasn't a peaceful sleep. Her lips were tightly pursed and she woke from my touch.

"Mom, what are you doing here?"

"Nothing, really. I just wanted to sleep at your side for a little while." She sat up. "Do you remember when you broke your arm as a kid? I think you were about five."

"Sure, near the dining hall." I was surprised she brought it up.

"You cried all evening and I didn't take you back to sleep in the children's house. When you wouldn't stop crying, I realized that there must really be a problem because you seldom cried. We took the kibbutz ambulance and drove to the hospital in the middle of the night. After several x-rays, they found a hard-to-detect fracture near your elbow. I told everyone that the doctors said you needed to sleep at home and not in the children's house until your cast was removed, and that you needed to be supervised so your arm wouldn't move at night. But that wasn't true. They didn't say anything of the kind. I just wanted to sleep beside you for a little while longer, hear you breathing at night, cuddle up next to you, and hug you while you slept. I had so little of that precious sweetness when you were growing up," she recalled through the haze of slumber.

Two days later, she announced that they'd found a professor, an expert psychiatrist who is also a psychotherapist, and had scheduled an appointment for me at his clinic in Tel Aviv. I felt so humiliated; I've reached a point where my parents

make appointments for me with a man who prescribes people brain medication. But honestly, I was looking forward to this appointment. Could this guy actually understand what I've been going through? Would he tell me something that truly matters? Maybe prescribe a medication that'll help me stop thinking about death all the time and start living?

There was an air of excitement in my house on the day of my appointment. It was strange. They both took a day off from work; my dad booked a car and explained to the foreman that he'd be needing it until evening and that it was important. We got in the car, they sat in the front and I, as always, settled in the backseat. I dug my nails into my seatbelt and felt as if I was in some nightmarish version of the birthdays I had as a child when we'd drive to the mall and watch a movie and I'd get to order anything I wanted at a restaurant. My father hummed along with the Stones playing on the radio.

As usual, the car ride made me dizzy and incredibly nauseous. When I couldn't stand it any longer, I sank down in the back seat and buried my head in the musty-smelling upholstery. I suddenly realized that I hadn't left the kibbutz since that day I came back from Tel Aviv with my tail between my legs a few months ago.

After an hour and thirty-three minutes, of which I counted every second, we parked in a quiet, upmarket neighborhood of private homes in a Tel Aviv suburb. We searched for the address, rang the intercom outside a wrought-iron gate, and entered. The metallic voice coming from the speaker directed us to head down a brick staircase. We reached the basement floor of a beautiful villa with every detail of its décor carefully

selected. The clinic itself was lavishly appointed with marble floors and reproductions of Kandinsky, Picasso, and Van Gogh in ornate gold frames. Beside each frame was a famous quote:

"*Everything has beauty, but not everyone sees it.*" - *Confucius*

"*A journey of a thousand miles begins with a single step.*" - *Lao Tzu*

A man in his fifties came out to greet us. He wore tailored slacks and a starched collar shirt. My parents shook his hand with reverence, and then he turned and offered me his hand.

"Liz, right? Let's go through."

A massive photograph of Rodin's The Thinker hung on the wall beside various degree certificates and awards. Two deep leather armchairs stood facing each other separated by a small wooden table with the expected box of tissues and a pad of wide-ruled paper. Behind the table, facing the door, stretched a wall of thick glass through which piercing rays of sunlight penetrated.

"Does this bother you?" He pointed to the huge, bright window when he noticed me squinting against the light.

"Actually, yes," I said. He pressed a button and the glass wall clouded and turned opaque. I've never seen anything like it.

He sat down in one of the armchairs, gestured for me to sit in the other, and said, "So, Liz, what brings you here today? I understand that your parents are very concerned about you."

"Ah... yes, I guess so," I awkwardly confirmed my role as a troublemaker.

"Tell me what's been going on with you," he asked in a pleasant, albeit obligatory, tone.

"Well, it's a little hard... there's a lot to tell," I squirmed uneasily in the huge armchair. How do you describe several years of hell to a complete stranger and how is he supposed to find a way out of it?

"I understand you've been in an accident." He attempted to offer me a lead.

"Yes."

"Maybe you should start from there."

"It's a little hard... I don't exactly remember it..." I replied hesitantly, hearing those galloping wild horses threatening to move in across my chest.

"Interesting. That's very typical of post-trauma. Did you know that?"

"Yes," I replied. "I'm studying psychology."

"Really?" He hummed to himself. "Tell me what you do remember."

I shrunk into my armchair and succinctly recounted the details of my birthday and the nightclub and the motorcycle and about Jazz and waking up in the hospital.

"I understand. Describe how this impacted your level of functioning."

"My level of functioning?"

"Yes, yes, functioning. If you're studying psychology, surely you know the criteria. Shall I refresh your memory? Do you have a healthy appetite?"

"Not really,"

"Do you sleep well?"

"Not exactly."

"Nightmares?"

"Yes."

"About the accident?"

"I don't know..."

"Working?"

"Yes!"

"Really?"

"Well... from home..."

"Yes..." He picked up the notepad and jotted down my answers. "You said you were studying at the university. How do you cope with classes? Assignments?"

"It's the Open University."

"Hmmm, I see. Do you drive?"

"No!" I blurted out loudly and then lowered my voice in embarrassment. "Ah... no." I felt like I was a cigarette butt tossed to the ground and crushed thoroughly under the sole of a shoe, ensuring no sparks were left in it.

"Sensitivity to voices? Sounds? Noises? Smells, sights?"

"Yes."

"Suicidal attempts?"

"No."

"Suicidal thoughts?"

"No," I denied it. I wasn't about to reveal my innermost thoughts to this man.

"Not at all?"

"You could say that I... sometimes I feel hopeless," I admitted.

"Have you always bitten your nails?" he scanned my fingertips.

"Ah... I don't know," I clenched my hands in shame.

"It's an expression of anxiety," he ruled. "Are you inherently prone to anxiety?"

"I don't think so," I muttered, trying to remember. I think I used to bite my nails even before the accident but I was never particularly anxious back then. I was actually rather reckless. I didn't know much about life back then.

He gazed at me confidently and said, "Liz, you're an intelligent girl. Let me be perfectly frank with you. You're undoubtedly suffering from a classic case of post-trauma, but beyond that, I'm afraid I also recognize certain narcissistic tendencies. Do you feel that your disorder allows you to make the world revolve around you and your problems? I noticed that both your parents accompanied you here today. How old are you?"

"Twenty-three, almost twenty-four," I replied in a muffled voice.

"Oh, I thought you were older. Do you recognize yourself in what I've said?"

"No, not at all," I fired back, ashamed of the tears that began stinging my eyes. "Well, it's true that I moved back in with my parents and asked for their help, but I honestly tried to avoid doing that and I definitely don't enjoy it. It's just that, lately, I realized that I can't cope with all this on my own."

"And yet, they're both here with you. They hover around you and worry about you. You're not exactly making an effort to spread your wings and fly."

"I did make an effort! I lived alone, and I work and support myself, I also rented my own apartment but then it was broken into and I had to return to the kibbutz –"

"Very well," he scribbled in his notebook. "Are you experiencing any sort of guilt following the accident?" He changed the subject suddenly.

"Ah... it's complicated."

"So, explain."

"Look... I don't think I'm to blame for the accident. But it happened when we went out to celebrate my birthday. On the other hand, we'd probably have gone out even if it wasn't my birthday. And then again, there were a thousand things I could have done to change what happened. If we'd only lingered a second longer, maybe Jazz would still be alive. But I didn't anticipate something like that could happen, so what could I have possibly done?"

"Were you two close?" He sent me an inquisitive look through his designer glasses, and I wondered if dirty images were now playing through his mind.

"As close as someone could get," I whispered. "Like sisters. More than sisters."

"This relationship – was it romantic? Sexual?"

You wish, I thought to myself, and replied, "No, it wasn't like that."

"But you claim she was the person closest to you."

"Yes. She was the most... special and beautiful person I've ever met. The person who understood me better than anyone in the world. We lived together in the months before the accident because she'd just come back from abroad and had nowhere to live." I fidgeted in my chair. I felt like I was under investigation.

"Forgive me, Liz. I'm about to raise a possibility that may be

unpleasant for you to hear, but, nevertheless, these things should be discussed. You're describing a very powerful symbiosis here. Stifling, maybe. Is it possible that your sense of guilt has been nurtured by the fact that a certain part of you longed to separate from your good friend? Perhaps you felt that your friendship was robbing you of your independence in the world? Is it possible that you harbored a certain fantasy that she'd disappear from your life? Perhaps you feel guilty because, deep inside, you realize that, one way or another, at some point you would each have gone your separate ways?"

"Is this some kind of warped take on the separation-individuation theory combined with an Electra complex?!" I fumed. I wanted to jump up from that pretentious armchair, lift it with some super-powered strength, and hurl it at his head. *Did I secretly wish for Jazz to vanish from my life?!* What I wished for at that moment was for him to vanish from the face of the earth, for him to choke on the insufferable words he was saying.

He was surprised by my reply and went on to say, "I see that you've studied developmental psychology. If you took a few additional courses, you'd probably also be aware that resistance is an almost integral part of any therapy."

It's also an integral part of any encounter with a pompous fart who thinks he can read minds, I thought to myself and said, "Call it what you want but write down in your notepad that I by no means whatsoever wanted Jazz to disappear. That was the last thing in the world that I wanted."

He looked at me with a somewhat bemused expression, and said, "Okay, Liz. I believe I've identified the situation and I'm

going to level with you. Look, I think this is a classic case. You're suffering from a significant post-traumatic stress disorder. I'm still not certain regarding the narcissistic tendencies. That's a matter we'll need to examine further. At any rate, your problem has but one solution. You must be exposed to the traumatic element and confront it head-on. That's the only way you can break free from this cycle. Treatment will be conducted in stages and you'll have to do exactly as I say at each stage in order to reach optimal results. For example, you'll need to achieve a completely calm state of mind and then imagine the accident, for all that it entails: Fire! Smoke! Bright lights, ambulances!" he exclaimed dramatically.

"We'll try to deal with the trauma and process it while probing your narcissistic tendencies. Perhaps, indeed, as you yourself have mentioned, you never completed the separation process from your mother and therefore formed a need for a symbiosis with others alongside an inexhaustible need for attention, love, and admiration with which you try, in vain, to fill the immense hole? We'll need to examine all these issues together. I'm recommending a bi-weekly treatment. Post-trauma therapy is usually short-term, about twelve to fourteen sessions. In your case, additional sessions may be needed in conjunction with psychiatric medications that I'll prescribe later on. In any case, I believe that, within a few months, we'll see positive results – if you cooperate with the treatment regimen, that is." He concluded his speech and I felt frozen in terror, my hands shaking with rage.

"Our time is up. I suggest you consider what was said here today, and since it's quite common for post-trauma victims to

resist treatment, let's call in your parents and I'll briefly convey the conclusions of our session. Do you approve?"

I stood there, stunned. All I wanted was to get out of that room, which grew more suffocating by the minute. He opened the door, called my parents, adopted his genial tone again, and said, "Liz and I had a talk and I've certainly understood the situation. I believe she's suffering from post-trauma and recommend that we conduct bi-weekly sessions. I think that you'll be able to see a significant improvement within two months." He talked about me like I wasn't standing in the room with them.

"Twice a week here in Tel Aviv?" my mother asked.

"Mrs. Fine, people come to my clinic from all across the country." He resented the question.

The session cost 800 shekels. My mother opened her purse and began counting fifty shekel bills out of an envelope. I looked at her and wished I could disappear. Their entire monthly budget was 2,100 shekels and the kibbutz had already made it clear that it would not subsidize my therapy since, technically, I had already left. My job wouldn't be able to cover the expense of two such meetings a week. How exactly were they planning to pay for regular sessions with this idiot?

After he accepted his payment, he walked us out. "You can be optimistic. This is good news. There's definitely something we can do." He bade us goodbye with his affected pleasantries.

So that's all I have to say about overpriced psychobabble. I'm too tired to write anymore. That's it for now.

Liz

Subject: "Two things are infinite: the universe and human stupidity; and I'm not sure about the universe."

Dear Liz, as you may have recognized, the quote above is not my own. It is a saying attributed to Albert Einstein that my father would mumble whenever a former colleague, acquaintance, or telemarketer would incur his wrath. The words resurfaced in my mind as I read your letter. Thanks to my parents, I never held much respect for those who boasted higher education. Various degrees never carried any expectations for me, not of the positive kind, anyway. I have a feeling that you still believe, or at least hope, that an academic education grants its students wisdom alongside the degrees and titles it bestows upon them. Well, let me save you from further disappointment. No faculty in the world offers a course that endows students with intelligence and takes away their foolishness. I don't suppose your spirit miraculously improved following the session you described and I'm sorry for the anguish it caused you. As for me, I certainly don't think you're a narcissist, if my opinion carries any weight in your eyes. I'm attaching a certain letter you wrote to Jazz. I recalled it as I was reading the diagnoses with which you were labeled. Tell me what happened after the session.

Warm regards,

Someone

Attachment: Hi there, my darling adrenal gland

Writing to you after a really long day. I planned to go straight to bed but I can't fall asleep and feel like I need to unburden myself from these thoughts. As you know, on Sundays I don't normally head to the base but conduct home visits instead. You know that the soldiers under my wing don't exactly come from the top income bracket (or even from the low mid-levels) but it doesn't usually affect me, as if there's a sort of wall between me and what I see. In most cases, I find myself observing even the most difficult circumstances with a certain distance, seeing without feeling – but, today, I had a really tough time. I feel it weighing on my insides now.

I conducted four home visits in the Ramla area and none of them were easy, but one of them disturbed me. It was the home of Dima, a soldier in my platoon, an incredible guy. He's a really special character, smart, and insanely talented. He carries a pen and paper with him in his pocket everywhere he goes and, whenever he has a free moment, he takes them out and starts drawing. While the rest of the soldiers try to drive their commanding officers crazy or just sit around cracking jokes, he's off on his own, sketching these crazy drawings. He's filled the barracks with drawings he taped to the walls. And yes, I can hear you asking, he's also pretty hot, but there's no way anything's going to happen.

Anyway, I already knew there was a record of domestic violence in the family and that he was the one protecting his mom, and I knew he was having a hard time with his dad, but I didn't realize how bad it was and I didn't think I'd actually see any evidence in their apartment. Like, how can you see proof of violence in a house? So, it turns out you can.

The family apartment isn't even in the worst neighborhood in town, but it's completely wrecked. I walked around like I'm supposed to during home visits. I followed his mother from room to room, asking questions for my report, and while we were walking and talking, I saw more and more marks of blows to the walls, holes in the doors, and broken things. It looked like a raging bull had been let loose in the house and destroyed everything that happened to be in its way, and we're walking through that house and talking about monthly budgets and not about the fact that there's a wild animal living there.

It was so surreal! You could easily imagine it being the set of some low-budget crime movie and not a real home where people actually live. The doors were perforated with knife cuts, there were punch holes in the walls, and the TV stood there in the middle of the living room, its screen smashed by Dima's father when he hurled it on the floor in one of his fits of anger! Do you get it?

The walls in Dima's room were decorated with his drawings, like the ones at the base, but here they were each slashed with a giant X. I could imagine Dima and his father screaming at each other in there and then I remembered Dima telling me that when he was younger, he wouldn't fight back but lately he'd

begun to stand up to his dad. He told me this, not out of pride, but with certain shame. Deep inside, I'm glad Dima's an only child. I don't know if I could have brought myself to leave that apartment if there was a little kid left to live there.

The wild animal, by the way, was home at the time, with a calmness that froze my blood with terror. Yes, his father was there, a stout, sturdy character, a former officer in the Russian army. I wondered if I should be scared or something, but in stark comparison to everything I saw around me, he looked completely cool and collected, composed and serene. He stood in front of me in the middle of this wrecked house and spoke with complete composure, without a shred of shame or apology. I think that was the most violent aspect of his behavior.

After the tour around the house, they invited me to sit down. I delicately asked about violence, and I could imagine the battered walls laughing around us as Dima's dad explained with perfect equanimity that his artistic son sometimes needed to have some sense beaten into him. They both admitted that the father drinks sometimes, and sometimes he gets a little angry, and yes, he threw the TV on the floor once. They talked about it like it was just a bad habit he couldn't kick, like when someone smokes too much or watches too much television.

I wanted to talk to Dima's mother alone, so I asked her to walk me to the bus station. The father objected to her leaving but I said I didn't know where the station was. He bought my excuse and agreed "to allow her" to leave. Once we were far enough from the house, I told her she needed to file a complaint with the police. I wanted to give her some phone numbers but

she wouldn't take them, saying her husband was just making a fuss and that he's a good man.

According to the law, I'm only obligated to report violence against minors, and Dima's no longer a minor. I know he'll be really mad at me if I report this to the police and I don't think it would do much good because, even if the police question his mother, she'll only deny it and this will endanger her even more. Her husband will probably punish her for it and Dima isn't home to protect her. I want to tell Dima to get the hell away from there, but he'd never leave his mother behind and she'd never divorce the father.

When I left that house, I still felt somehow okay but, on the way home on the bus, the day started closing in on me. My hands started shaking and I felt a heaviness on my skin. The sense of hopelessness became suffocating.

That's all, my darling ear auricle. I just needed to unload a bit. Going to sleep. Write to me soon!

Love ya,

Your Liz

Subject: Letter Number 21

Yes, as you imagined, the meeting with the famed psychiatrist didn't exactly encourage me. I left it feeling angry and frozen with humiliation and so enraged I couldn't even speak. I walked as fast as I could back to the car, got in, hurried to fasten my seatbelt and tighten it around me as I always do.

"How was it, Lizzielee?" My mother tried to draw the details out of me. I heard the strain in her voice.

"Forget it," I hissed. I was afraid that if I said any more than that, the tears would break out of my throat and flow along with the words.

"What he said sounds positive, overall. According to him, there's a solution to the situation." My father tried to sound encouraging.

"I'm not planning to talk to that man again. Come on, let's go," I urged them.

"But why, Lizzie? If he has a solution, maybe we should listen to him. He's a very esteemed psychiatrist." My mom questioned my decision with wonder.

"Because he's a pretentious idiot and he doesn't know what he's talking about and he's also a swindler and I don't want to see him ever again!" My voice was shrill and loud and my fingers dug into my seatbelt. I turned to look out of the window, making it clear that the conversation was over. All the way home, I

tried my best to conceal the fact that I was crying behind my sunglasses.

The next day, my mother approached me cautiously: "Lizzielee, I wanted to talk to you a little bit about what happened yesterday, during your session with the professor." I took a deep breath and we sat down at the table again. "Look, I know it isn't easy to talk about everything you've been through. Your dad and I weren't there when the accident happened. I wish we could have been there instead of you. I wish I could go back in time and switch places with you, but I can't."

"Stop it, Mom. Don't say silly things like that," I shuddered.

"You're right, it's silly. Because what happened can't be undone. I think it's natural for you to be upset with this man if he's asking you to relive those difficult moments."

"It's not that," I objected.

"So, what happened, then?" she wondered.

"Mom, do you think I'm too self-involved?"

"What do you mean?" She was surprised by the question.

"Someone who always wants to be the center of attention and wanting everyone to notice her?"

"I wouldn't describe you like that. You spent your entire military service taking care of other people's needs. And you always had friends you cared about very much until..." She fell silent. "Why? Is that something that came up during therapy?"

"Yes... sort of."

"Well, the professor doesn't know you yet and if he can help you, it would be a shame to dismiss him just because of this. Next time, he'll get to know you better and realize that you're

not like that at all." Her fingers danced nervously around her coffee cup. (I suppose she's the exact opposite of your father, putting her faith in authoritative figures with childlike trust.)

"It's not just that," I said in a strained voice and again felt my hands begin to tremble and the tears climb up my throat. "He said I subconsciously wanted Jazz to disappear and I feel guilty because of that."

"Are you sure that's what he meant?" She was skeptical.

"Yes!" I yelled. "And I will not see this man anymore, not ever! I don't care how many degrees he has or how well-known he is. He's not a good listener. He doesn't even see you when you're sitting in front of him. He interrogates like some kind of cop and then talks about how much he knows and catalogs you and makes you feel even smaller than you already do. Not to mention the fees he charges! I can't afford his rates."

"We've got this, Lizzielee. We talked about it – you won't need to spend a shekel on this."

"But where are you going to get that kind of money?"

"We've saved a bit each month," she said proudly.

I tried to quickly calculate how much they could possibly save from their meager budget... 200 a month? And only if they bought the cheapest essentials at the kibbutz store.

"Well, that's not the problem, anyway. Mom, believe me. I want to feel better, but he's not the man who can help me."

"Okay," she replied with uncertainty, "we'll look for someone else."

It was clear to me why the psychiatrist insisted that I should be exposed to aspects of the accident. I remembered a specific

type of behavioral therapy called Prolonged Exposure from my studies. It was developed as a specific treatment for combat-related PTSD, where patients are gradually exposed to trauma-related memories and it's supposed to somehow help diminish their anxiety. And even though this professor discounted me as a person, I had to admit that there was something in what he said. Ever since the accident, I've done my best to avoid anything that might remind me of it: roads, cars, driving. Even rapid movement makes me queasy, and loud voices and sounds make me want to disappear. And you probably remember my reaction to the smell of something burning from the story of the eggplants.

And though I've never stopped thinking and writing about her, I distanced myself from anything related to Jazz that exists outside my head. I haven't been to Mevo Golan since the funeral. I haven't returned to our usual hangouts. I haven't kept in touch with her family and I haven't been able to speak with our mutual friends.

After that frustrating therapy session, I realized that I didn't need to talk with someone who had a long list of academic degrees, but rather with the one person I had made a special effort to avoid.

My finger hovered over his name in my phone contacts for a long moment as I hesitated to press the call button. Ultimately, I made the call – to Michael. Mikey, Jazz called him. Her big brother. It had been at least a year-and-a-half since we last spoke.

The phone trilled several times before a familiar, yet different voice to the one I remembered, answered with the question,

"Hello?"

"Hey, Mikey, it's Liz," I said.

"Yeah, I figured when I saw your name on my phone screen. Long time, Dizzy."

The whole world knew us as Jazzy and Lizzie but he insisted on the charming nicknames Wheezy and Dizzy.

"How are you doing, Mikey?"

"Doing?" he hesitated. "You know, working... performing with my band a lot. And you?"

"Me? I lived in Tel Aviv for a while... and now I'm back at the kibbutz. School, work." The technical details were so far from portraying reality that I began to giggle.

"You don't say, Dizzy. Sounds like you're quite a busy bee," he responded in a strange cynical tone. "So how can I help you?"

"I... I need to talk to you."

"Okay, we're talking."

"No, not like this. Could we meet, maybe?"

"Sure, why not? My door's always open for dizzy bees. You're welcome any time."

"Where do you live now?"

"Forever a devout communist." It sounded as if he was taking a long drag from something. Michael smokes now?! "I'm still at the kibbutz."

"I... I kind of have a tough time going places. I don't drive." I didn't know how to explain.

"Got it," he hurried to respond. "Do you want me to come to Beit Katzir?"

"Can you?"

We made plans to meet.

The truth is that Mikey often tried to talk and meet with me after the accident, but I couldn't bring myself to see him. When he came here, I ignored him. I didn't answer when he called. I wanted him to stay away from me and never call again. He reminded me of her so much that it was intolerable.

Jazz had always seen him as the annoying older brother who tried to protect her from everything. She always made fun of him. After the accident, while I was lying on the couch at my parents' house unable to move, he came by quite frequently. Every time he sat beside me I could imagine Jazz making some joke at his expense. His face was the same shape as hers. I began to notice the similarities: how he drummed his fingers when he tried to think of something to say, just as she used to do. I began to hear her "umms" and "errrs" entwined in his speech when he was searching for the right words. I couldn't ignore that hint of an American accent in his voice, so much like hers.

I don't know if you'll understand what I mean, but beyond the way people are seen or heard, they carry a sort of impression with them. A certain air when they walk into a room. And the impression that Mikey brought at that time, I noticed, was almost identical to the kind Jazz would convey whenever she was around. Every time we met, it was as if she was sitting there between us in the room, an impression without a body. I couldn't take it.

I'm seeing him tomorrow. Wish me luck. That is, I hope I won't run away and find myself trembling with anxiety under some couch.

Okay, I've rambled so much. How about you help me get out of my head for a while and tell me about something else? If your wife moved out and took all the cats with her and you never leave the house, then what exactly do you do all day by yourself? Don't you meet any people at all?

Liz

Subject: Supporting player

Dear Liz, you can relax, you're not missing anything. My correspondence with you is the most interesting thing that has happened in my life lately. Your mention of Mikey has piqued my curiosity. I remember reading about him in your files. I'm very much looking forward to reading about your reunion. Since you're being a good girl lately, I'm enclosing the attached file you've previously requested – another letter from Yasmin in New York.

Warm regards,

Someone

Attachment: What's up, my darling bronchi???

We talked only yesterday and I'm already writing to you. I had such a brilliant night that I feel like I should get on a plane right now, sneak into your base, lure you away with a cup of gourmet coffee or any other drug of your choice, and kidnap you so you can be here with me – and yes, it's worth causing a diplomatic incident! (I can already see the headlines: American citizen abducts a young, female, Israeli soldier.)

Anyway. Remember Gary and the band I told you about? Theo's friends? So, yesterday they were supposed to perform in some open mic night. Theo and I went to see them and headed backstage to have a drink with the band before the show. We found Gary freaking out because their singer had pulled a disappearing act at the last minute. They were supposed to take the stage in thirty minutes and perform a couple of numbers and they'd been waiting for this shot for a really long time because this club, The Pit-hole, is one of the hottest places in town right now. We found him pacing the floor, mumbling to himself: "I can't believe she's done this to us again... what the fuck am I supposed to do now?" Apparently, it wasn't the first time she'd developed a case of cold ovaries before a show.

I looked at him with pity but didn't realize that Theo, that whack job, was plotting something. Suddenly he spoke up and said, "What's the problem? Jazz can fill in."

So Gary asked, "Can she sing? No offense, Jazz, but we've been waiting for this gig for ages."

"She sings like an angel on opium."

That's what Theo told him! Can you imagine?! That wretch had heard me singing in the art studio when I was bored.

"Do you want to?" Gary asked me.

"Hmmm, sure," I answered, while inside I'm jumping and screaming, "Hell, yeah! You bet your ass I want to!!!"

"Well, it's not like we've any other choice," he muttered. "I hope you're a quick learner." He called Sean and Louie, the drummer and keyboard player, who'd stepped outside for a smoke instead of stressing inside. They're strict around here about smoking inside clubs. They taught me their song in fifteen minutes, a really beautiful song. The key they played in for their singer suited my voice perfectly. Theo wrote down the words on my arm so I could read them while I was singing without anyone noticing. We rehearsed it once in the dressing room and I got the impression they weren't too bummed with how it turned out.

There was no time to teach me another song so we tried to think of a song we all knew and decided on one they could cover. We checked the key and it was time to go on. They were calling us onto the stage! At first, the spotlight hit me and I felt my heart slip down through my thong and crash to the floor, but then I heard the guitar and the keyboard enveloping me with their notes. I opened my mouth and remembered that this is a thing I fucking know how to do and started to sing, simply like I always just sing to myself.

I moved my arm around trying to read the words, which probably looked like the silliest dance move ever invented since "Walk Like an Egyptian" and let my voice just take control, adding improvisations that seemed appropriate and suddenly feeling better than I ever did. I felt like it was the real me up there on the stage, truer to myself than I'd felt in a long time. I felt like my voice was soaring in the air, gliding across tables and chairs, caressing people's faces, and soaking into the walls. I opened my eyes and caught Gary grinning at me and Sean nodding from behind the keyboard and harmonizing with my voice. I felt like we had such a connection, that we were moving together as one, ascending with the rhythm. It's pretty amazing how, in one moment, three people can reach the epitome of themselves in perfect sync without even talking much beforehand. It's like, for a brief while, we were all members of a secret cult only we knew about that would disappear as soon as we left the stage. My breath stopped quivering and I simply felt like I was making love with the microphone. I swear it wanted it, too!

The song ended and I heard applause. My eyes adjusted to the dazzling lights and I saw the crowd looking at us. No one had left or gone to get a drink at the bar or anything. We began singing the cover we agreed on – "Extraordinary Machine" by Fiona Apple – and I was really having fun now. I got into it and gave my own rendition of the song, the way I wanted to tell it. Cheers and applause filled the club as we left the stage. As soon as we reached backstage, Gary grabbed me, lifted me up, and started twirling me round and shouting, "Girl, you can sing!" Theo, who was waiting for us there, looked at me from

the corner of the room with a big smile across his face, and I just burst out laughing as the crazy adrenaline rush subsided.

When we finally calmed down, Gary said to me, "Listen, that was awesome. Where did you learn to sing like that?"

"I sang in a choir once," I mumbled.

"And did you ever sing with a band?"

"Hmmm, not really, just with my brother. He's a guitarist."

"Okay, what do you say about doing this again sometime?"

"Sure!" I said and held myself back from jumping up and down and screaming for joy and begging him to let me sing with them again.

I felt like I was in love, just not with a person but with something that I did, do you see? Like, for those fifteen minutes up on stage, I was just me, purer than I'd ever been in my life. I wish you could have been there with me and taken the stage with me... we'd have harmonized like we used to.

I think I'm going to call Gary in a couple of days and nonchalantly ask to join them for one of their jam sessions. Ever since it happened, I feel like I miss it. I mean, I miss the band but not exactly – more like the experience we shared together, the one we created when we went up on that stage.

So that's what happened. It's the middle of the fucking night for you but I just had to share this, so I wrote. Love you, miss you a lot.

Write to me and let me know when we can Skype.

From me, your vocal cord

Subject: Letter Number 22

Wow, that letter. I missed it so much. As I read it just now, I realized I almost knew it by heart.

Yes, Mikey and I go way back. He came to see me at my kibbutz as planned. You can probably imagine how I was shaking in my boots that day.

He looked different – limp and deflated, as if all the air had been taken out of him. He knocked on the door and stepped in with his restless, fidgety demeanor I'd managed to forget, and thick bristles covering his face. "Hey, Mrs. Fine! Looking fine." He shook my mother's hand with a smile.

"How are you, Michael?" she greeted him fondly. It was clear she was emotional. "I saw your picture in the paper recently. You play in a band, don't you?"

"Yes, we're on tour," he acknowledged awkwardly.

"Do you play heavy metal?" She was interested.

"Kinda. Alternative metal, if I want to sound pretentious."

"Sounds like you're very successful."

"We haven't filled Wembley Stadium yet but, hey, no one throws tomatoes on the stage during performances, so that's also a good thing." He rubbed the back of his neck in embarrassment.

"And you're still working at that place? The skydiving center? Remind me what you do there again?"

"Yeah... I'm still a skydiving instructor... and I also manage the place now." He drummed his fingers on his thigh just like Jazz did when she felt uncomfortable.

"Well," Mom collected herself, "sorry, I didn't mean to interrogate you. We just haven't seen you in such a long time. I'll let you two talk. I have to go, anyway. Take care of yourself, Michael. It's really good to see you." She bade him a warm goodbye and sent me a worried glance.

"Mothers..." I sighed awkwardly as we watched her dash away on her bike.

"Tell me about it." He shifted his weight from one foot to the other.

"Would you like something to drink?" I asked. "Coffee?"

"I was taught to never refuse a cup of Dizzy's coffee," he replied, and I felt a twinge in my heart. Jazz was addicted to the coffee I used to brew, but I hadn't made it for a while – the burnt smell, you know. If I was about to face my demons, I might as well give it a try. I headed to the kitchen and Mikey followed. I rummaged through the cupboards and found the small tin coffee pot, placed it on the stove, and added some ground coffee with cardamom. It wasn't the freshly ground coffee I used to buy at that special place in Haifa, but it was decent enough. I carefully measured out the coffee and water. As we waited for the water to boil, Mikey looked me over with concern.

"You've lost weight," he determined.

"Oh... thanks." I was surprised. Was he complimenting me now?

"No. I mean... no offense, but in a bad way. Let's just say that you don't look like you've enjoyed a good shawarma lately."

I noticed he looked rather thin under his baggy jacket, too, but I didn't say anything. The coffee boiled. I turned the heat down and let it simmer. I poured the hot liquid with a ritual that my trembling fingers hadn't forgotten and placed the cups on the dining table. We sat down facing each other and an oppressive silence hovered between us, mingling with the steam from our coffee cups.

"So, what's up, Dizzy?" He looked sideways at me and cradled the hot coffee cup in both his hands.

"You probably don't really understand what I want from you, hm?"

"Look. If you want to talk, I'm here, but let's just say that I get it. I know I wasn't exactly fun to be around. And at the end of the day, I can totally understand you. You've moved on with your life. It's pretty clear that my face was the last thing you wanted to see."

"Is that what you think? That I moved on with my life?" I couldn't believe it.

"Hey, I'm not saying that's a bad thing. Like, good for you for moving forward and leaving everything that happened behind you. Look. I had this urge to see you and talk to you after what happened, but now I realize why you didn't want to deal with it. We all do what we need to in order to survive."

Leave everything that happened behind me? I didn't know how to explain how far from the truth that was. I sat there quietly for a moment and then blurted out, "Actually, it's more like everything that happened left me behind. Suffice it to say, I'm not the most functioning person in the world right now."

"What do you mean?" He furrowed his brow.

"Do you want the checklist or the bottom line?"

"Both."

"I work from home and study with the Open University since I can't really manage to leave the house. And to say that I study is a wild exaggeration because my concentration sucks. So, I check the boxes for 'working' and 'studying' but I don't do either in reality. And I never sleep. And I... I'm, like, scared of everything. Even after I moved to Tel Aviv, I didn't really get out of the house or out of my head. On the other hand, I can't bring myself to contend with what happened. Talking with you, for example – it was too hard for me. But lately, all sorts of things have happened and I realize that I don't have a choice. I need to deal with the accident." I studied his reaction and continued. "I'm sorry for dumping all this on you right now. I know you're already somewhere else, with the skydiving and the band and all that."

"Dizzy, what I do all day, every day, is hold people while they jump off a plane to make sure they don't crash and die. Do you really think I'm not there anymore?"

"Okay, well... but the band, I've been hearing about you guys –"

"Yeah, my checklist sounds pretty good, too, doesn't it?" he chuckled bitterly. "Listen. After the accident, I was trippin' because I knew – I just knew – that one day something bad would happen to her, and I wasn't able to prevent it. After all, within our broken family it was always just the two of us, there for each other. Mom was all over the US with a fucked-up boyfriend, a house, and a clinic that she'd swap every couple of years. And Dad was always too busy to notice what Wheezy was

up to or to keep an eye on her. That was my job. And I failed. And I couldn't get over it. A friend who tried to cheer me up bought me a skydiving lesson for my birthday and I discovered that, during a dive, in those few moments of silence when I'm freefalling, I feel a sudden calm and my mind stops racing. It's the closest thing to a good night's sleep that I've managed to achieve.

"I started hanging around the skydiving center every day until the previous manager grew tired of me and offered to train me to become an instructor there. So, soon enough, I began instructing and... basically, I became the manager simply because I was always there. If they needed a guy to tandem jump with someone, I'd rather it was me. I'm a control freak now. I don't trust anyone." He took a sip from his coffee and continued. "Anyway, I needed to find something to do with myself at night, so each evening, after the center closed, I'd head to the underground bomb shelter on my kibbutz and jam on my guitar. Yanni, Ron, and Tzadok soon joined me. Later on, we wrote a few songs, and Yanni, the drummer, who's connected to all these clubs, started arranging shows and introducing us to agents and A&R reps. So, yeah, the checklist sounds great. But everything else? I don't know. If I said I've been sleeping well, I'd be lying."

I was surprised. I mean, I obviously knew Jazz was on his mind and everything, but I was sure he'd managed to move on while I remained stuck in the past.

"Say, why did you even want to talk to me after it happened? It seems to me that, if I were you, I'd be the last person I'd want

to see. If I were in your shoes, I'd be insanely angry at me," I said, but I actually wanted to ask: *Don't you hate me? She's gone while I'm here. I'm the one who failed to protect her.*

"I'm not mad at you, Dizzy. I'm just... sorry. You were, you still are, the closest thing to her I have left. At least you knew her as she was with you, as equals. She and I, we were the little sister and the big brother, the overprotective sidekick and the rebellious Wheezy. There's a sort of hole in my life, like a picture where someone's image has been cut out. We'd almost reached the stage where we were able to stop being a big brother and a little sister and just be siblings, but she died just before it happened. And I don't really know who she was or even how exactly she was killed. Not the details from the highway police, but those that truly matter. I chased after you obsessively, like I did everything obsessively after the accident because I thought you could complete the picture for me and tell me about her, you know. If she was in love at the time, and what was the last thing she said, and if she was happy that night, and if she was actually sober that night like the police said, and if anyone touched her that night or kissed her for the last time, and if she debated what to wear before she chose that black dress... and what was the last song she heard when she was dancing and what was she planning to do the next day and what was the last thing she ate..." He paused and took a deep breath. "In short, I had a lot of questions, but I got the feeling that it was hard for you to talk about it and I needed to respect that."

"I don't remember what happened, Mikey. I don't know why. I don't know how it's possible not to remember such a thing."

"I know. Some things are probably best forgotten."

We fell silent. We sat facing each other in draining silence until he said, "I'm dying for a smoke. Let's get out of here."

"Let's go there," I heard myself say before I had a chance to regret it.

"Where?"

"There. The scene of the accident."

"Forget it, Dizzy, you don't need that right now."

"What I need is to stop running away from everything, and I think, in order to do that, I need to start from where it all happened. And if I don't go back there now, I don't know when I'll have the nerve to ever do it."

"Are you sure?" he asked warily.

"Yes."

"Okay, but I'll drive slowly, and if you change your mind just tell me to stop."

We hopped in his pickup. For the first time since the accident, I sat in the front seat. I fastened my seat belt and dug my nails into it as usual. I reclined in the seat, shut my eyes, and tried to breathe.

"Are you okay?" Mikey asked as I battled against the intense nausea.

"I'm not good at riding in cars these days."

"Do you want to stop? Should I turn back?"

"No."

"You're sure about that?"

"Yes."

It's strange how little time it took us to get there. I was sure it would take us three-and-a-half years of driving. For me, that

place represents a moment where time was split in two, and not just another point on the map. But that's just what it was, and though I hadn't been there since that night, I felt as if I'd never really left. I suddenly realized that I visit this place every night in the dream that I can never remember. I assumed that, once we arrived, my whole body would tremble, that I'd freak out completely and want to run away but, strangely, it felt natural. Soothing, even. I felt at home.

Not much had changed there. A large street light now towered over the bend in the road. It didn't look particularly new and I wondered if it had been installed following the accident. The bushes on either side of the road were a little taller. They were green back then in late winter, and now, in mid-summer, they were golden-brown and brittle. The large boulder at the side of the road was still there. The dividing line separating the two traffic lanes was now bright white, apparently having been repainted.

Mikey stopped his truck at the side of the road. "Do you want to step out?"

"Yes," I nodded. I had a feeling that if I opened the door, I'd drop off the edge of the earth, but that didn't happen. Everything was so normal: the gray asphalt glistened under the afternoon sun, the scent of knapweeds mingled with the odor of worn tires, and birds perched on the power lines. Just a normal bend in a remote road. I don't know how, but I knew exactly at what point on the road the accident took place. We leaned on the truck and stared toward it.

"Have you been here since?" I asked him.

"Yeah... you could say that," he grinned.

"What do you mean?"

"After the accident, before I started skydiving, I came here quite often. Every day, in fact. At first, there were some stains on the road. On that first day, there were also shards of glass. Pretty soon, they dispersed but the stains remained. I had this thing where I'd come here every day to see if they'd faded. Gradually, they disappeared."

"It's strange that so many people drive down this road every day, and none of them know that a person ceased to exist here, isn't it?" I thought out loud.

"It's the strangest possible thing," he agreed.

"Do you think we should have set up a roadside memorial or something?"

"What for? So that whoever drives by here will see some name on a stone and just turn their eyes back to the road?"

"Or have an accident themselves for taking their eyes off the road," I added cynically.

"Yeah, huh? Honestly, the thought did cross my mind, but what would a couple of stones have to say about who she really was? I was her brother and I hardly know who she was." He whipped out his pack of Camels and chewed the tip of a cigarette. "And besides," he continued, "if you think about it, someone's probably ceased to exist in practically every place you go."

We stared at the satiated flies buzzing in the summer breeze under the crimson late afternoon sky. "She wasn't in love," I said.

"What?" He took a drag from his cigarette.

"Jazz. She didn't fall in love with people. Not with those she had sex with, anyway. She'd fall in love with her friends. She fell in love with Theo, the guy who painted her in New York – painted himself, that is, but he's gay. I guess she fell in love with me, too. And when that happened, it was as if a very special spotlight had been cast on me from above."

Tears began welling in the corners of my eyes but I didn't care.

"The last thing I remember her saying was some joke about a silly pair of pants someone at the club was wearing. She said she wanted a pair like that. Later, on the motorcycle, she sang, 'Happy Birthday to You' at the top of her lungs. And I yelled back that my birthday was already over, so she started singing 'A Very Merry Unbirthday' from the movie *Alice in Wonderland*."

"We were addicted to that movie when we were little," he said quietly.

"Yeah, I know. No one touched her that evening. She never paid any attention to someone else on my birthday. She had a purple dress on before we left but spilled some coffee on it so she changed into one of my black dresses. The last song she heard was some electro track by Underworld playing in the club to get everyone to clear out and go home. We were planning to sleep in the next day, meet up with friends who'd recently returned from India and ask them about the best trekking destinations. The last thing she ate was a Tim Tam – remember those chocolate-covered wafers she was hooked on, the ones you can use as a straw and drink coffee through? I think she was really happy that night. She drank one whiskey with me but that was when

we'd just arrived at the club, several hours before we got back on the motorcycle, and she didn't take anything. She was in a really good phase in her life, mainly waiting for me to complete my national service and for us to take that trip together. She was seriously considering studying music and wanted to volunteer at a sexual assault crisis center. I think she'd have been good at it." I tried to remember if he'd asked anything else.

"Thank you," Mikey said after a few drags from his cigarette.

"Sorry I couldn't tell you all this until now. Honestly, I never really thought about your side of it," I admitted.

"Enough with the apologies, Dizzy. No one but you expected that you'd come out of this thing undamaged. It's not your fault, you know."

"I know, but it's hard to accept that."

"All you two did was ride a motorcycle. Not the safest method of commuting, but you were twenty years old and it's not like you jumped from an airplane. Ultimately, you need to choose to either accept the fact that it wasn't your fault or lose your mind over it."

"Have you made that choice already?"

"Me? I'm somewhere in the middle. I think the hardest thing about it is the feeling of missing out... the sense that I didn't really know her. But what can I possibly do about that? It's not like my wheezy sister wrote a fucking diary or a blog like a normal girl her age. She was more about living life than writing about it."

"Maybe I can help you with that," I said hesitantly. "I wrote about her after she died. About things we did together. I wrote

quite a bit. A great deal actually. I documented her life. I also kept all her letters."

"Seriously?! Can I read it?" His eyes widened.

"So, the thing is... it's a little complicated. It's not all with me right now. But I'm working very hard on getting it back."

"What does that mean?"

"My apartment was broken into and my laptop was stolen along with all the files on it and the backups and everything. But maybe it can still be recovered."

"What?! Fuck! When did this happen?"

"A few months ago when I lived in Tel Aviv. That's why I moved back to the kibbutz."

"Shit, girl! They didn't touch you or anything, right?" His body tensed.

"No, nothing like that. I was just tremendously bummed because I lost all the things I wrote about her, but maybe I'll manage to get them back."

"What, like, data recovery?"

"Yes... something like that. It's a long story. Come on, let's get out of here." I avoided his questions. The sun had begun to set and I didn't want to be out there after dark.

"Yeah, I've had enough of this place," he said and we went back to his truck.

Liz

Subject: New York Epilogue

Dear Liz,
    Please find the attached.
    Warm regards,

    Someone

Attachment: My darling nostrils!

I've been writing this letter in my head for a week now, talking with you in my thoughts about everything that happens as if you're a ghost floating beside me. When we see each other, you'll have to constantly remind me that you weren't really here with me all this time.

I'm all packed and my room suddenly seems so bare. It'll probably take at least a month or two until a room becomes available for me in Mevo Golan and that's only once I get on the waiting list. At Dad's, I'll be banging my head for sure against the wall after a couple of days, so I guess I'll be bunking with you for a while. Do you think the kibbutz members at Beit Katzir will object? It'll be so much fun to hang around while you're at the base and spend the weekends together. I can't wait to go out dancing with you!!! Can you believe we're going to see each other soon???

Around here it's been quite a touchy-feely week. Hey, it's not easy to pack up eighteen months into a few cardboard boxes, tape them up and board a plane. Some boxes have loose stuff coming out of them and are so difficult to close that I have to sit on them and tape them up tight. It also doesn't help that everyone over here thinks that I'm moving back to some war zone and I'll need a bulletproof vest in the streets or something.

Theo's exhibition debuted this week. It was really draining. So

many emotions and everything we went through together... and the feeling that it's over since I'll be flying soon. Obvs, I'll miss him the most, but we already planned for us all to meet up when we come to New York together. We can stay in his apartment, for sure! I just know you'll be crazy about one another and he really can't wait to meet you after all those three-way Skype calls from the studio.

Along with the art exhibition and saying goodbye to everyone, the major thing that happened this week was that Theo finally showed me the last painting in the series. Well, he didn't have a choice anymore – the exhibition was the next day. And that's actually what I want to tell you about because it was such a weird moment. We both sat in his studio after the infamous table was no longer there. We hauled it out to the street the other day and, thirty minutes later, it was gone. Just try to imagine the kind of people who took it...

Theo said, "Well, I guess this is it." He took my hand and led me to the other side of the studio. I stood in front of the giant canvas and was amazed to discover that this time it wasn't a painting of his image but of mine. Not of my pussy, but of my hand, clenched tightly around the flesh of my thigh, my fingernails digging sharply into my skin.

I didn't understand what it was at first. "Didn't you notice?" he asked me. "For the first few weeks, your fists were clenched so tightly you pierced your skin." I wondered if he was making that up. "Sure, it was so striking that I had to paint it," he said and spread out dozens of drawings of my hands clasped around my thighs, gripping so firmly that the skin beneath them had

turned white. It's odd because I don't remember that at all. I don't remember it being difficult or stressful or anything like that. And then he looked at me strangely and said: "You have to take care of yourself, Jazz. You're much more fragile than you think you are. You're allowed to be vulnerable, you know."

Anyway, the debut was super successful, your typical New York pretension, flutes of champagne, mingling and small talk and all that shit. It was received with great reviews and I'm so happy for Theo. His paintings, though, are the saddest I've seen in my life. There's so much pain in those self-portraits.

Oh, yeah, and Jeff showed up at the gallery that night! It was so strange to see him there all of a sudden, among all the people and excitement. He gazed at the paintings for a long while, walking around the gallery and glancing at Theo now and then. When he came across the painting of my hand, he stopped and stared at it for a long time. We hugged. I told him I was sorry if I came off like a bitch the last time we met and I had a lot more to explore before I reached the point he was at right now. I'm glad I had the chance to see him again and tell him all that. TBH, I haven't treated him that well.

Of course, I also said my goodbyes to Gary, Sean, and Louie. We had one last jam session and it felt amazing to sing with them. I'll miss it so much! You know what? Lately, I've come to realize that music is something that makes me happy. It inspires me to be more myself than anything I've done before. I want to know more about it and get to know who I am when I'm singing. I'll talk to you more about it when I'm back in Israel.

And that's about it. I'll be on a plane the day after tomorrow. I've forwarded my flight deets. Talk to Mikey and my dad. Bummer that you couldn't get a pass from the base to meet me at the airport, but don't worry about it. See you very soon! I'm dying to see you already!!!

From me, your darling belly button

Subject: Letter Number 23

Thanks. That's one of my favorite letters. Do you think it's possible to take comfort in the fact that someone died when they were truly happy, or that it doesn't matter? Generally, I believe that life and death are rather meaningless, but when I read this letter, I can't help but be glad that Jazz managed to reach such a good stage in her life before she went and disappeared. But maybe that's actually supposed to make me sad? Forget it, these are just inconsequential questions for which there are no answers.

For a change, there were no dramas in my life this week. The mood at my parents' house has been a little calmer lately, like it's easier to breathe now there are no more invisible secrets between us and taking up all the space. Mikey and I chatted on WhatsApp for a bit. He asked if I was okay after our visit to the scene of the accident, and the truth is that, surprisingly, I feel lighter. Though I didn't realize it, that place has haunted me for the past three or so years. Somehow, once I went back there and saw that wretched little stretch of road, I felt I could stop running away from it.

Maybe there was a little drama this week after all. I discovered something that helped me make sense of certain issues. It wasn't anything concerning me for a change. Or maybe it was?

I met Nahum again. After that conversation about my grandmother, I felt a certain bond was forged between us. With

SNUNIT LISS | 291

this man, a million years older than me, I somehow managed to hold a more honest and profound conversation than I do with people my age. I found myself thinking about him, sitting by himself all day in his little room, making his usual rounds to the dining hall, the store, and the infirmary, riding his mobility scooter around the kibbutz to avoid the dreary nursing home. And all this time, there's a whole world alive within him, and no one to share it with. I wondered if that was the reason behind his grandchild hallucination. It's baffling to discover that a man who appears so sound and coherent sees and hears people who aren't there.

A few days ago, I went to visit him again. Sarah, the supervisor, was no longer surprised to see me. "He's in his room," she smiled at me.

He greeted me warmly as I entered. "Liza, what a welcome guest!" He turned off the TV, approached me, and put his arm on my shoulder as if to check that I was real. "So, what would you like to drink today, *maideleh*? I have a new tea! I asked Yaffa from the store to recommend something extra special. She gave me Apple Delight. What do you say about that? In my day, tea was tea. Today, we're delighted by apples!"

"Happily," I grinned, helping him to boil the water and arrange the snacks from the rustling bags that he enjoyed opening but never tasted.

"Tell me, Liza, do you happen to like playing chess?" he asked as we finished setting out the refreshments.

"I haven't played for a while, but actually, yes, I do like playing chess," I was surprised. He opened the bottom drawer

of his dresser, took out a beautiful board that exuded an antique hardwood aroma, and began to carefully arrange the intricately carved chess pieces. I helped him and when we were ready, he beckoned me to sit and play the first move with black.

"So, Liza? You're a psychology major, aren't you? How's that going?" he asked as he pondered his next move.

"Won't our conversation break your concentration when you play?" I tried to change the subject.

"*Maideleh*, conversation is the most interesting game of chess there is," he winked.

"Honestly, I haven't been doing too well with my studies."

"Why not? A girl like you? I'm sure you have more sense in your little finger than all your teachers put together!"

"Did you forget to take your medication, Nach'che? I think you're a little confused," I smiled.

"Oh, Liza, there are things that even this *farzhavert* mind of mine can't confuse," he laughed. I knew he'd get my humor.

"I... I'm not so focused lately." I tried to avoid the gritty details.

"Why, did something happen?"

"Umm. Yeah. No. Not recently." I was uncertain for a moment. Should I unload all my shit on this sweet old man?

"My dear girl, do you think a person my age needs a babysitter?"

"What?" I asked in confusion. "Of course not."

"So please stop trying to protect me and tell me what this is all about. After all, I have been through a thing or two in my lifetime."

"It's something that happened a few years ago," I hesitated.

"I'm listening." His eyes twinkled in anticipation.

"A few years ago, I was in a car accident with a really good friend of mine. And... she was killed and... I was injured. Nothing too serious but... ever since I've found it difficult to concentrate and do all sorts of things."

"Ahh," he gazed at me and mulled my words over in his mind. "I understand. So, in a way, you lost a life. Not your own life, but a lost life nonetheless," he said, half to himself.

"Yeah, exactly." I marveled as he articulated my feelings so clearly.

"Ahh, Liza. I, too, have lost some lives in my life." He placed his palm on my hand and we sat there, a broken young woman consoled by a confused old man.

"So how do you manage to stay the way you are – optimistic, that is? Waking up every morning, getting out of bed?" I wanted to learn from him.

"Look, I'll tell you something I realized when I was about your age. Just as a life can be lost, a life can be gained. Look at me. I lost an entire world in the war. Everything I knew before I came to this country went kaput and we weren't exactly picking daisies over here, either. And then one day, Malka'le arrived at the kibbutz. And she... with all the terrible things she'd been through over there – even I didn't know all the details – she had this energy within her. She had such a life force that, to this day, I can't explain its origin. She was altogether a miracle – for me, and as a being in herself. She, too, lost an entire world. And she soon became my whole world, and I was hers. And we didn't succeed in achieving everything we wanted together. But – what

can I tell you, Liza – a man and a woman together for forty years, it's not always Apple Delight. The togetherness we had, that was a life. An entire lifetime! And how bravely she fought against that cursed disease – like a lioness! And I lost her, too, but let me tell you a secret: the life I had with her, it continued to exist within me even after she was gone!" he proclaimed proudly.

"Tell me something," I hesitantly asked the question that had been gnawing at me since our first conversation, "what do you think of what my grandmother did?"

He sighed. "Think? Well. Eliza, God rest her soul. I thought quite a bit about what she did. Quite a bit." He took a deep breath and continued, "Look, my dear, unlike others around here, I'm not going to say that it was a reprehensible act. Well, there are certain circumstances in which a person's left with no other choice. But sometimes the 'no other choice' is the only alternative that can be seen by eyes blinded by despair. Sometimes, even when one believes they have no choice, they can rise above it if only they're offered a helping hand."

He paused again, narrowing his eyes as if trying to see through a thick fog, and continued. "But your grandmother... We didn't know how to offer her a helping hand. There were so many things we didn't know back then. She was probably convinced she had no other choice, but I don't think that was true. As life begins from nothing, it can be rekindled from nothing. Well, you'll see that when you have children of your own."

"Children?!" I choked on my tea. "What are you talking about? I can barely manage to take care of myself. I'm even getting tired of feeling sorry for myself."

"Ahh, Liza, Liza. So, feel sorry. Feel sorry for yourself. I'll tell you something that I once told my Malka'le: self-pity has long been wrongly perceived. Self-pity does not mean defeat – no, no! Feeling sorry for yourself means showing compassion for yourself when the world is unable to do so. It means being a womb, finding a warm place within yourself to rest and recuperate. You, my dear, are your own firstborn! Does a mother berate her baby when he cries? Well, I'm no expert but I very much hope not. She hugs him, sings to him, and feeds him until the crying stops. So take pity on yourself, *maideleh*, until you no longer require your mercy."

"And what if I lost too much, Nach'che? What if the crying doesn't stop?" I tried to process his words.

"Lost too much? How much is too much? I lost so many things, Liza. My childhood home, my family, Malka. I lost the kibbutz, too. After all, what we have here today is not what we dreamed of creating. We dreamed of reinventing the new socialist man. Well, what's new? And what man? The friends I had are gone, too. Loneliness is the tax you pay for longevity. Nevertheless, look at what can happen in the here and now, even when I'm old. Unexpectedly, you – Liza, the granddaughter of Eliza, God rest her soul, whom I also lost – appeared, and suddenly I gained a new friend after many years of being alone."

I blushed at his words.

"You're probably thinking that these are just the silly notions of an old *lemech*, but I do know this Liza: just as evil may come upon us, good may come upon us as well. And when the world outside is not good enough, your inner world can help. I'll tell

you another secret." He leaned toward me and whispered, "The grandchildren I told you about, they don't really exist. Malka'le, may she rest in peace, and I never managed to have children. Maybe it was due to what she went through back in the war. There's no knowing. The hunger, the diseases she suffered... Anyway, when it was just the two of us, I didn't feel the need for children. Well, there was nothing to be done. It was what it was. I was there for her and she was there for me.

"Yet, once she passed away, I began to miss the children we never had. And now I sometimes like to imagine that I have grandchildren. I like to think they exist and just don't have time to visit. After all, I heard David's grandchildren are all healthy and well and they don't seem to visit him much more often than my grandchildren visit me." He winked and pointed at his neighbor's room down the hall. "I just toy with the idea that I have children who live abroad. I try to imagine what our grandchildren would have looked like, what talents they'd have, and how they'd talk. And, oh, I love telling Sarah, the supervisor, about my grandchildren. Forgive an old man, but I deserve a little fun sometimes too, no? I tell her about the grandchildren I don't have and she squirms and cooperates with my story. She feels too awkward to confront me with the truth. Ha! She probably thinks I'm senile! And, also, Yaffa, from the store, I see how the two of them gossip. The least I can do is provide them with a topic of conversation," he smiled mischievously.

"And don't you get sad sometimes? Without your wife? Without the grandchildren you dream about?"

"Oh, Liza. I mourn all the things I lost and all the things I

never had, but I also live them. The grief of loss is balanced by the joy of all that I had, and the two live peacefully within me. At my age, that's a considerable achievement."

"Oh, Nach'che, you're really something special."

"That's what Sarah always says!" He winked at me again. "Now, Liza, you should try to concentrate a little. My queen is about to gobble up your queen."

Ultimately, he won the game. I should have known he didn't have dementia. The man plays like the Polish National Chess Champion.

So, tell me, what do you do with yourself all day if you don't leave the house? How do you pass the time hour after hour after hour?

Liz

Subject: What I do all day

In recent years, my waking and sleeping hours have shifted from the accepted norms. I sleep for a few hours, wake up and fall asleep again, all with no real awareness of daylight or darkness. One thing remains constant: every time I wake up, I feel as if an imaginary chokehold is being tightened around my neck by a disembodied figure standing above me. It does not offer me any final requests, and no words are spoken between us. And I know it's not just me it haunts. People marry each other, chase after money and fame, even post nude pictures of themselves online, all in an attempt to escape the debilitating sense of loneliness they encounter every morning. Me – I release the chokehold from my neck and shake hands with the disembodied figure. I've formed an alliance with loneliness. It's my only companion. I'll never have another. The bottle will keep us both company.

I woke up quite early this morning, stretched, and stood In front of the mirror. I was clad in just a pair of old boxers. I examined my appearance. My penis and testicles appeared to be sagging within the grayish, worn fabric of my shorts. My plump belly looked as if it were mocking my scrawny arms and legs that seemed to me like two pale toothpicks. I felt a deep aversion toward the pallor and degeneration looking back at me from the mirror, but I continued to stare at my reflection for a long while.

Later, I propelled myself to the bathroom, brushed my teeth until my gums became tender, and put on some clothes. I stepped out of my apartment, took the elevator to the lobby, sat on the bench, and gazed at the passersby through the one-way mirror at street level. I examined them: their movements, their dress, the manner in which they carry their belongings. I sat there for about an hour. The occasional neighbor would walk past me and glare at me with contempt. My neighbors are not fond of my presence.

I waited to see if Hanan would pass by. When I saw no sign of him, I approached the lobby door and cracked open a slit. The bright daylight blinded me. Without stepping outside, I cried out several times: "Hanan! Hanan! Hanaaaan!" Sometimes he hides and waits until I get discouraged, then suddenly jumps up at me. When I realized he wasn't around, I headed back to my apartment, sat down at my desk, and switched on my computer. A message from a client regarding a deadline I haven't met was waiting for me in my inbox. I read the first two lines of her email: "Hey there! What's up? We're about to launch the campaign and I simply must have the copy for the web banners ASAP. When will you send it? Have a fantastic day!" Her words sent bile rushing up my throat. I turned to the safe, took out your laptop, and turned it on. I checked on your whereabouts. I hope you're aware that anyone who knows your Google password can do that now. I saw you haven't gone far today and, in fact, seem to still be at your parents' house. Later, I logged into your email and browsed through your recent correspondence. I read some of the SEO articles you sent to your employers and wondered if

you, too, are often overwhelmed by a sense of utter futility when compelled to write thousands of words about such nonsense. I checked to see if you've taken any photos with your cell phone in the last few days and found a picture of a tree stump.

After that, I tracked Ella's whereabouts in the same manner. For several hours, I drifted between your digital footprints and Ella's. Eventually, I forced myself to perform the task my client requested. I came up with some silly slogans and supplemental text for a trivial sales campaign and sent it.

For several days now, my computer's power charger has been showing signs of deterioration. I was concerned that it would stop working altogether and that I'd no longer be able to charge my laptop. My need for Hanan had become urgent. I hadn't seen him for a few days and wondered where he was. I picked up the charger and headed back down to the lobby. It was afternoon by then. Parents and their children walked past the window – rambunctious human cubs scurrying around their mothers and fathers.

Suddenly, I saw Hanan, straggling as usual down the street in his gawky body and worn-out clothes, dragging his long legs in the used shoes I gave him several months ago. He was pulling a pink, floral shopping cart, the kind little old ladies like. He must have found it in the trash. He headed forward purposefully, his long arm gripping the cart handle as it trailed after him like a faithful pet. I sprang toward the door, opened it, and called out, "Hanan!"

He froze in place for a moment and then kept walking, pretending he hadn't heard me. "Hanan!" I called again. He ignored me. "Hanaaaan!" I called out for the third time.

He stopped, turned, and looked at me with a hint of a smile, and then began to pace slowly toward me, stopping a few feet away from the door. "What?" he said, taunting me.

"How are you?"

"What? I can't hear you," he said smiling.

"Enough, Hanan. Come here. I haven't seen you in a while. Are you okay?" I hoped he would stop his silly tricks long enough to listen. He enjoyed teasing and coercing me to exit the building. "What??? I can't hear you! Come closer!!!" he yelled over to me, his smile spreading across his face.

"Enough, Hanan. I require your services."

"So come closer, then."

"Oh, come on," I pleaded. He moved a little closer and stopped five feet away.

"How are you? I haven't seen you in a few days," I said again.

"I've been around. I had some business in the south side of the city," he blurted out, and I noticed he was chewing something. What business could he possibly have? "Why? Did you miss me?" he continued teasing.

"My laptop charger," I handed it to him. "It's faulty and I need a new one. It's urgent. I need you to go to the computer store, show it to them, and ask for a new one of the same model."

"Which store?"

"It's on the corner of Ibn Gavirol and Jabotinsky Street." I pointed in the right direction.

"And how do you know that's the right store?" he persisted in provoking me.

"I looked it up online."

"200." He named his price for the errand.

"100," I said. It was our usual negotiation dance.

"150," he replied.

"I'll give you 50 now and another 100 when you return with the new charger. Tell them to call me when you're there and I'll take care of the payment. And you must return within thirty minutes because the laptop needs to be recharged."

"Must?" He deliberated.

"Please."

"Okay." He reached out for the charger. He was too far away to take it from my hand even though I stretched out my arm as far as I could.

"I can't reach it," he grumbled.

I sent him an imploring look, but he ignored it and repeated, "I can't reach it."

I pushed the lobby door wide open to make sure it remained ajar, took one step outside my building, placed the charger in his hand, and hurried back inside. "Satisfied now?" I asked.

"You're so fucked-up. When will you stop living like a snail with a house attached to its back?"

"When will you stop living like a homeless slug?" I retorted.

"In another life, I guess," he said thoughtfully.

"Yes, in another life," I agreed and, for one odd moment, we stood there facing each other like mirror images until I urged him, "Quickly, my laptop battery's running low. I'll be waiting for a call from the store. Ring the intercom when you get back." A neighbor entering the building looked at the two of us with disgust.

I went back to my apartment and counted the minutes as I watched my laptop battery slowly draining. Finally, the store representative called and Hanan returned soon after. I paid him and climbed back up to my apartment for the third time. It was evening by now. I ate leftovers from the take-out I ordered two days ago. I picked up a half-empty bottle of Johnny Walker and sipped from it. I stared at my computer and browsed through the news websites with their already familiar headlines. My apartment felt suffocating. My long, self-imposed quarantine had taken its toll like an unbearable itch. For the most part, my conversations with Hanan dispel this feeling, but not this time.

I logged on to Tinder and gazed at the photos of women. One by one they appeared before me, hungry for validation, pairs of eyes behind which I recognized that same distressing itch that was spreading through my body. I swiped right and left: this one looks too cheerful, this one has a hollow gaze, this one's attractive, this one's pictured at a party... . The party girl might be deterred by my reclusive lifestyle. It was an infinite library of loneliness soliciting more loneliness to be alone with.

I swiped right on the profile of a brown-haired girl who had swiped right on my photo. We chatted.

"What do you feel like? Coffee? Drinks?" she asked after agreeing to meet with me.

"I'd be happy to host you at my apartment."

"Forget your apartment. I feel like going out."

"I'm interested in you, not the rest of the world."

"Let's start by going out and if we hit it off, we could end up at your apartment –"

"I'm not interested in going out."

"There's no way I'm coming over to your place right now. We don't even know each other..."

"Whatever."

There was another woman who wanted me to come to her place. I ended that chat swiftly and continued swiping through the field of hungry, carnivorous flowers. And then I came across her face. She wasn't particularly pretty but there was a demure charm to her features. Her eyes betrayed a formerly youthful spirit that had been replaced by the plea of a woman who had not been told she was beautiful in a very long time. I examined her photo; she was wearing a dress a size too small in an attempt to project contrived sexuality. Her arm awkwardly covered her abdomen, trying to conceal the folds of fat exposed by the unforgiving fabric. Her light-colored curls framed her face in fearless abandon in stark contrast to the apprehension in her eyes. Her name was Aviva. "A-Vi-Va." I rolled her name on my tongue and enjoyed how it moved between my front teeth and my lips. I swiped right and, within a few seconds, I received confirmation that she had stroked my photo in the same manner. This is how courtship is conducted nowadays – two strangers, stroking each other's photos in the same direction on a screen.

"I like your name, Aviva," I typed.

"I don't," she replied.

"May I ask why not?"

"It means springtime in Hebrew, and I'm always cold. Aviva is a silly name for someone who always has goosebumps. Do you like your name?" she asked.

"My name is of no interest to me. It's not indicative of who I am, just as I'm not indicative of it."

"Even so, the word 'apple' implies something about the taste you'll feel when you bite into an apple. Your name says nothing about you?" she persisted.

"Bite me and find out," I typed. I know. It wasn't very witty, but it was late and I was drunk and craving physical contact. "Why don't you come over?" I was worried she would shy away from my blunt language and hurried to add a more delicate suggestion.

"And how do I know you're not some kind of pervert or just plain repulsive?"

"I'll tell you what. Johnny the red Walker and I are waiting for you at my apartment. When you arrive, I will open the door, fully clothed. You shall look at me for as long as you wish, and if you don't like what you see, you can leave just as easily as you came." I cast my net into the water.

"You made me laugh with that bit about Johnny the red Walker."

"I'm glad I made you laugh." I gave her directions to my address and took another swig from my bottle. I went through my closet, wondering what was appropriate for such an occasion, but the need to put on a metaphorical costume evoked a sense of disgust in me. I decided to stay in the clothes I was wearing.

About an hour later, there was a knock at the door. I walked over, looked through the peephole, and saw Aviva. The curved glass distorted her image. Her head looked disproportionally large and round and her body seemed thin and lanky. Her lips

were painted with bright red lipstick and her body was squeezed into a short, overly tight dress. Her eyes, which seemed huge through the peephole, betrayed a glimmer of shame and hope. She waited, turning her head from side to side and a couple of minutes later rang the doorbell. I kept peering at her through the peephole. She took out a cell phone from her purse to use as a mirror while she fixed her makeup. She then gazed suspiciously at the peephole and texted me: I'M HERE. The message alert on the phone I was holding broke the silence. Her eyes narrowed in confusion. It was clear that she had heard my phone ping and was aware of my presence. I stood in front of her with the door between us and continued watching her, one hand on the door handle, the other gripping my phone. I sensed the despair in her red lipstick seeping through the door and penetrating my skin, attacking me, soaking through me, and I couldn't bear it. I longed to open the door but couldn't bring myself to do so. Her fingers fluttered over her phone again. ARE YOU THERE? Another text. My phone beeped again, sending a resounding echo through the air between us. She glared at the peephole in anger, waited for another moment, and typed DROP DEAD! She turned and walked away.

I remained standing there, watching through the peephole, shocked and defeated, until the timer on the stairwell switched the light off and the sound of the elevator faded.

I picked up the whiskey bottle and sipped slowly, went to the bathroom, and took off my clothes. Intense nausea overwhelmed me. The bile burned my throat as I vomited into the toilet. I filled the tub with the hottest water I could bear and soaked

for two hours, maybe three. Perhaps I fell asleep. By the time I stepped out, the water was cold. I wrapped myself in a towel and headed to my computer. Thankfully, it was fully recharged by now. I felt thoroughly relieved upon discovering a new letter from you. I opened it, read it several times, and then replied with this very email.

This is what I did today.

Warm regards,

Someone

Subject: Letter Number 24

Okay, you win. Your life is even more miserable than mine. And you tracking my location is the most pathetic thing I've ever heard. I barely go anywhere! The fact that you chose me as the object of your obsession reflects very poorly on your stalking skills. If you wanted to live vicariously through someone, you could at least have chosen someone with a more active social life.

You once asked me why I don't go to therapy. So, what's your excuse? Why don't you even try? And no, stalking doesn't count as trying.

And speaking of trying, something unexpected happened to me recently. I saw another shrink – a woman therapist, to be more precise. And she was surprisingly normal! I think I'll even see her again.

After that fiasco with the pretentious psychiatrist, my parents consulted with the kibbutz social worker and she suggested a newly-opened HMO clinic for anxiety-related disorders. She told my parents they're quite busy but well worth a try. Mom asked my permission to call them but I was tired of them calling and making appointments for me like I'm a five-year-old. I made the call myself and, luckily, someone had just happened to cancel and there was an appointment available the next day.

So, my dad took a day off work again and drove me. I think he needed to resist the urge to rub his eyes in shock when I sat down in the front seat beside him and not in the back. He watched me anxiously throughout the drive as I performed some breathing exercises I saw on YouTube.

We arrived at the gray and drab HMO building on a side street in downtown Haifa. A strong scent of disinfectant and bureaucracy filled the air. We waited a while until the door to our assigned room opened. A woman in her fifties with white, curly hair stood at the door. She bade a warm farewell to the previous patient, picked up her list, reviewed it, and scanned the corridor. Her eyes focused on me. "Liz?"

I stood up. "Yes, hello. Doctor Pillar?"

"Mariana!" She stretched her arm out and we shook hands. "Come on in," she invited me into her office. "Would you like some coffee?" she asked and lingered beside a homey-looking cabinet that held a kettle, instant coffee, sugar, and milk.

"Ah... sure," I agreed. I felt uncomfortable for the doctor to be making me coffee.

"Don't worry," she noticed my uneasiness, "you're doing me a favor. My coffee enjoys having a partner. How do you like it? Strong? Weak? Milk? Sugar?"

She walked over to her desk with the two coffee cups and sat down.

"Yes, Liz. What brings you in to see me today?" Like a game of Chutes and Ladders where you always end up sliding back down to the starting point, I was once again in front of a total stranger and debating how to begin.

"I... went through something a few years ago and... recently I realized that maybe I wasn't coping with it so well and that I probably need some help. Professional help."

"That's a difficult question to answer, isn't it?" She surprised me.

"Yes!" I let out a sigh of relief. "Actually, I've been trying to tell my story to some people lately and it feels so strange that I need to recap my entire life in just a few moments. Like some sort of job interview in a tragedy factory."

"Ha! A tragedy factory – what an appropriate description! Maybe one day I'll put that up as a sign on my door," she said with a smile. "So, let's take into consideration that it's impossible to recap your life in a moment or even in an hour, and have you try telling me just as much as you can about what you're dealing with."

So I told her. Hesitantly at first but then, gradually, the words began to flow. I spoke in detail about almost everything: about Jazz and how much I loved her, about the motorcycle accident and the pain and my parents' couch and the incidents in the kibbutz kitchen and the clothes warehouse and the shame and the tears and all the days alone in the darkness of my room. I spoke about the bouts of nausea and the horses galloping in my chest and the crippling fear and the food I have no appetite for and the sleep I can't seem to embrace. I spoke about forgetting, and writing in an attempt to remember, and about Tel Aviv where I tried to escape and discovered that you can't escape from yourself, and about the break-in and the missing laptop, my return to the kibbutz and what I found out about

my grandmother and my conversations with my dad and with Nahum. I talked and talked and she listened, tilting her head a few degrees to the right in thoughtful attention, occasionally sipping from her coffee or offering me a tissue. The only subject I left out was you.

Once I was done, we sat facing each other quietly for a moment. "You've been through quite a lot, Lizzie."

"Yes."

"You've suffered a difficult blow, and the road since then hasn't been easy, either."

I nodded. It was weird to hear someone discuss my life like we did during army staff meetings when reviewing problematic soldiers.

"You know, Liz, our mind and body have limits of their own. When those limits are crossed, our systems become overwhelmed. They want to put up a defense but don't know how to. For example, you know how when a car takes a fast turn, we might feel as though we're being pushed away from the direction of the turn due to the centrifugal force?"

"Yeah," I nodded.

"So, the accident, for the purpose of our analysis, was a sharp turn taken too quickly and your mind and body were subsequently thrown off track."

I cringed. It was still hard for me to think of driving fast and taking sharp turns. "I don't think I'll ever be able to get back on track... get back to who I used to be." I voiced one of the fears that persistently haunted me.

"You won't be who you once were. You'll be a different Liz. Perhaps sadder, perhaps wiser, certainly more experienced, but you'll still be Liz," she said with a gentle smile.

"Sometimes it seems that I've drifted so far from myself that I'm no longer sure who I am. I look at myself and what's become of my life and I hate what I see."

"Maybe one of the things we'll need to work on here is your ability to accept yourself, even when you're not functioning as you believe you should. When you're grieving, when you're hurting, in everything you do and feel, Liz, you always remain you."

"Could we maybe... I've read about Prolonged Exposure Therapy. You know, repeated exposure to traumatic memories and the related stimuli until the anxiety gradually dissipates. I read that it's very effective. Maybe we should try it?" I just wanted a quick solution.

"Easy there, Liz. You experienced an invasive event that unexpectedly tore away everything you knew and loved. I'd like our sessions to be a redeeming experience. This is your opportunity to be heard, to do things at a pace that's right for you, your emotions, and your physical well-being. Prolonged exposure is certainly an effective technique, but I think we should also discuss your perceptions of yourself and your life, and together we can process what you went through and what it means to you."

"Okay," I said and let out a giggle.

"What?" she asked.

"Nothing. I just honestly never thought I'd find a doctor I could talk to about these things, but I feel that you somehow understand what I'm going through."

"I'm a clinical psychologist, Liz, not a doctor, but let's not worry about titles now. I'm a therapist. And hopefully, a friend. Your experience is your own, but yes, I think I can identify with what you're going through."

"Have you lost a life through the course of your life, too?" I recalled the words Nahum wisely said to me.

"Yes. I too have lost a life in my life," she admitted, and I didn't ask her to elaborate.

"Now, since this clinic is part of the HMO's services, there are some forms we need to fill out together," she said and ran through the standard questionnaire with me: living situation, work, school, eating and sleeping habits, reaction to sights and sounds. At the end of the list, the anticipated, much-dreaded question about self-harm lay in wait.

"Yes, I've thought about it," I admitted for the first time to someone other than you.

"I want us to continue these sessions regularly, Liz, but I need you to promise me something. I want you to assure me that, once we begin this process, you will not hurt yourself in any way and, if any such thoughts surface, you will share them with me, and together we'll consider how best to deal with them. Do you agree?"

"Yes," I nodded and couldn't help recalling you and your deals.

We scheduled some sessions. Before we parted, she insisted on giving me her cell phone number and email and warned me that sometimes she forwards jokes she receives and asked if that was okay with me.

I left the room feeling a strange kind of relief. Someone else now knew some of my most horrible thoughts – someone who isn't you, someone who isn't virtual. And the world just kept on going as usual: random sounds of people coughing filtered through the building's corridors, lost patients still looked for the right room number, rays of sunlight flickered through the old shutters, and no orderlies in white coats came to drag me away in a straitjacket.

My father greeted me with concern. "How are you, Lizzie?"

"I'm okay," I said and, for the first time in almost four years, I didn't feel like it was a complete lie.

Liz

Subject: Letter Number 25

My phone rang and an unidentified number appeared on the display. "Liz? Liz Fine?"

"Yes," I replied. I don't get many phone calls nowadays.

"I'm a messenger from Same Day Couriers. I have a package for you."

"What package?" I was surprised.

"Beats me. I'm just the delivery guy. It looks like a laptop or something."

What?! I gave him directions to the nearby road and hurried to meet him outside. He handed me a carefully wrapped package and asked me to sign a delivery receipt. I hurried to rip off the plastic wrapping, opened the bag hidden inside, and there it was. My laptop.

"You okay, sweetie?" The delivery man was startled when I sat down on a nearby rock trying to regulate my breathing.

"Who sent you?" I asked as I held on to my computer and tried to switch it on.

"The courier company."

"Yes, but who ordered the delivery?"

He scanned the documents in his hand. "Don't know sweetie, it's not mentioned on the order. You can call my supervisor if you want. Gotta go, tons more deliveries to make." He hurried

to his truck, slammed the door, and drove away before I had a chance to protest.

I remained sitting on that rock near the side of the road, the laptop on my knees and the bag at my side. I called the courier company whose name was printed on the address label. "Yes, I have the shipper's name right here," the woman on the other side of the line said in an indifferent voice. "Hanan."

I paused for a moment and asked, "Hanan what?"

"Hanan Hanan," she replied impatiently.

"Hanan Hanan? Is there an address?"

"No, I don't seem to have that information," she replied with blatant disinterest after a few additional keystrokes.

"I don't understand. Don't you ask whoever's sending the package to provide some form of identification?"

"He identified himself."

"Hanan Hanan? Does that sound like a real name to you?"

"I don't know what to tell you, ma'am. Those are all the details I have."

I asked to speak to a manager, but he couldn't supply any additional information and wasn't too bothered by the outrage I expressed over their sloppy business procedures. "We allow anyone to send anything provided it isn't offensive or illegal," he recited dryly.

I headed back to my parents' house, placed the laptop carefully on the table, and plugged it in. On the desktop I found a folder labeled "Letters from Jazz" in which you kept all the emails you deleted in perfect order. Everything was there, including what you said you'd permanently deleted. All my other folders were

arranged exactly as I left them. All the files were there, nothing was erased. So why didn't I feel relieved?

"Hi, Lizzie, you okay?" my mother greeted me as she came in. "What's that? Is that your laptop?"

"Yes, it's my laptop," I replied distractedly. "It was delivered here."

"What? How wonderful! How did that happen? Did the police find it?"

"Yes," I lied. I didn't want to bring her and Dad into this whole sordid story with you. I didn't want to cause them any unnecessary worry and complicate the whole matter.

"Really? And they just sent it over?" she wondered.

"Yeah... they raided this apartment that belongs to someone who breaks into people's houses, found my laptop, and cross referenced it with the details from the complaint I filed." I went on lying.

"And it works?! All your files are intact? Work and school files?" She was ecstatic.

"Yes..." I tried to conceal my confusion.

"How remarkable, Lizzie. That's fantastic! What a happy ending to this whole story."

Liz

Subject: Letter Number 26

Hi, I'm not sure you received my previous email. You didn't reply.

You surprised me. I wasn't sure you'd ever return my stuff, definitely not before I've finished paying the entire "ransom" you demanded to begin with. I don't know why you did it but – thank you. You already know how much this means to me.

I still have your "hostage," your sad little diary. I kept it safe and secure and you deserve to have it back. Give me your address and I'll send it back to you. I promise to keep my word and never tell anyone about any of this.

Liz

Subject: Letter Number 27

Hi. You didn't reply to my last emails. You don't have to disclose your address if you don't want your diary back, but why did you suddenly decide to return my computer?

Liz

Subject: Letter Number 28

So this is how it's going to be with you? You coward! Pestering and harassing when you feel like it and disappearing when you feel like it? Well, why does that even surprise me? Rather suits you perfectly. Everything happens according to your rules, through the one-way fucking mirror with which you surround yourself. Could you maybe get your head out of your ass just once in your miserable life and answer me?

Liz

Subject: Letter Number 29

Okay, it's not funny anymore. I know you think I hate you, and that's pretty much true, but we're no longer strangers. You revealed some aspects of your life to me and I'm a bit worried about you. It's not right for you to ghost me like this! At least write something so I know you're alright. You can't just disappear like this, it's troubling.

Liz

Letter Number 30

I won't be sending you this letter. What's the point? And yet, I continue to write to you, just like I continue to bite my nails, a disgusting and inane habit already ingrained in my system. Without it, my teeth begin to chatter and the tips of my fingers feel restless.

I tried to locate you. While diving into the sea of my familiar files, I tried to discover who you are. I collected and cross-referenced the details I thought I knew about you but didn't Google while you were still writing to me, so you wouldn't somehow find out, get spooked and delete my memories. Oddly enough, nothing seemed to match. The facts you occasionally mentioned about yourself didn't pan out to form one specific person: I couldn't find any copywriters, advertisers, sons of linguistics professors, or spouses of psychologists who have also authored two books and whose details correspond to yours.

I suddenly realized that everything I know about you stems from what you've told me, and it's quite possible that every sentence you wrote to me was a lie except, perhaps, that sad diary of yours that looked too authentic to be fake – but go figure. The further I searched, the more my perceived leads seemed to slip from my grasp.

Now that I have my laptop back, I've discovered that I'm different from the person I was when it was stolen. The files

in it hold less fascination for me. I hurried to back everything up then. This time, it's all in the Cloud as a new user, but the sense of calm I envisioned would envelop me once the files were in back my possession paled in comparison to the restlessness that your mystery has induced in me. Who are you – the man who brusquely thrust himself into my life, wallowed in my soul, and forcefully saved my life against my will? What made you suddenly and unilaterally end this strange game we've played? I have so many questions and not even a sliver of an answer.

Though I couldn't draw any comfort from my beloved letters, I knew someone who desperately needed them. I called Mikey and told him that my long-lost computer has been returned.

"What? Dizzy, that's amazing!" He was thrilled. He hurried to meet me and surveyed my archive of letters and notes. It felt strange to see someone else reading through all that extremely personal correspondence between Jazz and me but, oddly, there was also something comforting about it.

"Wow, it's crazy what you've collected here. It's a fucking doctorate! When did you manage to write all this?" he wondered as more and more letters and diary entries appeared before his eyes.

"Let's just say that, for a long while, I did nothing else but write."

I chose the entry where I wrote about the first time Jazz and I met. "Here, read this," I offered.

His eyes were glistening when he finished. "How old were you then? About fourteen?"

"Yeah," I confirmed.

He leaned forward, his elbows on his knees: "Listen, Dizz, I'm not sure how much of this I can process all at once. It's hard, you know, feeling her like this, so intensely."

"Take your time. Whatever you'd like to read is yours. No secrets." I was all too familiar with the sensation he described.

"What's up with you, Dizzy?" he looked up at me with a sudden suspicion. "You just got your laptop back. You should be on cloud nine, but you don't seem happy. What happened?"

"It's nothing." He reminded me of Jazz again. I could never hide anything from her, either.

"Don't try to bullshit me. Something's going on with you."

I didn't reply.

"You said no secrets."

True, that's what I said. And come to think of it, why should I keep the whole situation with you hidden from Mikey? He deserves to know where all this info about his sister was held and why I couldn't show him her letters earlier, while I deserved to stop lying to the world and living behind a mask. And why should I continue to protect you anyway?

I found myself detailing everything that happened since my apartment was burgled: that first creepy email from you and our weird agreement for forty letters, and your sad diary and your sad life, and the laptop that was returned to me out of the blue, and how you suddenly vanished.

"Wow, do you get what you're saying here, Dizz?! This is crazy!" He gaped at me with disbelief.

"Yeah, I know."

"And you don't know who this person is?"

"No, I've no idea."

"Do you have any crazy exes or anything? People you once knew? Someone with an obsession for you?"

"I don't think so. I thought of several people I've met but I find it hard to believe that anyone found me that interesting or that anyone could be so... how should I say it? Like this man. He's quite an unusual character."

"Fuck! We have to find out who this son-of-a-bitch is!" Mikey jumped to his feet and began pacing the room in agitation.

"Look, I know I'm the last person in the world who should stand up for him, but he's not exactly a son-of-a-bitch. Like, he kind of is, but he's also a very troubled person. He's not a bad man, he's just really, really tragic," I squirmed.

"Are you listening to yourself? Who isn't troubled and tragic in this world? Since when does that give him the right to steal or blackmail?"

"Well, I guess he also basically watched over me. He recognized I was in a pretty bad place and he made sure I didn't... that nothing would happen to me."

"Seriously, Dizz? Do you have an online version of Stockholm Syndrome?"

"Yeah, probably. I just don't want him to get hurt. I don't want anything to happen to him."

Mikey sat down, thought for a moment, and said, "Listen, my blood's boiling just thinking about this dude and I feel like beating the crap out of whoever he is, but I promise not to do anything without your consent."

"Okay, it doesn't matter anyway. I've tried to find out who

he is. I researched every detail I have on him, but I didn't get anywhere."

"There's no one who doesn't leave a footprint," Mikey determined. "According to what you said, this dude wanted to tell you about himself. There's no way he didn't clue you into something real we can track. Let's review everything you know until we find it."

"Okay." I was skeptical but decided to cooperate and told him everything you revealed about yourself or let me assume: your approximate age, where you live, what you did for a living, your books, Ella, and your parents.

"Well, there's not much to go on," he agreed with me. "Even an eighty-year-old woman living in some southern suburb with her sixteen cats could have written all that. Try to think in a different direction, Dizzy. Not about something that he told you about himself, but something that you'd really know."

I debated whether or not to show him your diary. Did I have the right to expose the deepest secrets of the man who confiscated mine? Eventually, I took out the small notebook from my bag and peeled away the wrapping I keep it in. "He sent this to me and said he wrote it as a young boy. Theoretically, he could have made this up too, but it looks really old and authentic."

Mikey carefully turned the yellowing pages filled with faded, child-like handwriting and confirmed my sentiment: "This shit does look legit."

Together, we reviewed the details in the diary and I slowly realized that the answer was here in my hands all along. The only things that haven't changed since you wrote this journal

are the ones related to your father, who died at its conclusion – his occupation and his death. You wanted me to find you. Maybe not easily or swiftly, but you handed me the means to find out who you are shortly after you first wrote to me.

After searching for a long hour, we came across the In Memoriam pages on the Tel Aviv University Physics Department website, in which he appeared among twenty or so names: Dr. Alexander Stern. He died in 1980 at the age of forty-five. His short biography didn't indicate why he stopped teaching in the faculty a few years before his death. The cause of his death was also not mentioned. The final line noted that he was "a brilliant staff member whose dedication to his field knew no bounds. His death was an unfortunate loss to the School of Physics and Astronomy and to the field of research in which he was active."

"It fits, huh?" asked Mikey. "Is there a chance this could be his dad? Doctor Alexander Stern?"

"Yes," I took a deep breath. "It fits perfectly."

"We're almost there. It should be just a short step from here. Are you ready?"

I pulled the laptop toward me and Googled: "Dr. Alexander Stern's son."

There were no results. I tried: "Author, his father, Dr. Alexander Stern." Hundreds of hits appeared on the screen, all related to one name: Adam Stern.

Adam Stern. You've made a superficial effort to hide from me. The major elements you described were, apparently, true. The persona you portrayed was not a figment of your imagination,

neither were your life story, your family, or your interests. You only altered some minor details to make it a little harder for me to track you down. You didn't write two books, but one: The Power of Words, which covered the life and death of your mother – a doctor, not a professor, of linguistics – Stella Stern. You weren't a copywriter but a marketing executive, and your ex was not Ella, but Anna. You were born in 1970, you grew up and lived in Tel Aviv, you were never officially married, and you have no children.

Your book stirred up quite a bit of interest, mainly because of your mom, who was quite famous in her time, but it never received the accolades as you claimed. I didn't find any reviews that claimed you were a "rising star in the Israeli literary world." Several articles were written about your departure from the marketing agency you worked for before you became a freelancer. You were described as a brilliant man who wasn't easy to work with. I found some older entries related to lectures and book readings you participated in while promoting your book. You were mentioned in several articles that explored what had happened to authors who published their debut novel and were never heard from again. Nobody mentioned that you're an agoraphobic hermit or that your father used to lock you in the closet. There was no reference to the fact that you're a messed-up son-of-a-bitch who doesn't know how to communicate with people, yet can somehow be a really good friend.

After combing the web and reading through a few dozen pages that mentioned your name, I Googled your image and zoomed in on the clearest ones. I saw a man, neither young nor

old, neither handsome nor ugly, with hair that was once black but is now streaked with gray, and dark eyes that penetrate the camera with their gaze.

"Do you know him?" Mikey asked.

"I don't know. It's definitely not someone I know well, but his face isn't exactly unfamiliar. I need to see him face-to-face to be sure."

I thought it would take another deep dive to search for your address, but the 411 directory quickly located it: 31 Sokolov Street in Tel Aviv. I stared with astonishment at the address on the screen.

"So what's the deal with all those details he faked if I could just find him out so easily?" I asked Mikey as I searched for the address on Google Street View and zoomed in on the building whose front entrance was sheathed in mirror-like glass.

"How should I know? Maybe he doesn't really live there. Maybe he wants to play this game of cat and mouse with you because he has the hots for you. And maybe he's just so fucked-up that his behavior can't be rationalized. What would you like to do now?"

"I need to take a breath. Let's go out for a cigarette."

"When did you start smoking again? I thought the smoke made you anxious."

"Just now."

We left the house. The hours had flown by as we conducted our strange detective work and, before I knew it, evening descended. We wandered along the cobbled lanes of the kibbutz until we reached the playground that was now empty of children. We sat

on the swings and Mikey took out two cigarettes, lit them, and handed one to me. I inhaled my first cigarette smoke in years, held it deep in my lungs, exhaled, and watched the blue swirl climb toward the dark skies.

"An angry dragon." I remembered a game that Jazz and I used to play by looking for shapes in the tail of the smoke plume.

"Wait, I've got a sedative for it." Mikey blew a perfect ring of smoke toward my dragon.

"I need to go there. I have to see him," I resolved.

"I'm coming with you."

"I need to see him alone, Mikey. It's between him and me."

"I can't let you go there alone. This man could be dangerous. No way."

"We'll go together and you can wait for me downstairs, in the stairwell. If anything happens, and I don't think it will, you can come up in a second and help me."

"Sounds like a plan," Mikey said pensively and took another long drag from his cigarette.

We continued sitting there, staring at the smoke swirling in the night air. Later, we walked back to my parents' house, I gently returned your sad diary to my bag, and we headed out.

I knocked on the door and heard a faint rustling sound inside.

"Adam, open up!" I shouted. The rustling drew closer.

"Adam, it's Liz. I know you're in there. Open the door!" I banged on the thick wooden door with my fists.

A key turned in the lock, followed by the slow twisting of additional locks, and the door opened wide.

I had a feeling I'd seen the hunched, gangly figure in the doorway before, but he looked nothing like the man I'd Googled. "You're not Adam," I said. The man shook his head, clicking his tongue. "So who are you?"

"Hanan."

"Where's Adam?"

"Who knows?" he shrugged. "You're Liz, then?"

"Yes," I nodded, confused.

"I've been expecting you," he declared without elaborating further. He turned his back to me and drifted into the apartment wordlessly, leaving the door open. The sound of objects being moved could be heard from inside the apartment, followed by echoes of shuffling feet approaching the door again.

"Here. This is for you." He handed me an envelope bearing a handwritten inscription in small, black, erratic letters:

"To be opened by Liz (Eliza) Fine only."

Dear Liz,

If you are reading this letter, you have likely chosen to seek out my true identity, arrived at my apartment, and met Hanan, who lives there now. For over three-and-a-half years, I've been writing you this letter in my mind. My hand is trembling, so forgive me if my handwriting is unclear. I'm drawing on words that I've kept silent for too long and now I must tell you the truth.

Three years, seven months, two weeks, and one day ago, I was invited to a book reading at a community center in Haifa. Later, I had a drink at a local bar and was compelled to wait for several hours for the alcohol to clear my system before I returned to the road. Shortly after four that morning, I drove my car around a sharp bend on a narrow and remote section of a road you know only too well.

I have rehashed the ensuing turn of events countless times and tallied my sins: the alcohol in my body had metabolized and legally, I was sober, yet traces probably remained in my blood. My mind was preoccupied. An intolerable song began playing on the radio just as I approached the turn, and I reached over to change the station.

Suddenly, a tremendous thud reverberated around me, objects I didn't recognize hurled through the air and in a flash landed on the asphalt with a crushing sound unlike anything I've heard before. A flame ignited. I slammed on the brakes

and my car came to a screeching halt. I ran onto the road. Just a few feet away, a pile of metal enveloped in a ball of flames emitted explosive, crackling sounds. It was your motorcycle. A rustle at the side of the road caught my attention. I ran toward it. It was you. Your body had landed in some shrubs that, I suppose, saved your life. I stared at you, dressed in a skirt and sweater, resting on a bed of tangled foliage, a helmet on your head. Completely detached from the turmoil around you, you looked like an astronaut who had landed on the wrong planet. Through the helmet, I could see your half-closed eyes, your lips quivering, mumbling something indecipherable. I didn't detect any open wounds or bleeding, only scratches on your legs from the shrubs.

Further down the road was a puddle of fluids with flames reflecting on its surface and a figure lying in its midst. At the time, I didn't know it was Yasmin. I ran to her and bent over her body. She was sprawled on the road in an unnatural position and the pool of blood that surrounded her was spreading wider. Her helmet-clad head was tilted to one side. I called out to her over and over again, begging for her to wake up. More popping sounds came from the motorcycle as chaos erupted all around me.

I have no interest in justifying what happened next, Liz. As opposed to the random sins I counted earlier, my subsequent actions did not occur by chance. This is my greatest sin, the badge of shame that I will bear forever. Every fiber of my being cried out unmistakably: I could not stay there a moment longer, once again standing by helplessly watching a human

life drain away before my eyes. Without thinking or planning, mechanically and automatically, I guided myself to my car and drove away, shaking, sweating, and mumbling, "What are you doing? What are you doing?" as I tried to process what had happened. I noticed a payphone at the side of the road and brought the car to a screeching halt again. While disguising my voice and wiping away any fingerprints, I called the police, reported the accident, and drove away from there.

I drove and drove, disregarding the road or the hour. After a while, it occurred to me to check my car for damage and I was shocked to discover that our fate-altering encounter had left almost no telltale marks: a slight dent in the bumper, a few cracks in the front left headlight, and nothing else. Thoughts raced through my head: *I must turn myself in to the police. And if I turn myself in? One of the girls I hit has died, and I fled the scene leaving the other (you), to meet her fate. In the blink of an eye, I've become a killer. I'll probably be sent to prison. Once again, I'll be locked away in a cell, unable to escape.*

I couldn't bring myself to drive to the police station to confess my crime and accept the penalty I legally deserved. I neither condone my decisions nor hope for your forgiveness. These were the circumstances and I am responsible for them.

As I continued to drive later that morning, I realized that I must return home to avoid raising suspicion. I called Anna (you probably already know that this is Ella's real name), told her that fatigue had taken over and compelled me to nap in my car after my lecture and I was now on my way home. I assume she sensed I was hiding something but likely thought it concerned alcohol.

She couldn't possibly guess that this lie hid a far greater sin.

Once I reached our apartment, I sat glued to my computer, searching for any information about the accident. Newsflashes appeared on several websites: "One killed and one injured in a motorcycle accident near Haifa."

Anna noticed I was unwell. "You look pale. Stay home and rest." She made me some tea and excused me from our mutual plans for the day. I stayed home and continued to follow any posts regarding the previous night's incident. That Saturday night, I stayed awake until dawn, went out to the corner market, bought all the daily newspapers I could find, and searched them for news on the matter. I found a brief report in two papers: hit-and-run, one young woman dead, one survivor, the identity of the driver at fault still unknown, police continue to investigate and are requesting the public's assistance in locating a suspect.

I have spent every day since anxiously awaiting a ring on the doorbell, a knock on the door, or a team of detectives to finally trace my identity but, to my amazement, this has yet to occur. No one but I knows the truth, and this knowledge has consumed my life.

The fear of being incarcerated paralyzed me, but I was soon trapped in another kind of prison. I was stricken with bouts of intense anxiety every time I left my house. Daylight scorched my skin like the flames from that night. People around me looked at me accusingly, their glances dripping with justified hatred. I felt like everyone knew. I imagined hearing their thoughts echoing around me: "Girl killer. Liar. Coward." Sleep eluded me. Every time I shut my eyes, I was tormented by the

sights and sounds of that night. I gradually stopped finding meaning in daily trivialities: changing clothes, shaving, small talk. I stopped going to the office. I was unable to manage my employees or conduct daily nonsensical communication with my clients. None of these held purpose for me any longer.

And Anna. I couldn't stand the thought of the look in her eyes when she discovered the depravity of the man she shared her life with. I preferred her to think of me as incompetent or for her to hate me – anything but find out the truth. I wanted her to abandon me as I did not deserve her. If I had ever thought of bringing children into the world, after the accident it became infinitely clear that I would never sire offspring. I kept my distance from her just as I described to you. It took very little effort or theatrics to become an intolerable person. I was just being myself. She recognized the change in me, knowing that I was not as I once was, only the *deus ex machina* remaining hidden from her eyes.

Another course of action was set in motion on that horrible night when our paths crossed: a slow current began drawing me into your life. I felt a strong urge to discover what had become of you and track your recovery. I hungrily followed every post about the accident. I soon found out your name and searched for any speck of information about you like a person possessed. I realize there was no logic behind my reasoning, but I felt that I must watch over you in some way and that I could not abandon you again as I deserted you on that road.

While my life and relationship crumbled around me, I immersed myself in your life. I drifted away from my daily

routine and dived into your past. I searched through all your digital profiles on social media and followed you. I tracked your screen name and traced every word you wrote in presumed anonymity. But it wasn't enough.

The internet is a stalker's paradise. You don't have to be an expert to gain access to another's innermost secrets. Once I got to know you, I was able to easily guess your Google password – Yasmin's birthday, and from there I could track nearly all of your actions. Much like me, your interaction with the world at the time was mediated by the internet, and thus I was provided with a portal into your life. Rather than leaving my house, I tried to imagine what you were doing. I spent my days shadowing you. My conversations with Anna were now replaced by a one-sided dialogue with you.

For over three-and-a-half years, I've been reading every one of your emails and posts on social media. I know your list of favorites and browsing history by heart, the sites you visit often and those you'd never enter. Even before your computer came into my possession, I was thoroughly familiar with your financial and medical records. I've read all of your gradually dwindling correspondence with those who were once your friends, your kibbutz offices, and various federal institutions. I've followed every awkward flirtation initiated by men who were not worthy of you, every romantic encounter and the dialogue that faded in its wake. And through the old emails that lay in your inbox, I became acquainted with Yasmin and shared your pain at her loss.

When you moved to Tel Aviv, I couldn't resist. Once a week, I would leave my house late at night and find myself with a

bottle of booze in my hand, gazing at the open window of your ground-floor apartment.

During those weeks, I hardly left my house anymore except for the times I observed you. On one such occasion, as I returned home, drunk and stumbling, Anna decided to leave me. Once she was gone, I was alone within my walls. No wife, no pets, no expectations of redemption. Just me, my memories, and your life.

In the months following your move to Tel Aviv, I noticed a considerable change in your behavior. If, at first, you used to vigorously type and email your work-related articles, you then spent the following weeks typing for hours on end without ever emailing your writings to anyone, and I longed to read those files. I noticed you rarely left your apartment, which, through your window, seemed like a world falling into chaos. You stopped paying attention to the manner or place in which things were organized. You no longer gazed at your pretty reflection in the mirror or listened to the music that you had so enjoyed in the past. You no longer corresponded with anyone but your employers. Instead, I saw you weeping bitterly alone all night. You spent your waking hours typing feverishly, words that were never sent to anyone, and thus I could not gain access to them. These were later revealed as the chronicles of Lizzie and Jazzy.

On one of my late-night surveillance expeditions, I recognized various objects from your apartment placed outside your building – pictures you had removed from the walls, kitchen utensils, and trinkets. Week-by-week, your apartment became emptier. I later discovered an unsent email in your drafts folder in which you informed your employers of your resignation. I

found no evidence of a search for another job. You didn't seem to be planning a new career and I saw no signs of you moving back to the kibbutz. You began to neglect your schoolwork, failing to submit papers that were due, not replying to letters informing you of missing credits, and not registering for the semester's final exams.

One evening, I read a post you had written in the Bereavement and Loss forum you've visited several times since the accident: "If you could isolate one moment from your life and turn it into a cocoon where you could curl up and nestle whenever you wanted, which moment would you choose? If you could isolate one moment in time and remove it from your life, like a tumor that jeopardizes an entire body and whose extraction could change the entire picture, which moment would you extract? I know exactly the moment I'd like to remove, but I can't extract my tumor without sacrificing the entire body. I also know to which moment I'd like to return. Will I succeed? Who knows?"

The other forum members weren't too bothered by your abstract post. Some of them wished you luck, others added words of encouragement, and many just ignored it, while I stared at my computer screen in horror. This was the last piece in the disturbing puzzle you had assembled before me. I hurried to check your search history and I felt the blood drain from my face. You looked up things such as, "Ways to commit suicide," "What floor do you need to jump from to die," and, "Potentially fatal medication."

It was then that I realized that I could no longer maintain my position as a mere observer of your life and that I must

340 | SOMEONE'S SECRET

take on a more proactive role, one that would enable me to protect you from self-destruction. I couldn't consider making an anonymous call to the police. The thought of exposing your secrets or being unwillingly institutionalized was intolerable. I had to do something myself – and quickly.

I enlisted Hanan's help and hurried him to your building in the middle of the night. We situated ourselves behind a tall hedge a short distance from your window. The lights in your apartment were off and I was afraid I was too late.

"Go in and check if there's a girl in there, and see if she's asleep, not dead," I urged him.

"Are you crazy?" Hanan objected. "Who's in there? Your girlfriend?"

"No. A woman I'm worried about."

"An ex?"

"No, Hanan. Hurry up! I'm afraid she's hurt herself."

"So, you go in!"

"I can't. She mustn't see me." I didn't have time to explain.

"You and your quirks," he hissed in disdain. "How much are you paying?"

"A thousand shekels." I tried to think of an amount he couldn't refuse.

"Hahahaha!" He rejected my offer with contempt.

"Three," I blurted out. He stared down indecisively.

"Your shoes, too," he insisted.

"Okay, I'll buy you some shoes, but go in, already! The window's quite low here and there's probably no alarm system," I hastened him.

"No. I want your shoes," he pointed at my feet.

"Why?"

"They look comfortable."

"Okay, I'll give you my shoes, just go in! I'm afraid something happened to her!"

"Right now. Give me the shoes now and I'll break in."

"You're not breaking in, you're just going in through a window to check if everything's alright. Oh, very well..." I cursed under my breath, removed my shoes, and took the tattered shoes he handed to me. Surprisingly, our shoe size was identical.

He climbed onto the windowsill, removed the torn mosquito screen that likely no longer protected you from bugs, effortlessly slid open the window, and crawled inside. About thirty breath-stopping seconds later, he peered out of the window, signaled that you were okay, and began to climb back out.

"Wait! Check there aren't any empty pill bottles near her bed!" I whispered to him. He went back inside and immediately returned, shaking his head, again starting to climb out.

I had no time to formulate a clever plan but an idea popped into my mind. Though I didn't know what it was that you spent all those hours on, writing alone in your little apartment, I hoped you considered it of value, maybe something to do with Yasmin. I assumed you wouldn't hurt yourself if you were compelled to rescue all your files or if Jazz's letters were taken from you. And thus – impulsively and carelessly – "Someone" was conceived.

"Wait! Grab her computer!" I whispered an order to Hanan.

He gave me the finger.

"Take the computer or you can forget about the money!" I urged him to hurry before you woke up. "And take the external drive as well. It should be just beside the computer!" I remembered watching you faithfully backing up your work every night.

He made another obscene gesture at me, turned back inside for the third time, his lanky frame disappearing into the darkness of the room. A few seconds later, he climbed out of the window with the laptop and drive in his hands. He shoved them into my arms and whispered, "Let's get out of here! She woke up!"

Two days later, I wrote my first email to you. I told you I was a frustrated author who saw you as his muse. It wasn't a complete lie. Indeed, I hadn't written anything of value since the night of the accident, but the true purpose of my correspondence with you was to ensure your safety, and that purpose became my reason for being. The idea I offhandedly devised on the night you wrote your parting words on that forum was formulated into a plan of action. I would use the memories you composed as bait, flaunting them before your eyes and making you work to salvage them. I would assign you tasks that you'd need to undertake in order to get back your files. I would give you a purpose for existence. I deleted Yasmin's letters, which I knew well, from your inbox and added them to the deal as well. If your own words wouldn't serve as a convincing enough incentive for survival, I hoped her words would fulfill that role.

As our correspondence ensued, I was relieved to see how your spirit was gradually replenished with the essences of life.

Factors unrelated to me encouraged you to relinquish your plans for self-harm: your discoveries about your family, your newfound intimacy with your parents, your friendship with Nahum, and your conversations with Michael. When you described your first session with Mariana, I felt you had found a new, far worthier confidant who would fulfill the role I had taken upon myself. Once the threat of you hurting yourself was no longer valid, there was no excuse left for our relationship. I had to acknowledge the fact that I must let you go. I returned your computer. My demand for forty letters was irrelevant, in any case. It was merely a ruse meant to ensure that you continued writing long enough for me to dissuade you from your suicidal intentions.

From the very beginning, I acknowledged your right to expose my true identity, but I didn't want to force it upon you. Therefore, I modified a few identifying details, obscured some traces, and scattered a few clues that would help you to track me down if you wished.

I don't suppose the following will bring you much comfort. Nevertheless, it's important for me to write it: though you and Yasmin were the victims and I the perpetrator, my life was also lost that night. I was also thrown off my trajectory by the terrible force of the event. Just like you, I will never be who I was before that moment. My former life went up in flames along with yours.

I could not muster the courage... I am not brave enough to face you, Liz. I have no defensive argument and I don't expect your forgiveness. I've sentenced myself and now I shall begin serving

344 | Someone's Secret

my penance. As you see, I no longer live in my apartment. Yes, Liz, I finally left my house. I will not be returning.

I will reveal no further details. I hope to allow you to disengage from me, not to chase after or run from me. However, if you seek me out, you will not find it very difficult to locate me. This confession is now in your hands. If you wish, you can turn me over to the police, who will trace me and bring me to court to face your accusations. I leave this choice in your hands.

I miss you, Liz. The pledge we made to each other through no wish our own has rendered you the person closest to me since our destinies crossed. I cannot describe how sorry I am. For Yasmin. For Yasmin. For Yasmin. For you. For everything I took and was unable to give back. For that moment in time I would give anything to extract from my life, like a tumor. I am sorry for the horrible repercussions of that night, for my carelessness and my terrible weakness. I am sorry for the fears I failed to conquer and the methods I used to play a role in your life. Yet I will never be sorry for thwarting your plans to end your life. Please take care.

Warm regards,

Adam

I sit in a corner on a bustling street. Jerusalem is more crowded than Tel Aviv and its aromas are more intense. I couldn't risk her running into me in the street, so I was forced to travel further east. What are the chances that she'll ever reach this part of the capital? The street odors creep across my skin and latch onto it. The commotion overwhelms me. During the past few weeks, the dust from the city's alleys has clung to my body and clothes until it seems I can never shake it from me. It all goes according to my plan.

Evening begins to fall and I know I can't spend the night on this street. As darkness descends, it fills with groups of teens inundated with alcohol and violence. I stand up, dragging the pink, floral shopping cart I received from Hanan in return for my apartment, and move myself with self-loathing through the sea of humanity. People glare at me with accusing eyes. I'm humiliated by their looks. The buzzing that grips my senses is unbearable. I double over amidst the crowd and vomit, accompanied by the protests of passers-by. I rinse my mouth out with vodka and continue walking. I don't know how much longer I can go on like this and I don't care. This is the penance I have imposed on myself without her knowledge: I will never have a home. If she seeks further retribution, she'll see to it. Now, finally, her fate is in her hands, as is mine.

The End

Thank you to the dozens of friends and colleagues who have advised, supported, and encouraged me through the four-year process of writing and editing this book: my confidants, my family, my editor, Michal Heruti, for being my guide and companion on this journey, and my beloved Geva.

Please feel free to share with me your impressions, reactions, thoughts, and comments about this book at:
Snunitliss@gmail.com

Made in United States
Orlando, FL
29 July 2023